The wind has been p........ ...., ... now it whooshes through the open windows...

One of the men has turned on the radio, because the next thing I hear is a woman with a French accent, probably broadcasting from Monserrat, calmly announcing that a force three hurricane is expected to land by nightfall.

"I better close the shutters," says Spike's buddy. *Damn, I should have hidden behind the couch.*

"I hope you've got a backup generator."

"It's in the basement."

The sound of their footsteps going down the stairs provides a glimmer of hope that my life will not end as abruptly as expected. Slipping off my shoes, I take the steps two at a time, pass through the unlocked gate—this time with no need for gymnastics—and make a run for the jeep. I release the brake, let out the clutch and start rolling downhill, amazed at how much noise the tires make on the rough road.

As soon as I'm sure the jeep is out of earshot, I start the engine. The wind competes with me for the steering wheel, pushing the vehicle towards the edge of the narrow road. The rain, beating ever harder on the flimsy roof of the jeep, reminds me of how thirsty I am.

One thing is clear, parched and dry as my mouth may be, I'm up to my neck in water far deeper than the lagoons encompassing this lovely island.

Ask the Dead
by
Joyce Yarrow

Ask the Dead

Joyce Yarrow

Martin Brown Publishers ● Kokomo, Indiana
www.mbpubs.com

Published in 2005 by Martin Brown Publishing, LLC.

Set in 12 pt. Times New Roman by Sharene Martin.

Printed in the United States of America.

Ask the Dead
ISBN 0-9765409-1-6

For Lanac,
Long live nepotism!
Warm regards,
Jna

This book is for Ian.
Love 'ya.

Acknowledgements

Many thanks to Pete MacDonald for his belief in this book and his unflagging devotion to the craft of writing.

Much appreciation to my brother, Rick Smith, for sharing his expertise, to Tom Willis for his devious mind, and to Robert Brown, my editor, for his enthusiasm, sharp eye, and hard work.

Also, thanks to Don Murray for letting me pester him with questions about all things legal, and to Jon Clark for shedding light on the mysteries of air traffic control and regulations.

And lastly, heaps of gratitude to my husband Gary, for his help, encouragement and buoying sense of humor.

cells divide
cultured in dishes
they mimic creation
cells divide prisons with inmates
in deep isolation

Chapter One

She's waiting in front of the store, a large African-American woman, mature, perhaps in her mid-fifties. Her ample figure is comfortably draped in a long skirt and flowing caftan, a symphony of muted tones in violet and spring green. Her heart-shaped face is a mellow shade of cocoa, making her a beauty if it weren't for the gaunt and haggard eyes.

"Jo Epstein?"

I nod.

"I'm Shondrea Johnson. I need to talk to you. My son has got himself into some deep trouble."

"Who referred you to me?"

"Tony Sanchez. He said you were a godsend."

It's two years plus since I got Tommy Sanchez off the hook. Still, they find me. The ones with brothers, sons, and nephews who swear they're innocent, no matter how damning the evidence.

She watches me as I unlock the door and then follows me inside. "If you would just give me a few minutes of your time, I'm sure you'd find a way to help. Or at least tell me what you think I should do next." She's not going to be an easy brush-off.

I hit the light switch, and *Ted's West Side News* illuminates in red neon, bathing the front shelves inside the store, as well as the drab facades of the adjoining brownstones. Opening the register, I count the cash. Happily, it matches Ted's reconciliation from last night.

I'd like to tell this anxious woman that I'm retired, that nowadays when I can't sleep it's because I'm reading a mystery, not solving one. But my dream of supporting my writing habit by

1

working part-time is rapidly dissolving, along with the proceeds from the sale of my agency in Los Angeles.

"What's your son's name?"

"Gabriel, Gabriel Johnson," she says, and the story floods out. "He's a photographer. Last week he got a phone call, somebody wanting a print. Gabe went up to the Bronx and made the sale, but on his way back he was jumped in broad daylight by some hoods, just three blocks from the subway. He said that he was tryin' to disarm the one who had the knife. He said that what happened was an accident. The police didn't believe him, but they should have. Because he didn't run away. He waited for them so he could tell his own side of the story. Didn't make any difference. They charged him with manslaughter, when his only crime was defending himself. That's not right, is it?"

These last words bring on the tears, and I hand her a tissue from the box I keep near the register. "Do you know who called about the photograph?"

Mrs. Johnson wipes her eyes while she scans her memory. "I answered the phone and gave it to Gabe. It wasn't a familiar voice and later Gabe wouldn't tell me who it was. Said I was better off not knowing. That got my curiosity up, like I told the police, and that's why I remembered the call. But when I went to the station to make a statement, I could tell they thought I was covering up, telling lies to protect my boy. Please, you've got to help me find out what happened. Gabe needs someone to take his side."

"Look, Mrs. Johnson. I'll be honest. You should go with someone who has better contacts in the Police Department. I could give you a few names."

She looks around the newsstand with a disparaging frown. "Woman, from what I've heard you're a competent professional. Why are you working *here?*"

It's a long story, and none of her business, but she does have a point. "Has your son been in trouble before?"

"Just once. Last year, when Sean was staying with us. Sean's a street kid, a runaway, and Gabriel brought him home. He does

2

things like that. One night the two of them went to a party and the next thing I know Gabe's calling me from jail. He said he was gonna leave—it was getting too wild—but then the police broke down the door, and it was too late. They arrested everyone. Gabe had a small bag of cocaine in his shirt pocket, but he swore he wasn't using. Said Sean bought the drugs at the party and insisted on a two-way split. Wouldn't take no for an answer."

"So your son has done time before."

"No, he hasn't, but that's only because Silas Harding came on as our attorney. Because of him, Gabe got a six month suspended sentence, with the one condition that he go to rehab, upstate. When he came home, he went to New Beginnings, a re-entry program downtown, and they were the ones who convinced him he could turn professional and sell his photographs. Gabe was doing fine, right up until that phone call came."

These last words are accompanied by direct eye contact, and I get the message. All those years spent trying to keep her son out of trouble, and now he's headed down the tubes.

"Tell you what, Mrs. Johnson. I've gotta go to Rikers Island tomorrow to deliver some books. While I'm there, I'll have a talk with your son. I charge three hundred bucks a day plus expenses."

She digs through her purse. "Take this as an advance. You'll have to work quickly. The trial is set for September."

The five hundred dollar check she presses into my palm seems to like it there. Maybe it has some friends that will help me cover the latest raise in my rent.

"No promises, Mrs. Johnson."

"Please, call me Shondrea. I'm not expecting any miracles, but to have someone looking out for my son, someone who knows the system, that's what I been prayin' for." She hands me a crumpled business card. "I've written my phone number and address on the back, as well as Mr. Harding's private number—you can call us anytime." She leaves the store briskly, and through the window, still a bit misty with spray from an afternoon shower, I watch her progress down the street, her shoulders a bit straighter than before.

3

It's a slow night, just two people inside the store—an elderly woman half asleep in a wheelchair and her Haitian caregiver, browsing the magazines. From my perch at the counter by the window, I cover the outside kiosk, while minding the interior as well, keeping one eye on the cash register and the other out for customers with bulging pockets. According to Ted, thefts are outnumbering sales by two to one. More people must be reading *Steal This Book,* now that it's on the Web.

By the time Ted comes in at 11:40, my arms are aching from the strain of unpacking the hundreds of pounds of periodicals we display out front. Some are slick and glossy, smelling of sickly sweet perfume samples, others recycle their stiff paper as well as their literary pretensions.

You'd think, at his age, that Ted would give me the grave-yard shift and stay home to get some shut-eye. Maybe he thinks I can't handle the late night weirdos, or maybe he likes hanging out with them himself. Ted's a hard one to read.

"We need shelf space. I'll take some returns to Riker's on Saturday," I tell him.

"Isn't it a little early in the month?" he asks, his suspicious nature aroused by my unusual display of conscientiousness. Ted is straight and tall, what you might call rangy, with a full head of white hair and a high forehead that would make him look distinguished if it weren't for his bulbous nose.

"I've got an aunt in Queens I haven't seen in a while," I improvise. Telling Ted that I've taken a case is not a good idea. He thinks I've retired from dangerous endeavors.

Before my boss can question me further and catch me in a lie, I slip into the storeroom. The floor is covered with stacks of naked books, stripped of their covers to prepare them for their one-way trip to prison—rejects soon to be read by other rejects. We're supposed to trash unsold books, after returning the covers to the publisher for credit, but Ted's got a soft spot for those he calls "throwaway people." He's owned this place since the '40s, Mayor LaGuardia's time, which makes him prehistoric. In a rare mellow mood, he once told me how the Mayor, whose nickname was "The Little Flower" (from his first name, Fiorello), went on the radio during a newspaper strike to read comic strips to the kids.

On the dot of midnight I grab the paycheck that Ted hands me, as well as a newspaper to read on the bus, and head out the door. I'm feeling pretty good, having been paid twice in one night.

The Number 2 drops me off at 98th and Broadway, and I walk over to the yellow brick apartment building on West End that I've called home for three years. Picking up my mail in the lobby, I take the mahogany-paneled elevator to the ninth floor. It was the classy elevator, combined with the ridiculously low rent, that overcame my initial squeamishness when the landlord disclosed, as he was legally required to do, that a suicide had taken place in the bathroom of apartment 9G. I took the bait and moved in. Since then of course, the bastard's raised my rent three times.

Opening the door, I'm greeted by a blast of hot air. The southern exposure is great for growing basil on the windowsill in winter, but when summer rolls around, I know what it's like to be trapped in the boiler room of a tramp steamer. I dial the air conditioner to High Cool, and it starts up with a growl. Hunting around the fridge, all I can find is a tofu-veggie pot pie I must have bought during one of my health food crazes. While the pie is in the microwave, I pour myself the last of last night's chilled white wine, put my feet up on the kitchen table and relish my solitude.

Living alone has taken some getting used to, since I've always had a knack for skating off the thin ice of one relationship directly onto the newly formed surface of another. On the other hand, I've learned to treasure the minor freedoms found on the flip side of loneliness. These days, I can order takeout from the Cuban-Chinese place on the corner without considering anyone else's taste buds, and, if I've got a poem working in my head at 3 a.m., I can turn on the light and write, sans fear of provoking muffled screams under the covers.

* * *

On Saturday morning, I call Silas Harding at home. He's got a solid reputation as an aggressive defender, especially on civil liberties cases. I explain who I am and that I'd like to interview Gabriel Johnson.

I've never met Harding but his voice has a patrician quality, suggesting cashmere and loafers. "Yes, it's a tough case. So far no exculpatory evidence. Shondrea told me she hired you, which means you'll be working for me, too."

I get ready for him to inquire about my license, but the question never comes up. If asked, I'd have told him that New York law allows me to work without a license as long as I confine myself to taking one case at a time. My California investigator's license might still be valid, but I wouldn't know, having burned it in the ash tray of the car I drove to the airport on the day I moved back to New York.

"Can you tell me the name of the arresting officer?"

"Lieutenant Saleh, at the 42nd in the Bronx," he says, no hesitation.

Some instinct makes me ask. "How come you remember?"

We share a full five seconds of dead air, before Harding comes up with, "He's a client of mine. Can't say any more."

He doesn't have to. Khurram Saleh's case was plastered all over the papers a few months ago. He was an Egyptian grad student at Columbia University whose friends from Pakistan were detained and deported for collecting funds for a charity that had vague connections with the ill-defined shadow world with which we're supposed to be at war. Khurram went underground before he could be arrested, or so the tabloids said. Occasionally they run his face on the evening news, asking anyone who has seen him to call the police. Lieutenant Saleh must be one of Khurram's relatives, but I know there's no use inquiring further.

Harding clears his throat and moves on. "Here's what I'll do, Ms. Epstein. There's a corrections officer at Rikers named Larry Tollway who acts as a liaison with some social workers I know. He's that rare breed, a CO who actually believes in rehabilitation. Tollway knows Gabe. I'll ask him to meet you in reception."

Outside, the air is more liquid than gas. There's another

suffocating inversion on the way but it's still cool enough for me to jog the mile to the newsstand, where I stack the boxes of stripped paperbacks onto a dolly and wheel them to the subway.

On the N train I kill time trying to guess which passengers will get off at Queens Plaza to take the Q-101 bus to Rikers Island. I look for morose parents or gloomy girlfriends, those who sit alone with their thoughts, anxious and sad. As it turns out, almost everyone on the train boards the bus. I take a window seat near the back, next to a petite blonde wearing denim cutoff shorts and high heels. Nobody talks.

When we reach the top of the Buono Memorial Bridge, the gigantic detention complex rises to meet us—ten different jails on 414 acres, surrounded by coils of razor wire and an electric fence. Only minutes from Manhattan, it's a sight that most New Yorkers have never seen. Up to 16,000 inmates take up space on Rikers Island, most of them awaiting trial and too poor to make bail. The ones who are sentenced to less than a year stay here. The rest will be transferred to state prisons.

A CO is waiting for me at the registration desk in the Control Building. Slight and wiry, with thinning brown hair, Larry Tollway has a bulldog quality that I imagine serves him well in his line of work. "Silas told me this is your first visit. He asked me to take you through security."

"I'm not used to this kind of red carpet treatment."

Larry grins. "No problem, glad to help. I've been up all night doing intake, so forgive the wrinkled look." His blue uniform looks serviceable, if not dapper, and except for blood-shot eyes and a sunburned face to match, I see no signs of fatigue.

"Looks like you stayed too long at the beach," I observe. His welcoming committee smile gives way to a 'what's it to you' look for an uncomfortable moment and then the jovial Larry is back. We chat about what a hot, miserable August it's been, while I submit to the labyrinthal process of gaining entrance to one of the largest jails on earth, culminating with my enclosure in a dazzling red cylinder, where I'm scanned for metal from head to toe. Larry surprises me by offering to deliver the donated paperbacks to the library, while I take the bus over to the Motchan Detention Center.

Several layers of security later, I'm waiting in a window-less room where prisoners are allowed to communicate with their loved ones. Next to me a young girl wearing a gold cross over her green tank top snaps her gum while listening to a tirade of affectionate curses and caresses flung so loudly by an Asian teen that I can hear them through the telephone receiver she holds six inches from her ear. "You make me bust a nut just looking at you, bitch," is the closest he comes to a compliment. His arms are covered with snake tattoos, and I'm fascinated by the way they're magnified in the glass partition.

The husky build and shaved ebony head of the young man who now enters and sits down offers a sharp contrast to his delicate facial features. He avoids eye contact, waiting for me to make the first move, so I pick up the phone.

"Gabriel, my name is Jo Epstein, and I'm a private investigator. Your mother hired me to look into your case."

"Leslie's already doin' that."

"And who might she be?"

"Leslie Corning. She works at New Beginnings as some kinda intern. Came by a few days ago. A real wise head. Shoulda' been a lawyer. 'It was self defense, not manslaughter.' That's what she said when I told her how it went down."

"Would you mind telling it again?"

Gabriel's expression says otherwise, but he complies. "I did some business, and I was on my way home."

"What kind of business?"

"I sell prints of my photographs. It's what I do." He gives me a challenging look, to let me know his talent is to be taken seriously. "These three gangbangas tried to jack me. One of 'em pulled a knife, so I grabbed the handle and twisted it back. I didn't mean to stick'em. When the others saw what happened, they done a rollout."

"You gonna tell me what gang?"

"Since you're dumb enough to ask. They were Scorpions—one of 'em was flying the flag."

8

"Any witnesses?"

"Like I tol' Leslie, just a sleepwalker from the neighborhood."

"I'd like to talk to him."

"Save your breath. Why should he say somethin' gonna give him a rep as a snitch?"

"It's worth a try. Can you give me his name? Tell me where to look?"

"Sure. But if you go up there, you betta' take a bodyguard."

"I know you'll find this hard to believe, Gabriel, but I grew up in the southeast Bronx."

The ghost of a smile visits his eyes. "Fo' sure you don' live there no more. The junkie's name is Sonny Rodriguez. He hangs at the bodega on the corner of Tremont and Washington."

"What does Sonny look like?"

"He wears Hawaiian shirts and has a white streak in his hair that makes him look like a skunk. If you find him, ask him if he still has that thing I gave him."

I know better than to ask what this *thing* might be. "Sure. I'll let you know if I find out anything that could help your case."

"Don' worry 'bout me. I got my own plans for gettin' outta' here."

These are definitely not the words of a desperate man, wrongly accused and facing a long prison term. Maybe he's blowing hot air to hide his fear. Hard to tell. There's more than a pane of glass dividing us.

"Is there anything you need?"

"Besides my freedom? Keep an eye on Leslie. If somethin' bad came down on her because she was on the lookout for me, that wouldn't be right. And when you see Silas, tell him I've got some information I wanna use to make a deal."

"I'll do what you ask. But if you're not being straight with me, *you're* the one with the most to lose."

"Yeah, well straight hasn't done me much good, has it? I coulda' fled the scene but I waited for the police and what did that get me? Handcuffs and a railroad job unless I can swing a deal."

Riding back to Queens Plaza, my seatmate is a thin, talkative woman with a slight Irish brogue. "I work at the drop-in center near the Plaza," she says. "We try to help them before they hit the streets. Imagine, being released at three in the morning and all you have in your pocket is a buck fifty and a Metrocard."

* * *

During the twenty-one years I lived in Los Angeles, my old neighborhood in the Bronx was the setting for recurring nightmares in which California sun and sand were replaced by dimly lit side-walks, and I was forced to walk the shadow-filled streets. Today my bad dreams have a chance to mesh with reality, but when the train leaves the tunnel, emerging into bright sunlight and running parallel to the pre-World War II rooftops, I enter a world that's more pathetic than frightening.

It's not the drug deals in doorways or the sniffling kids running half naked through the streets, although that's bad enough. It's not the sickening smell of garbage or the ever-present graffiti that gets me down. It's the claustrophobia, and knowing that the only way most people leave this place is in a box or in a uniform provided by a prison or a branch of the military.

Descending from the elevated station, I pass a pack of teens partying on the steps. They're busy sharing an after school joint, but take time out to sneer at my Birkenstock sandals and stretch jeans. No wet smacking lips and obscene gestures, just curious stares aimed at the lady with the kinky red hair and freckles.

Among the boarded up tenements on Tremont Avenue, there are several bodegas, including one that used to house an evangelical church. The signs are still in Spanish, but the owner is Korean—no surprise given how often these little stores change hands. He's reloading the soda machine, and I purchase a Dr. Pepper.

"Maybe you've seen my friend. His name is Sonny Rodriguez. Has black hair with a white streak."

"Don't think so. Hard to say."

That's the best I can get out of him, and the same goes for

10

the clerk at the Dollar store. I try the bodega two blocks down, which dares to carry fresh vegetables and a modest selection of wine. A skin-and-bone, white-haired apparition skulks behind the cash register, a cigarette dangling from her mouth. "You mean the Skunk," she hisses, in response to my inquiry. "Hold on to your purse if you go near that low life. I was out for a smoke about an hour ago an' I thought I saw him in the park."

Crossing the street, I walk up the steps leading into Crotona Park, where the stately trees provide a welcome haven from the relentless sun. The meadows and hillsides make a beautiful setting, but the original designers would roll over in their graves if they could see their exotic trees and shrubs providing perfect cover for sex offenders and druggies. On the basketball court, a game is in progress and one of the players, a twenty-something Tony Banderas look-alike, makes a jump shot, catching my eye on the way down. He trots over to the fence and the face that looked so good at a distance turns out to be a pock-marked landscape with a few scars thrown in for good measure.

"Lookin' for somebody?" He's still a little out of breath.

"Sonny Rodriguez."

"You off duty?"

"I'm not a cop. I just want to talk to him."

"Try the chess tables." He points behind me. "The Skunk doesn't play, but he likes to watch the action."

"Thanks."

Four chess tables, cast in concrete and mounted on pedestals, are squeezed in between the swings and the baseball diamond. Only one game is in progress, a match between two geezers smoking cigars, the earth around them already littered with three empty cans of malt liquor. A third man nurses the fourth can, stretched sideways on a bench, his face a light shade of jaundice yellow. There's no mistaking the neon blue Hawaiian shirt and the hairdo that's made him famous, but I put the question to him anyway.

"Sonny Rodriguez?"

Over the beer can raised to his lips, eyes like two expressionless puddles examine me. I've seen this stagnant water before, dead to everything, craving only short-lived euphoria. I wonder if I'll get through to him.

"My name is Jo Epstein. I'm a private investigator working for the mother of a friend of yours, Gabriel Johnson."

Sonny surprises us both by pulling himself up to a sitting position. "He no friend a mine."

"Gabriel's been charged with manslaughter. Says the fight was three to one, and that he was the one. Did you see this?"

"I didn't see nothin'." He starts to scratch his neck, stirring memories of a hophead I had a crush on in high school, a boy who seemed to inhabit a cool, far off universe where the laws of physics were pleasantly different. Jason wrote junkie poetry that made me fall half in love with him. Luckily for me he had no sex drive and rejected my awkward advances.

"Your evidence could be grounds for having the charges against Gabriel dismissed."

"It could also be grounds for gettin' me shot." His brain may be cooked, but his instinct for self-preservation appears to be intact.

"So an innocent man goes to jail because you're chicken shit?"

"Thas' what that social worker girl said, but I tol' her it wasn't her ass be put on the line. She was here last week, quacking some line about Gabriel needing my help. Yeah, I know him, but he's not my brother—not somebody I'd get smoked for—and that's what you be askin'."

I give it one more try. "Gabe must consider you a friend, because he told me he gave you something to keep for him."

"Musta' been some other body."

"Okay, Sonny. Have it your way. Let me know if your memory improves." In the bottom of my purse I find one of the old business cards that I keep forgetting to throw away and scribble my New York number on it. Sonny takes the card and makes a show of stuffing it in his shirt pocket. "You people gotta stop buggin' me."

I walk over to a pay phone, cursing the Parks Department for installing it next to the men's room. Sonny's laughter follows. "That ringer hasn't worked since the President's daddy was president.

Don't you have a cell?" I wish I did, but I cut back on all unnecessary expenses when I quit this screwball profession.

I leave the park and walk two blocks before finding another phone in front of the Boys and Girls Club. I flip through the war torn pages of the thick book chained to the kiosk and punch in the number I want. The precinct operator connects me.

"Homicide. Lieutenant Saleh speaking."

"This is Jo Epstein. I'm an investigator working for Silas Harding, and I'd like to talk with you about the Gabriel Johnson case. I'll take no more than ten minutes of your time."

"Have Silas call me." Click.

It infuriates me, but there it is: the typical "fuck you, everybody's a criminal unless they can prove otherwise" cop attitude. Well, I'm not going to let him obstruct this investigation. That is, if I can come up with four more quarters for this stinking pay phone. Looking around for a store where I can get some change, I see a run down van parked across the street, day-glo cones and sundaes painted haphazardly all over its mustard yellow sides—easily the funkiest ice-cream truck in the city. I buy a Nutty Buddy—seems like the safest bet with the least food coloring—and get my change from the five in quarters.

Back at the pay phone, the late afternoon sun has me sweating, and it gets worse when Silas Harding's voice mail picks up on the first ring. This means that someone—probably him—is in the office and on the phone. It also means that if I call back too soon, I'll loose two more quarters. I take a leisurely ten minutes to eat the ice cream cone and try again.

"Harding here," he says.

"It's Jo Epstein," I reply. "I'm five minutes from the precinct but that cop from the Bronx you referred me to is giving me a hard time. Wants you to call him to verify that I'm worthy of his precious time."

"No problem, Jo. You can head over there right now. I'll take care of it."

The teens are still hanging out at the train station and this time I get a tentative smile from one of the girls. I ride one stop and walk two short blocks to the precinct, which is squeezed in between the

Hard as Nails salon and *Jessie's Barbecue*. My own nails could use a trim, and my stomach is growling.

Lieutenant Saleh keeps me on a bench in the hallway for an hour before inviting me into his microscopic office on the second floor. The décor is a testimony to the versatility of gray metal—the desk, the chairs, even the picture frame showing off his kids—all have the same dull sheen. His suit, however, is a dark maroon, set off by a mustard yellow tie. I stand awkwardly in front of his desk as he shuffles through some papers. His eyebrows are delicate, above wide almond eyes, but his broad cheekbones and square shoulders give him a solid look.

Without glancing up, he says, "I owe Silas Harding a favor, and it seems you're it. What can I do for you?"

I can see he's going to be a pleasure to work with. "There seem to be some unanswered questions about the Johnson case."

"Really?" His tone clearly says that talking about a closed case goes against his grain. Like most cops, he thinks he's infallible, and in spite of what he said about owing Silas a favor, he won't hesitate to throw me out. A weak hand is better than none, so I play it. "Are you related to Khurram Saleh?"

The Lieutenant finally looks up.

"That's none of your business." He pauses, and I wait for the other shoe to drop. "It's the Johnson case you're here to talk about. Let's get this over with, shall we?" he says, crisp as a Pringle. Then he walks over to the hotplate in the corner and offers me peppermint tea in a styrofoam cup. "We only drink overcooked coffee on TV shows," he says, rolling a chair across the floor. "Have a seat."

"Did you interview any witnesses at the scene?" I ask, thinking of Sonny Rodriguez. I sip my tea, trying not to show my amazement that Saleh has added some honey.

"We cover all the bases. What makes you think we've overlooked something on this one?" He runs his fingers through his dark, razor cut hair as if expecting it to be longer.

"It never hurts to be sure."

"Did we catch him on the scene with blood on his hands? Yes.

14

Were his fingerprints on the knife? Yes."

"Gabriel says he was jacked by the Scorpions, that he grabbed the knife from one of them and used it in self-defense. I have a potential witness, but he's too scared to talk."

"Or he's stringing you along."

"Mr. Johnson also said that his social worker, Leslie Corning, has been trying to verify his story."

"She came in here with some half-baked ideas, but as I'm sure you know, one foot isn't enough to walk with."

"Maybe so, but self-defense isn't manslaughter."

Saleh glares at me and starts pecking at his computer keyboard. When he looks up, there's a smile on his face, and it's not a pleasant one.

"According to the DOCS database, Leslie Corning posted Gabriel Johnson's bail this morning. Two hundred thousand, the whole amount in cash, not the usual ten percent. Last I heard, social workers didn't make that kind of money. She must be sweet on this guy."

Before I can waste any more of Saleh's time, I find myself on the street, nursing a cold cup of tea and a bruised ego. One day on this case and already I'm feeling like a yo-yo, walking the dog to nowhere. I flag down a gypsy cab that's defiantly cruising for passengers near the police station. There's no irksome meter involved, just a flat fee of $15 paid to the Sikh driver. Although she's paying my expenses, I don't want to bill Shondrea for any more than I have to.

* * *

Saturday night, and another busy shift goes by at the newsstand with little time to think about the Johnson case. We have a small section of literary magazines and during a lull I copy down some editorial addresses. I submit my poems occasionally and every now and then one gets published.

At home after midnight, I relax and talk to Ellie-the-ghost about the day's events while soaking in the tub. I got in the habit of chatting with her shortly after I moved in here. The landlord never told me her name, so I came up with one myself. Some people might think it strange, talking to a dead person in the room where

15

she took her own life, but conversing with Ellie seems like the most natural thing in the world. She's a great listener and since she never objects, what I say always goes.

Improve your English
do not lean on the door
turn your dreams into reality—register now!
meet thousands of other singles
subway ads
enlivening the tunnels
with debt solutions for a better life

Chapter Two

On Sunday afternoon I make a long overdue visit to Mom. Car service would be faster, but the D-train suits my budget and I use the time to collect my thoughts on the way to Brooklyn. Seems like all those years doing homework on the subway still have me convinced that I need the sound of rumbling wheels, squeaky brakes, and the congested breathing of densely packed commuters to reach my deepest levels of concentration. Buses, trains—name anything that moves and chances are I've written a poem or pondered a case while riding on it.

I stop in at Luigi's for a slice of pizza, happy to see that he's still in business. When I moved back here from Los Angeles in the late '90s, the Cyrillic alphabet was just beginning to dominate the storefronts in this neighborhood, a few miles north of Brighton Beach. Today the only remaining sign in English is *Luigi's Ristorante*, which technically is in Italian. Go figure.

At Luigi's the customers eat standing, belly up to the counter. I spill enough tomato sauce on my blouse to attract the attention of the fashionably dressed Russian woman next to me, and she looks over with amused disdain. This must be one of the women that Mom talks about, the fashion plates who stir up the shoppers at the Stop 'n Shop by wearing their mink coats in the check out line while purchasing tuna fish with food stamps. "Nikolai says that in Russia it's so cold that even the poor people have fur coats," is Mom's take on this.

She's always had a soft spot for Russians. So much so that

she named me Jo when she still had the hots for Stalin. She couldn't believe he was a mass murderer, not until she fell in love with an émigré musician who claimed to have conducted for the Kirov ballet. Nikolai lost his entire family, all purged from the pure body of Soviet Russia. He's also the jealous type and refuses to acknowledge that my father ever existed. Probably thinks I sprang like Athena from the head of Zeus.

Halfway down East 15th Street I'm assaulted by the abrasive sound of heavy sandblasting, accompanied by loud Cuban music. Peering upwards through a cloud of dust, I see the silhouettes of two workmen in gas masks. Confidently perched on a scaffold suspended from the roof, they're strafing the red bricks of the 5-story building where Mom has lived for thirteen years.

I take the stairs to 5H and ring the bell. By the time she unbolts the three locks drilled into the battered door, I've put my backpack down on the pink checkered tiles of the hallway floor and am considering doing my nails. Mom's overjoyed to see me, and I try to focus on the brightness in her pale blue eyes instead of whatever new signs of aging have appeared.

"What's that on your blouse, honey? Is it blood?"

I head for the bathroom to remove the offending stain, but Mom cuts me off. "Here, see if this fits." The sleeveless tailored shirt is bright pink, my least favorite color, but I put it on. It's strange how clothes take on a wearer's identity. Wearing Mom's blouse feels like slipping into her skin.

In the kitchen I pour myself a glass of much needed water and Mom tells me that Nikolai, who usually does the shopping, is out of town and the cupboards are bare. Given that the windows are vibrating with noise from the sandblasters and the air is full of questionable particles, I'm happy to take her over to Avenue M to do some shopping.

Like most elderly women in the neighborhood, Mom uses her shopping wagon as a combination grocery cart and walker. When I remind her of the cane that the hospital provided after she broke her hip last year, her gentle blue eyes turn gray and flinty and she indignantly exclaims "I'm not a little old lady!" What she means is that canes are for the vulnerable, marking their users as

18

ripe for robbery.

During our slow crawl around the neighborhood, Mom points out the new restaurants that have opened and praises the architecture of her favorite churches, as if this were the first and not the hundredth time we've taken this walk. We fill up the wagon with canned junk and frozen food dinners that she loves to eat when Nikolai isn't around to cook for her. On the way back, we stop at a used bookstore, and she lets me buy her a copy of *The Good Terrorist* by Doris Lessing. The sardonic nature of the title, given current events, isn't lost on either of us.

By the time we get back, the sandblasters have gone. In the only bedroom of the apartment, which also doubles as an art studio, Mom shows me her latest paintings, pulling them one by one from a tall stack balanced atop the ironing board. Some are neatly matted, but most of them need work. There's one piece—a lone, hooded figure walking on Rockaway Beach with vigorous waves pounding the shore and monolithic buildings rising in the background—that I particularly like. "Maybe I should redo this, make it a night scene, add a full moon," she says. I tell her I love the picture the way it is. Mom took up painting in her 70's, and she swings between the surreal and the ordinary with ease. My favorite is the series of acrobats, dressed in orange and brown, suspended in space.

I help her return the canvases to their precarious perch on the ironing board. "Why don't you put some of these up on the wall?" I ask.

She looks around the stark bedroom and smiles. "Nikolai thinks he's an art critic. Whatever I choose to put up, he'll want something different." I know better than to question their unique relationship.

"Written any poems lately?" she asks.

"Actually I've taken on a case, a mother trying to help her son beat a manslaughter charge."

"Hmmm," she says. Vocations other than the artistic have always been dismissed by Mom as irrelevant. Maybe she's right. "I think you got your love of words from Derek," she says. "Did you know he wrote short stories?"

When Nikolai isn't home my father's name has a way of

cropping up in conversation. "He let me read the one about the super who goes crazy and torches the garbage at the bottom of the dumbwaiter shaft." Mom looks wistful. "Sometimes I think that you became a detective so you could search for him."

I swallow my reply. It's not a question of where my father is, but of why he doesn't want to be found.

Soon it's time for dinner. It always amazes me how fast time flies here, given the agonizingly slow pace of my mother's movements. I cook up some spaghetti with marinara sauce and fresh asparagus on the side. Afterwards, we stay up late, munching on sardines and crackers while drinking Merlot, exchanging chit-chat, catching up on things. I'm happy that we're staying on the surface. Since I moved back to New York, after my second divorce four years ago, every visit with Mom has included a quarrel about my bad taste in men. Tonight's different.

Maybe it's because she's a bit tipsy from her second glass of wine, but when the subject comes up, she says, "If I'd been a better role model you'd have acted differently." I vehemently deny this, but at the same time recognize a grain of truth—Mom's been married three times. Before she can fall asleep in the lazy boy, I guide her to bed.

With Nikolai gone, I can camp out in the living room and hang my rinsed out underwear in the bathroom without embarrassment. Fire engines erupt periodically, the station being two blocks away, so sleep is intermittent.

In the morning I try not to make a face at the instant coffee Mom insists on brewing with hot tap water and flavoring with non-dairy creamer. Like the cane, the paper filters and French roast coffee I gave her will never be used. When she starts making noises about cooking us breakfast, I put my foot down and tell her I'm taking us out. She may be a fine water colorist, but when Mom steps into the kitchen all creativity is abandoned. So much for the stereotypical Jewish mother. It's a good thing she raised me to prefer fresh ideas to fresh bagels.

When we get back from breakfasting at what I'm sure must be the only Kosher-Brazilian restaurant in New York City, I call Shondrea Johnson. No word from Gabriel, and she's astounded when I tell her that his social worker posted his bail. I tell her that I'll stop off at New Beginnings to see if Leslie Corning can tell me where Gabe is.

* * *

At the height of the Monday morning rush, it takes more than an hour for the Q train to crawl from South Brooklyn to Manhattan's Lower East Side, also known as Losaida. The train slows down while crossing the Manhattan Bridge, and some of the passengers sitting on the left side twist their heads to look out the windows at the empty space where the Twin Towers once stood. I make eye contact with one of them, a Hispanic in a business suit, and we share a quiet moment before he goes back to his newspaper.

The train descends into the blackness of reverberating tunnels, taking me back to the days when I was fresh out of high school and commuted to a job as a clerk-typist at a big publishing house. I don't know which I hated more, the job or the train ride. Some mornings I'd sleep late and dream that I was already packed into a crowded subway car, with all the usual elbows, hips and other body parts pressing against me. It was no fun waking up and realizing that the whole miserable journey was still to come and would end, as usual, with me arriving at work drenched in multiple brands of cologne and deodorant, all supplied by other people.

I get off at Cooper Union Station and walk east, past the historic brown building where Abraham Lincoln gave the "Right Makes Might" speech that got him elected.

These days, when I visit the East Village, I miss the smell of borscht and pirogues with onions that used to greet me on my youthful excursions in search of marijuana and entertainment. Like everyone else, the folks here are getting used to drinking espresso from cups with corporate logos. Sad to think that on East 6th Street there will be no dancing at the Polish Social Hall tonight.

The storefront windows of New Beginnings are covered with spray painted slogans and could use a good wash. On the other hand, maybe the staff likes to see *Guns Don't Kill, Multinationals*

21

Do every time they walk through the door. Inside, I hear a chorus of voices rising above the partitions that divide the large space into cubicles.

"So you're interested in getting a GED?"

"Lady, I need a job, not a piece 'a paper.'"

"How long have you been out?"

There's a small reception area, a silver-haired pixie on duty behind the desk. "Can I help you?"

"I'm looking for Leslie Corning."

"Sorry, she's not here. Hasn't been for a week or so. Maybe Daniel knows where she is." She points towards the back of the room, and I walk in that direction. An open door, covered with cracked varnish and marked "Director," leads into a dingy office with jaundice-yellow walls. A man stands with his back to me, his dirty blond ponytail streaked with gray, one foot on a desk chair near the blackboard. "Okay, I'll see you at ten," he says, before hanging up the phone.

I knock on the door jamb to get his attention. The 40-something face he turns towards me is thin and sun-baked, more the wizened farmer than the social worker. He walks over, his hand extended, and looks up at me, half a head shorter than my five-nine. His grip is firm when we shake, followed by a slight squeeze. "Daniel Rose. Can I help you?"

"Jo Epstein. I'm a private investigator. I need to speak to one of your interns, Leslie Corning, about one of her clients, Gabriel Johnson. Can you tell me where I can find her?"

"Not likely, given the confidentiality regs, as well as the fact that Leslie flew the coop last week with no notice. I'm trying to line up a replacement, and I can tell you, it's not easy."

"So it's a tough gig working here?"

"The staff has a high burnout rate—fact of life—but I should have known better than to hire someone from Beverly Hills. Leslie's father is a well-known movie producer. She's probably sulking on an airplane right now, on her way back to California."

"She may not be flying solo," I inform him. "Leslie posted Gabriel's bail on Saturday. I visited him at Rikers on Saturday, just a few hours before he was sprung. It's strange. He didn't say a word about making bail."

He frowns, the concerned professional, picks up a pencil, looks like he'd like to chew on it, then puts it back on the desk.

"This is not good news. I make a point of keeping tabs on all our clients, and, from what I've heard, Gabriel would be a lot safer on the inside, where the Scorpions don't have any push. He killed one of their own."

"Then why would Leslie put him on the street and make him a target?"

"She's as hip to his world as an angora cat doing research on life in the dog pound."

"Mind if I see where she worked?"

"Suit yourself." Daniel ushers me into one of the smaller cubicles and leaves me to it. The thin partitions offer no real privacy but after the close quarters of prison, the people who come here probably find them an adequate illusion. Seated in Leslie's chair, I envisage a seasoned ex-con dying for a smoke and smirking at me while I tell him to get a high school equivalency degree, land a minimum wage job and stay off drugs. Climbed Mt. Everest lately?

Leslie's desk is crammed in between a small bookcase and a filing cabinet, leaving just enough space for two chairs. A framed photograph of a boy riding a bicycle leaps off the cubicle wall, a vivid street scene, worth a second look. Is it Gabriel's work? I search the drawers, finding the usual office supplies, government forms, a nail file and some high-priced fabric samples looking out of their element. The desktop calendar pages are blank. If she's like me, she carries a day-timer in her purse. A photo is taped to the top of her computer monitor. Carefully, I pull it free.

Against a background of bare cinderblocks, Leslie's toffee colored face is framed by a halo of micro braids. Even in the dim light her brown skin radiates a healthy glow. Seated at a desk, her fingers on the keys of a laptop computer, she looks up at Gabriel. Her expression says she thinks highly of this thickset young man. Dressed in brown slacks and a green plaid shirt, he looks like

23

an up-and-coming college student.

I hit the redial button on Leslie's phone and after two rings get a recorded greeting. "Alicia here. At the tone, you're on." The voice is young and flippant. I jot down the number glowing on the display screen just as Daniel squeezes himself into the other chair, rotating his shoulders, as if demonstrating he knows how to relax. "I would have done that myself, but I respect people's privacy."

"Then you must be glad there are people like me around when you need information."

His response is drowned out by a screeching disembodied voice. "Daniel! I'm in your office, right on time, but where the fuck are you?"

Laughter emanates from several cubicles nearby, and Daniel jumps to his feet, eager to placate this person before further embarrassment occurs. I follow, out of curiosity and because the loud, nagging voice is disconcertingly familiar.

In Daniel's office, a woman struggles out of the over-stuffed visitor's chair and wobbles to her feet. Why is it that just when you think the past is safely on the shelf, like a hastily read pot-boiler you'd rather forget, up pops a sequel? Dressed in flowered overalls and an overflowing blue tank top that she's probably owned since puberty, Gloria Kelly exhibits minimal changes since college. The sandy hair I remember is dyed jet black and her arms are thicker above the elbows, but her bangs still need a trim to keep them out of her green eyes. At the sight of me, she raises her eyebrows like a quizzical clown. "Jo! I can't believe it!"

These five words break a mutual silence of—could it be twenty-two years?—that began on the day she vowed never to talk to me again. I didn't blame her at the time. I had stolen Zachary, her boyfriend, and what's worse, married him. The guilt lasted longer than the marriage.

"I'll understand if you're still not talking to me."

Gloria waves her hands in denial, her silver and turquoise jewelry flashing. "Nonsense. We're not children anymore." True. Time has marked us as day old bread and turned Gloria, who once parked herself atop the campus flag pole to get a headcount during demonstrations, into a middle-aged woman.

"So…you work here?"

"I volunteer, two mornings a week. They call it counseling, but it's more like bandages for brain tumors. They don't need therapy. They need jobs. Are you still gum-shoeing?"

"Yes and no. When it's yes, I freelance."

"So it's business that brings you here."

"I've been retained by Gabriel Johnson's mother."

"What a tragedy."

"I'm not that bad of a detective."

Gloria sniffs derisively. "I was referring to Gabriel. He was looking at a bright future as a photographer."

"You make it sound like all hope is lost."

"Fifteen years to life isn't a scholarship to NYU." As I recall, that's where she did her graduate studies.

"Any idea why Leslie Corning would post his bail?"

"What a sucker. Probably bought his hard luck story. Leslie was a spoiled brat, and we're better off without her." Her voice is harsh, more brittle than I remember. She turns to Daniel. "We'd better get on with our meeting. I don't have much time, and I can't keep them waiting, not the ones who pay by the hour." Then, talking over her shoulder, "Jo, let's do lunch sometime." The casual rudeness is new, too.

"I'll walk you out," says Daniel, ignoring Gloria's annoyed "Tch!"

On our way to the front door, we encounter a tall spider of a man with an athletic build. His curly black hair is paired with a goatee. "Jo, this is Sal Salvatore. He runs our drug rehab program upstate." In spite of the sweltering heat, Sal is impeccable in an expensive looking light-weight business suit. He takes my hand, like he's about to kiss it, then changes his mind in what appears to be a fit of political correctness. We both find this funny.

Sal turns to Daniel. "I need to talk to you."

I walk ahead, intending to give them some privacy, but can't help staying within earshot. "We've got an audit coming up, Daniel. It's important we look at the books together."

"No problem," I hear Daniel say, "just take a number, and I'll be right with you."

He catches up to me. "Sorry about that."

"Can you give me Leslie's phone number and address?"

"Try the phone book. If she's not listed, I can't help you."

"If she helps Gabriel skip, she'll be out a lot of money."

"They say girls in Beverly Hills like expensive toys." For a social worker, he's quicker to judgment than a cop on steroids.

"Why did you take her on as an intern, if she's so hopeless?"

"Her father is a friend of Sal's. When she heard about the program, she wouldn't take no for an answer."

I agree to keep Daniel posted and, five minutes later, I'm in a taxi, courtesy of my client, headed for the Upper West Side. Through blasts of static on the radio, a woman complains about the latest increase in subway fare.

flesh blends with the earth
when parted from the soul
thought continues its flicker
from pole to pole

Chapter Three

I fix a peanut butter sandwich and wash it down with apple juice
before calling Silas Harding. "Are you aware that Gabriel Johnson
was bailed out on Saturday by Leslie Corning? That she's an intern
at New Beginnings?" No hesitation in his answer to the negative.

"At Rikers, your client asked me to tell you he was ready to
trade some information to make a deal. Has he contacted you since
his release?" Again the monosyllabic response.

"Leslie's phone number is unlisted, but I've got a lead on
one of her friends who might know where she and Gabriel
went."

This information jars some words out of Silas. "Gabe is
pretty smart," he says. "He knows better than to leave town. I'll
call Shondrea and see if she's heard from him."

A minute later I'm into my running shoes, loping down
the stairs. Waves of heat wash over me on the sixteen block
jog, trailing me as I hustle up the steps to the library on West 100th.

Using her phone number, it's a cinch to find Alicia's upper East
Side address in the reverse directory. After jotting down this
information, I decide to indulge a long standing curiosity about what
went down in my apartment four years ago, when the woman I call
Ellie took her own life. I search the *Daily News* archives and up
comes a 1999 article entitled *Teacher's Death Ruled Suicide*.

"A kindergarten teacher reported missing last week was
found dead Thursday of an apparent suicide. According to
police sources, Beverly Ellis failed to show up to teach her
kindergarten class at P.S. 78 in Manhattan. The school secre-
tary reported that Ms. Ellis never failed to request a substitute
when she was ill or needed a personal day off. After one of her
co-workers failed to gain access to her apartment, he decided

to call the authorities. Ms. Ellis' body was found in the bathtub
of her Upper West Side apartment. She died of a suspected
drug overdose. An autopsy is pending."

I search the obits and find that Beverly Ellis was born in
Cincinnati and survived by a sister, Chloe Sterling of Hoboken,
New Jersey. Although not a superstitious person, I feel a definite
chill while writing down these names on a miniscule slip of library
paper. Ellis is just one letter apart from Ellie—how did my subconscious make this connection? No matter. The world is full of hap-
penstance; otherwise, how could psychics make a living? Maybe I'll
give Chloe Sterling a call and offer my condolences. Or maybe not.
Do I really want her to know that I have lengthy, one-sided conversations with the ghost of her departed sister?

Back home, I change into my own version of suitable East
Side attire—black pumps, a short denim skirt with embroidered
patches and a yellow blouse. I catch the cross town bus, which cuts
through Central Park on 86th Street, just north of the Great Lawn—
scene of many picnics with my father in the days when we fre-
quented the Delacorte Theater. At ten I was too young to appreciate the soliloquies, but I can still taste the disappointment I felt when
King Richard offered his kingdom for a horse and neither of the pair
of mounted policemen in attendance chose to seize the chance of a
lifetime.

A short time later, I'm climbing the front steps of a three-
story brownstone. The first floor windowsills are crowded with
pots of well-tended purple and yellow pansies. I press the bell
and a perky "Who's there?" leaps out of the intercom. "I'm
looking for Leslie," I say, and there's a long silence before the now
less than enthusiastic voice replies, "Third floor," and buzzes me in.

The stairs are creaky in spite of the thick carpeting. The smell
of fresh paint and the unmistakable sound of Brazilian music
(Caetano Veloso singing *Um Tom*) both grow stronger as I climb.
Alicia waits on the landing, barefoot, jeans and a fuchsia T-shirt
covering her thin frame, topped by an elfin face with dark eyebrows
and short neon green hair. Add my crimson curls and we're a
Christmas tree. She's plainly worried. "Have you seen Leslie?" she
asks me. "Is she staying with you?" Not a good sign.

The upscale apartment was probably a maid's room when the house was first built and is now retrofitted for young professionals who serve the rich in other ways. Sunlight pours in from two floor-to-ceiling windows, warming the sage green walls and the white satin sofa with matching overstuffed armchair. The doors to the bathroom and bedroom are closed.

"I need to talk to Leslie about one of her clients, Gabriel Johnson. His mother hired me to try to clear him of a manslaughter charge. On Saturday, Leslie posted bail for Gabriel. Do you have any idea where they are?"

"Have you tried calling her apartment?"

"Her employer wouldn't give out the information, so I used the redial on her office phone and got your number."

"I think that's very clever," she says, scribbling an address on the back of a blue envelope and handing it to me. It smells of lilacs.

"How did you and Leslie meet?"

Alicia motions me towards the puffed up armchair, and I resist the urge to check my skirt for dirt particles before sitting on the pristine white cushion. She sits on the couch and leans towards me.

"I'm an interior decorator at *The House of Art* on Lexington." The words come out in a husky, conversational whisper that I assume she uses to good effect at the store.

"Leslie came in to buy slipcovers for a loveseat she was fixing up. I could see she had an eye for fabric. We talked about mixing up antiques and modern, whether or not to use textured wallpaper, things like that. She ended up inviting me to her place for dinner. I'm not one to make friends with customers. I mean they're usually just looking for free advice, but I could see that Leslie was lonely."

"So you started hanging out together."

Alicia pops up and shuttles a small Chinese bowl from the coffee table to the top of the bookcase; it looked fine where it was to me. When she sits down again, she continues her story, while I try to guess which part of it she was adjusting while moving the porcelain.

"It was difficult for Leslie, living alone in New York after growing up in Southern California. We usually met on Sundays for a movie matinee or lunch in the park. Then last week, I think it was Monday night, she called me in a panic. She said she needed a place to stay, that her boyfriend was hounding her after she broke up with him. I told her to come right over, but she never showed. When I couldn't reach her on the phone, I thought maybe she'd left town for a while."

"Did you ever meet her boyfriend?"

"No. It created some tension between us. I mean, how could she act like I was her best friend and not even tell me about him? I asked her if he was married or was a rock star, and she just laughed it off. Of course, when he gave her trouble, I was the first person she came to. Except she didn't. She never arrived. Maybe she didn't trust me to help her out. All those upper class twits she went to school with, they were a bunch of back stabbers, raised to keep an eye out for number one. If you ask me, that's why she went into social work. To spite them."

I give Alicia my number to call, day or night, if she hears from Leslie or gets any ideas about where she might be. With her hand on the doorknob, ready to let me out, she tells me to wait while she opens a small drawer in a refinished antique desk. "Leslie gave me a spare key to her apartment. I think you should have it until she turns up. I hope she's not mad at me for giving it to you." Along with the key, she hands me a yellow sticky note on which she's written Leslie's address.

Leaving her self-consciously elegant apartment, packed with African art, Victorian furniture and '50s kitsch, it occurs to me that Alicia, and not Leslie, might be the lonely one.

I'm way overdressed for work, but there's no time to go home and change into my usual outfit of sneakers and jeans. Munching on a hotdog, I decide to walk back through the Park, forgetting that I'm wearing heels. Halfway across the meadow a stinging blister on my left little toe reminds me. When I get to the newsstand just before six, Shondrea is waiting inside.

"I've been looking at this thing for half an hour, and I haven't read a single word." She puts the copy of Vogue back on the rack.

"Silas told me that Gabriel's out of jail, so why hasn't he called me? He wouldn't worry me this way, that's one thing I'm sure of."

"I can go over to Leslie's apartment after work and see if Gabe is there. A friend of hers gave me the key."

"Do you want me to go with you?"

"That's okay. I'll give you a call when I get home and let you know how it goes."

"Don't worry about waking me. I don't sleep much these days."

Shondrea leaves just as Ted comes in, and he lays on the sarcasm. "At it again, are we? What some writers won't do to avoid the blank page."

* * *

The cab drops me off at Leslie's yellow brick apartment building on East 21st, just one block from Gramercy Park. A private refuge, the park is owned by the residents of the surrounding square and few New Yorkers enjoy the privilege of opening its locked gate. In the 1920s, the residents of Irving Place threw wild parties, causing Ethyl Barrymore to say, "I went there in the evening a young girl and came away in the morning an old woman."

I'm sure Alicia would agree that whoever decorated the lobby of Leslie's building lacks a discriminating eye. The clashing tones of the peach and gold stiff-backed chairs seem designed to discourage any inclinations to make yourself comfortable. In spite of the heavy bag of Purina under my arm, the doorman, who has a distinct Cockney accent, is skeptical but resigned when I tell him that Leslie asked me to feed her cat. I take the elevator to the third floor, wondering if the gaudy wall covering has ever actually attacked a passenger.

As soon as I open the door to 3C, I have to remind myself that Leslie has no cat, and that even if she did, no feline—no matter how neglected—could emit a smell like this. I back up and take a deep breath of relatively fresh air in the hallway before gathering enough courage to enter the apartment. One corner of the dark living room is softly illuminated by a gurgling fish tank, tinged green with algae. I flip the switch near the door and two couch-side lamps light up. Walking through, I get a quick impression of inexpensive but stylish furniture. Several bookcases are filled to overflowing, but this is no time to sample Leslie's reading habits.

On the bedroom's threshold, the appalling smell gets stronger, in spite of the open window with its curtains billowing in the summer breeze. The wall switch doesn't work, but I can make out a lamp on the bedside table and slowly make my way towards it. I stumble over something on the floor and carefully walk around it, already suspecting what it might be.

With a click, the lamplight reveals Gabriel sprawled on the floor next to a dark stain on the bright red carpet. He's fully dressed, and there's a bloody gash in his shirt directly above his heart. The detached part of me makes a note to look around for the knife that made it. Then my un-numbed senses kick in with a rush of heart-pounding adrenaline.

The walls, covered with graffiti, scream in undecipherable defiance. The window gate is open, and I climb onto the fire escape, gulping in fresh air, clutching the railing. Below me, treetops in the back yard sway in the slight breeze, oblivious to the violence perpetrated above them. On the platform, a canvas beach chair and a towel hint at better days. A glint of metal in the corner catches my eye. Pulling a pencil from my purse, I use it to retrieve the chain, which is attached to a miniature replica of the Empire State Building and a small key. I insert the key into the padlock on the outside of the window gate and it turns with a smooth click. I know I should leave this evidence where it is, but on impulse I place the key chain my pocket. How easily years of training can go down the drain.

I force myself to re-enter the bedroom, knowing I have only this one chance to investigate before the police secure the scene. I'm calmer than I'd expect, but all my experiences tracking deadbeat dads and scam artists haven't prepared me for the ugliness of violent death. This is my first murder victim, my first corpse.

Minus the energy of life, it's impossible to tell if Gabriel's eyes were expressing fear, surprise, or acceptance before he died. He had made some bad choices, but I don't think he'd chosen to be bad. He'd been concerned about Leslie and touched by her concern for him. *Gabriel, I'm going to find out who did this.*

I give myself three more minutes, hoping the doorman's memory isn't that sharp and the police won't notice the time lag between my arrival and the call I'll make when I finish searching the apartment.

If Leslie's into jewelry, she's wearing all of it on her person. There are no velvet boxes or earring stands on the dresser. Judging from the scarcity of clothes on the hangers in the walk-in closet and the large number of textile samples on the shelves, it looks like she cares more about decorating her living space than adorning herself. In this neat-as-a-pin environment, the unmade bed stands out. Maybe the rumpled sheets and blankets signify that Leslie and Gabriel were more than friends.

The fridge in the kitchen is as poorly stocked as my own. The only sign of indulgence is a half empty bottle of plum wine from a New York State winery that I've never heard of. The trash is loaded with non-fat, plain yogurt containers. In the cabinet above the stove, some spaghetti sauce jars are filled with white rice and yellow lentils. I bury my hand in a tin of flour, but my fingers come up empty. If it's still here, the murder weapon has eluded me.

In the top drawer of a small desk in the living room, I find two airplane tickets for the Saturday night redeye to San Francisco on United Airlines. There's one for Leslie and one for Gabriel. Two empty seats. One passenger dead and the other missing. My three minutes are up. It's time to call the cops.

Your first picture
taken with an instamatic
from the window in the attic
into the frame came a blurred bicycle wheel
no big deal, until you saw the silhouetted face
above the handle bars
racing against the stars

Chapter Four

It's 1 a.m., and Lieutenant Saleh has arrived on the already crowd-ed scene, summoned by one of the two detectives from the nearby Chelsea precinct—one male, one female, both red-eyed and tail-dragging tired—who responded to my call.

Detective Aimes wears her thick dirty blonde hair cut short and slowly paces the apartment as if modeling her uniform on a fashion runway. She and her rotund partner, Detective Jackson, questioned me at length about how I got into the apartment and my involvement in the case before agreeing to call the Lieutenant to check out my story.

"Yes, sir, forensics is sending someone. No, we won't collect any evidence until you get here." He hangs up the phone, directing a wry, "wouldn't you know it" grin at Aimes. They're obviously not happy about having to turn the case over to a Lieutenant from the Bronx.

Saleh takes charge as soon as he walks through the door, assigning each detective a room to search. Then he turns to me. "The doorman works nights—there's no day shift—and he doesn't remember anyone who looked like Gabriel entering the building over the weekend. You, he recalls, as a bit unsavory."

A pair of men in black vinyl coveralls wheel a stretcher through the front door and disappear into the bedroom, one of them carrying a body bag. A few minutes later, they make the return trip, with Gabriel on board on his way to the morgue. The forensic technician, covered from head to toe in white, starts to report to Detective Aimes but is sent over to Saleh. He pulls off his hair net before speaking. "One traumatic knife wound to the chest. He struggled—that much is obvious. I'll tell you more in a few hours."

Detective Jackson emerges from the bedroom. "No sign of forced entry, sir. The window gate was open, but we haven't found the key." The key that's burning a hole in my pocket. The key that I can't give up now without losing whatever minimal stature I have in the Lieutenant's eyes. Before he can notice my discomfort, Detective Aimes walks over, grace personified, and hands him the plane tickets that I wisely left in place in the desk drawer.

As Saleh examines the tickets, I venture an opinion. "It looks like the plan was for Leslie to bail out Gabriel in time for them to catch a flight to California."

He nods in agreement but doesn't answer until Aimes has resumed her search of the living room, out of earshot. "I've put out an APB. We need to find her as soon as possible. We also need to talk to the man you say witnessed the attack on Gabriel in the Bronx."

"You weren't so interested in him on Saturday."

Lieutenant Saleh bristles. "I know I should have followed through on the information you gave me, Ms. Epstein, but at that time we thought Mr. Johnson was alive. Not that it's your concern, but I've been working overtime on thirteen other cases."

So he is man enough to admit his mistake.

Saleh instructs Aimes to call on Mrs. Johnson and break the news of her son's death. I'm grateful it won't be me. I'll need some time to work through my remorse at not having found her son sooner, and alive.

The Lieutenant turns back to me. "Jackson told me you have a key."

For a second I'm wondering how the hell Jackson knows I found the key to the window gate, and then I realize he's talking about the key to Leslie's apartment. I dig into my purse and hand it over. Saleh's giving me a curious stare but doesn't pursue it. He's got more important things on his mind. "Dwight Davis, the banger that Gabriel killed, was a hard core Scorpion, and from the looks of the wall decorations left behind, this was a gang execution. I can understand why your witness is keeping his head down, but the guys in the gang unit need to bring him in."

In our game of give and take, he's making it clear that it's my turn to give. "His name is Sonny Rodriguez, and he likes to watch the chess games in Crotona Park. Try not to lean on him too hard, or he'll clam up for good."

"Thanks for your cooperation, Ms. Epstein."

"Please, call me Jo."

"As you wish."

"You're not going to ask me to call you Hasim, are you?"

His throaty laugh makes the technicians turn their heads in disapproval. "I'm waiting to see how helpful you'll be. Even the hand of compassion is stung when it strokes a tarantula." He catches my skeptical expression, "Not the cop shop banter you're used to? Sorry to disappoint."

The man's got hidden depth.

* * *

I'm so tired my eyelids ache, but more in need of a bath than sleep. The candlelight calms me and tense muscles relax. Washing my hair with aromatic green tea shampoo, I discuss the case with Ellie, aka Beverly, confiding that not only have I broken my latest vow to abstain from detective work, I've stumbled into my first murder investigation.

Hell, maybe you've already met the victim in the afterlife, or wherever you are. Gabriel Johnson, one more young Black male arriving in a body bag. Except that before he became a murder statistic, someone named Leslie believed in him enough to risk her own neck. Which is more than anyone did for you, isn't it? What was it, I wonder, that was so painful that it couldn't be balanced by daily contact with five-year-olds who still believed in Santa Claus?

As if trying to answer, the dying candles flicker and sputter, creating shadows on the damp tiles before they go out.

* * *

On Tuesday morning, I wake up to a case that's gone from obscurity to national attention, thanks to the fame of Leslie's father. The press is selling paranoia, especially the *Daily News*,

36

which I borrow from my neighbor's doorstep while picking up my own *New York Times. Gang Invades Gramercy Park, Hollywood "Princess" Missing.* Leslie's the star. Gabriel's an extra, relegated to second and third paragraphs—*the victim was released on bail on Saturday and may have been trying to flee.*

I call New Beginnings and get Daniel Rose. "I was about to call you," he says. "The police have been here, looking for Leslie."

"Have you contacted her parents?"

"Gloria's working on it."

"Mr. Rose, I need you to be straight with me. What was Gabriel up to?"

He answers after a slight pause, a professional giving his assessment. "According to Leslie, he was selling photographs, lots of them, and putting the money away in the bank so he could go back to school. Then he had the bad luck to tangle with a gang member. They have long memories and a mandate for taking revenge. End of story."

"Is that what I'm supposed to tell his mother? End of story? She deserves more of an explanation than that."

"Blame it on society or blame it on an individual, what difference does it make? He's dead. When you see Mrs. Johnson, please give her my condolences."

Give them to her yourself, is what I want to say, but I may need his future input. I settle for putting as much ice as I can into, "I'll be in touch," and hang up the phone, none too gently.

* * *

Approaching East Harlem in a taxi, I marvel that Gabriel would need to go to the Bronx to get into trouble when there's so much of it to be found in his own neighborhood. I'm wrong. The streets are clean, the local businesses thriving, and the red-brick apartment building where he lived with his mother is almost as well kept as the woman who answers the door on the fourth floor. The pastels are gone. She's dressed in black, with the exception of a simple white head wrap, her eyes shining wells of pain.

"I'm very sorry to disturb you at this time, Shondrea."

There's a barely perceptible nod of her head, as if she's

remembering who she is. "You'd better come inside."

The living room serves double duty as an art gallery, the deep gold walls almost entirely covered with black and white photographs. Scenes of street life captured by a discerning eye—girls jumping rope, a saxophone player serenading passersby, break dancers showing off their stuff in front of a hip-hop record store. Mrs. Johnson follows my eyes. "This was Gabriel's work. His calling."

"Your son was talented."

"Everybody said so." I wait as she composes herself. "He once told me that if people could only slow themselves down, they'd be able to appreciate life one frame at a time. He was a peaceable child. Never meant to hurt a soul. No drugs, except for that one party. Said he needed his eyes clear to take pictures."

She seats me on the couch and then slides a photo out from under a book on the coffee table. Leslie stands at a boat railing, her skirt blown tight against her legs. Behind her, a classic view of the downtown skyline, as seen from the Staten Island Ferry.

Shondrea sits down beside me. "She believed in him, even after he got in trouble again, and I appreciate that. But if Leslie had left well enough alone, Gabriel might still be alive."

"Maybe she had reason to think he wasn't safe at Rikers."

"Maybe so," she says, but then shakes her head to the negative. "The girl wasn't streetwise. Gabriel told me that." She takes the photo from me and examines it closely, as if looking for an answer. "I never met her face to face, but he talked to her on the phone all the time. She wanted him to learn computer skills so he could market his photographs on the Internet instead of selling them on the street."

"Did your son have a bank account, Mrs. Johnson?"

"His statement came yesterday. I put it in his room, on the dresser."

"Would you mind if I have a look? It could be important."

"No harm in that I suppose. His room is just down the hall."

There are no photographs on Gabriel's walls, instead a

diploma from Music and Art High School and a poster for Jazz at Lincoln Center. The single bed is neatly made up by a mother's hand. From the knotty pine dresser, I retrieve a business envelope that's buried under a pile of lenses, camera straps and empty film cans. The Chase Manhattan account is in the name of Gabriel Johnson aka Sharp Shots Photography. The current balance is $450.00, but five wire transfers, each in the amount of $8,400.00, came out of the account during the month of July. I put the envelope in my purse and make a quick return to the living room. No sense intruding further on Shondrea's grief by asking if I can search her son's room.

"May I take this with me? I'll be sure to make you a copy."

"I guess so. What good will it do him now?" She hands me a glass of water, which I gulp down gratefully.

"Maybe no good at all," I admit, "but it may help me to find Leslie, who has probably made some people angry by knowing more than she should."

Shondrea sinks into the cushions of an upholstered chair, all at once looking small and frail. "I know the girl meant well. If there's anything I can do to help, please let me know." To throw off the grip of despair and make an offer like this has to take a lot out of her. It's obvious she wants me to leave before she breaks down.

"I promise, you'll be the first to know when I find out what happened to your son."

"Bless you, child."

I walk down the stairs, thinking about all the times she must have said 'bless you child' to Gabriel, encouraging him to have faith in life and in himself. Words she still miraculously believes in. I admit that beneath my admiration there's a touch of envy. The two things I've tried the hardest to avoid throughout my life are hard drugs and religion.

* * *

I call Lieutenant Saleh from my apartment, and I share the gist of my visit with Gabriel's mother, including the irregular bank statement. In return, he tells me that the coroner is willing to say that

Gabriel died sometime on Saturday, but it will be a day or so before he's able to narrow down the time frame. "There's no sign of forced entry and no sign of the knife. We're questioning everyone in the building."

Since he appears to be in an expansive mood, I take a chance and ask the Lieutenant if he can get Mrs. Johnson's phone records for the day that Gabriel was attacked in the Bronx. To my surprise, he agrees. I'm not sure why he's decided to cooperate, but it's a boon I intend to enjoy while it lasts.

Saleh calls back two hours later, by which time I've eaten a tuna sandwich with some potato chips, paid a few of the colorful late notices from my stack of bills, and opened all my neglected junk mail. "Only two calls came in that morning," he says. "One from Leslie Corning's apartment, the other from a pay phone in Peekskill."

I remember what Shondrea told me. "Isn't there a drug rehab center up there?"

The pause tells me Saleh is running his computer through some paces. Then he's back on the line. "You're right. The call was made from Sunflower House. It's a 30-bed residential facility, affiliated with the New Beginnings program in Manhattan. One of Gabriel's buddies must have called him. Maybe they arranged to meet in the Bronx and score some drugs."

"His mom maintains that Gabriel didn't do drugs, and, according to Gabe, the phone call was from a prospective buyer of his photography."

"The call was from a buyer all right, but not of photography." Hasim's tone actually asks, *how I could be so naïve?*

"I'm going up to Peekskill to check this out."

"Suit yourself. A day in the country might put some color in your cheeks."

"What are you, my cosmetologist?"

"I'm here 'til six. Stop by on your way back. There's something I'd like to run by you. And don't forget to bring that bank statement." Accustomed to giving orders, he hangs up before I can respond. He's trying to put me in my place, or he's nervous about working with a free agent. Either way, it's something

40

I'll have to live with.

Much as it irks me to ask for her help, I call Gloria's office at New Beginnings and leave a message on her voice mail. "Daniel tells me you're in touch with Leslie's parents. Can you find out how she raised the bail money she put up for Gabriel? Two hundred thousand is a lot of cash—maybe she got it from them."

I unearth my New York State map and for the first time since leaving Los Angeles, regret having sold my car. True, you've got to be rich to keep up a car in Manhattan, and I was happy to be released from the tyranny of repair bills and the responsibility for creating tons of smog—but how can you tail a suspect from a bus?

I get Ted on the phone and brace myself for a lecture.

"I hate people who are too environmentally conscious to drive but still expect their unprincipled friends to provide transportation."

"There's a lot at stake here, Ted."

"I own a newsstand, Jo. I read the papers."

"Please."

"It's on the east side of the street, just south of 87th and Riverside. As I recall, you've still got the keys from last time."

"Thanks, Ted. You're a sweetheart."

"If you don't show up for work, I'll call it in stolen." Then, "Watch yourself, Jo."

* * *

It's a long time since I loaded a thermos with coffee and headed up the Henry Hudson Parkway. Coltrane blowing through Ted's great sound system calls up memories of the night, so many years ago, when I went out on my first surveillance. I had moved back in with Mom after the disastrous marriage to Zach, determined to finish school. She had finally moved from our East Bronx neighborhood, the one with the highest crime rate in the entire city, to a respectable one-bedroom apartment in the West Bronx. Mom's new apartment was on the second floor of a well-kept building near NYU's uptown campus. With her working full time as a secretary downtown and me holding down a job and going to school, our shared moments took the form of hurriedly scrawled notes, left for each other on the mahogany telephone table directly below our only family heirloom:

41

An ornately framed, round mirror that my grandmother left me.

It took me two years of night classes to earn my Criminology certificate, working days as a waitress at the Brighton Café on Burnside and Jerome, serving coffee more bitter than Nixon's resignation speech. After graduation, I was psyched to be offered a position by the Adept Detective Agency. They specialized in industrial crime, thefts from assembly lines, missing spare parts—what Zachary would call the revenge of the underpaid worker.

For my first assignment, Adept sent me to keep watch on a Brooklyn warehouse where an electronics company was hemorrhaging inventory on a nightly basis. I parked a block away from the warehouse. Within the hour a guard opened the gate to admit a milk delivery truck, followed closely by two police cars with headlights dimmed. Nonchalant was the word that came to mind as I watched the cops help the burglars unload dozens of boxes onto the milk truck. After the police cruisers took off, I tailed the truck deep into New Jersey, where the stolen goods were stashed in a junk yard. The next morning, I told my new boss what had happened, and he took me off the case. "Great job, but it's too dangerous," he said. "Forget about it." Shortly afterwards I left for the west coast, where at least the corruption occurs in a warmer climate.

Suffering for an hour in heavy traffic, I turn with relief onto Route 9 from the Saw Mill River Parkway, following South Street into Peekskill. The food at the Chinese luncheonette is surprisingly good, setting me up for the drive west. In the distance, green rolling hills offer a pleasant contrast to the flatness of passing farmland, while cornstalks cook in the heat next to roadside stands. I promise myself some cherries and peaches on the way home.

The map guides me down a gravel road that snakes through a dark tunnel of irrepressible blackberry bushes for the next mile or so, until an incongruous Tudor mansion, painted a shade of yellow brighter than fake buttered popcorn, comes into view. If built with real bricks instead of stucco and plywood, the house might have been classy. Absurdly large and ill-proportioned, the overall effect is Neo Tacky.

Rolling up to a closed security gate, I lean out the window and push the call button. In response, footsteps crunch on the gravel path, followed by a familiar looking man in shorts and a T-shirt. Minus the business suit he wore when Daniel introduced us at New Beginnings, Sal Salvatore takes a few moments to register. His round, good-humored face, dark curls, and powder blue eyes suggest Dublin bar keep, not Italian millionaire. He pulls on his goatee, scanning the Protegé's interior.

"You come all this way yourself?"

"Are there bandits on the road I should know about?"

Using a remote to open the gate, he slides into the passenger seat, and I drive us through. "That's sad news about Gabriel. He showed a lot of promise." The grief in Sal's voice sounds genuine, but this man is smooth as single malt and probably just as sneaky.

The grounds have the manicured look of a country club— the lawn furniture expensive, the green grass an extravagance to maintain in this heat. I park next to a volleyball net strung between two elms in front of the house. Sal gets out and moves quickly around the car, opening the door for me, still playing the self-deprecating gentleman. "We don't usually allow visitors, but you're in luck. It's movie day. All of the residents are in town for a matinee."

We climb the steps of a wraparound porch. The green metal sign above the front door displays *Sunflower House* in yellow letters. Inside, the pretentious exterior is more than matched by the speckled marble floor of the lobby and the wide carpeted staircase, straight out of a British horror movie, without the cobwebs. I shiver, perhaps from the chill of the air conditioning, but more likely at the thought of where all the hardwoods come from. "Tough life," I comment. "Deluxe accommodations. Weekly movies. What about the brutal behavior modification methods I've heard so much about?"

"We keep the cattle prods in the basement." Sal shows me around, obviously proud of the well-equipped office, the cedar paneled lounge with its pool and ping pong tables, and the comfortably furnished group therapy room.

"Where are the bedrooms?"

"Upstairs and off limits to you." The mammoth dining room is worthy of a Governor's mansion and prompts a history lesson.

"This place was built by my father. It was his pet project. He intended to live here in baronial splendor after he retired, but he died a few weeks after the last window was framed. As the eldest son, I inherited a house that I hated. I was planning to sell, but then I heard from Daniel that New Beginnings was looking for a location for a treatment center. I decided to donate the property."

"Just like that?"

Sal's not that easily offended. "I was an addict, Jo, but in my case there was a family that could afford to pay for a residential program in Arizona. Donating Sunflower House was my chance to give something back. '

"What a guy."

"Why so cynical?"

"In my experience rich people don't give things away unless there's an ulterior motive, like a tax write-off or an honorary degree."

"He's not like that." The eavesdropper is a thin, blonde, post-adolescent male with the slouch to prove it. "Sal's here almost every day, has his own chair in group therapy, helps out in the kitchen, you name it. He's even finds jobs for some of us and drives us into the city for interviews."

"Why aren't you at the movies, Mokie?" Sal asks.

"I slept late. Why didn't you wake me up?" Another innocent with a talent for deflecting blame.

Sal glares, sending the kid back upstairs in a hurry. "I'd introduce you, but we have a 'no contact' rule for residents."

The tour ends in the library, where Sal parks me in a comfortable leather chair and offers to get us something to drink. The room is dark, and when I open the drapes, the summer light illuminates the intricate patterns on the thick Persian rug. The stained glass window looks out on a line of neatly trimmed box hedges that frame a vegetable garden—broccoli looking healthy, lettuce wilting in the late summer sun. A baseball diamond abuts a grove of trees that I assume marks the property boundary, and a flatbed truck is parked nearby, possibly used to ferry produce to the local market.

I browse the library shelves filled with self-help books touting solutions every bit as fabricated as the science fiction and fantasy crammed in beside them. The photographs on the wall look like Gabriel's work. There are no computers, not even a television, and when Sal returns with a pitcher of lemonade, I ask him why.

"The people who come here don't need outside distractions. What they need is to take a good look at themselves."

"But they're not completely cut off? I mean you do have a pay phone?"

"Using the telephone is one of the privileges they earn as they go through the program."

"I need to know who called Gabriel Johnson on the morning of August 2nd. Do you keep records of who uses the phone and when?"

"This is a treatment center, not a prison." Sal opens a blue folder he carried in with the lemonade, his manner now formal, his back straighter in the chair. "We had high hopes for Gabriel. Talented photographer, supportive mother. Some arrogance he needed to work on, but when he left here I was sure he'd make it. The last thing we expected was for him to get tangled up in a gang fight."

I sip my lemonade, too sweet to be refreshing. "Did Gabriel make any enemies while he was at Sunflower House?"

"None that I know of.'

"Did Leslie Corning visit him?"

"Look, I told you we don't allow visitors. They might have spoken on the phone."

I flash back to the vandalized pay phones in Crotona Park and a question I hadn't planned to ask pops out. "Was Sonny Rodriguez in treatment here?"

There's a brief flash of surprise in Sal's eyes before they revert to their normal opaqueness. "Not a familiar name, but I'll look through the records and give you a call." He doesn't seem comfortable with telling such an obvious lie, and I'm not overjoyed to hear it.

Sal stands up. "It's a damn shame when someone like Gabriel dies before his time, but he's not the first, and, sadly, not the last. What we do here is to try to change the odds that people like him face." This stock speech is my cue to leave, and I take it.

In Peekskill, I stop on Main Street, where a run down movie theatre with a crack in the marquee has somehow survived the march of the malls. A pimply girl is reading a comic book at the ticket window. "Slow day?" I ask.

"Nothin' new in that," she says, the gold stud in her tongue catching the light.

"What about the Tuesday crowd from Sunflower House?"

"Only nine of 'em this week. Maybe the rest are out playin' miniature golf or something. The next show's at four. Wanna buy a ticket?"

"No thanks. One performance a day is my limit."

Ask the Dead

Miles from the ocean
beach umbrellas protect the fruit
on Coney Island Avenue
from the cold rain

Chapter Five

As far as I know, I'm the only person who has ever landed a job as a private investigator through the *Little Nickel* classifieds. The yellow weekly, with its black and red print and funny little clip art graphics, is a great source of used cars, fish tanks and sailboats, but to say that its employment ads are dubious would be too kind. *Work from your home and earn $3,000 a month* translates to *get sick from licking the glue on 10,000 envelopes.*

I was kicking myself for wasting my time perusing these pathetic offerings, when *Trainee wanted by reputable detective agency* caught my eye. At that time, getting a PI license in California required a three-year, full-time paid apprenticeship before you could take the test, and I'd been in town for two whole days. I decided it was time to get started.

Stan Reese ran his agency out of a modest, faux adobe home in Torrance, which meant low overhead for him and afternoon breaks in the swimming pool for me. He interviewed me on a Saturday, dressed in a white polo shirt, one of the three he wore on alternate days, tucked into silk basketball shorts that showed off his muscular legs. His shiny black hair was under strict mousse control. Stan asked if I liked dogs and was I a Dodger fan—these being the most important things in his life. I pled guilty to both counts and was told to report for work on Monday.

For the first three months, I typed surveillance reports, sent out invoices, and used a lint brush to remove copious amounts of dog hair from my clothing every night. I was beginning to think I'd never get out in the field, when I got a call on a Monday night, right in the middle of a Star Trek re-run.

"I need someone for a black bag job," said Stan. "Are you willing?"

I didn't ask him what a black bag job was because I knew this was my chance to join the club. At 10:30, I took a cab and had the driver drop me off in front of a darkened house in Brentwood. Stan appeared out of nowhere. He asked me to keep watch while he broke in. "Don't worry," he said. "They're at the movies. Stay in one place—a good lookout doesn't pace around or call attention to himself, er, I mean *her*self."

It was a quiet neighborhood, and I was familiar with the voice of every cricket on the block by the time Stan came out. "I've got it," he said. "Pay dirt." He showed me a small black picture frame containing a diploma from Johns Hopkins medical school. "You can still smell the smoke on it," he gloated, handing it over for a sniff test. I must have looked totally confused. "Let me buy you a drink, and I'll tell you a story."

We drove east through Hollywood to Los Feliz. Rubbing elbows with the regulars at the only bar for miles around without a sawdust floor, Stan told me about the arson case he was working. The insurance company was preparing to pay off a two million dollar claim, convinced that a disgruntled patient had burned down Dr. Knox's upscale clinic. When Stan visited the site, he found several burned up picture frames in the remains of the doctor's office. Each charred frame lay directly below a light pink rectangle, indicating its former place on the dark red wall behind the doctor's desk. Stan noticed there was one smaller rectangle for which there was no corresponding frame, and from its size and shape, he deduced that a diploma or certificate of some kind had graced that particular spot on the wall.

"He burned down the clinic without batting an eye, but he couldn't bring himself to cremate his medical degree," Stan chuckled. "We've got him now."

Knox eventually signed a release, absolving the insurance company of any obligation. The doctor knew that Stan's evidence was probably inadmissible, having been obtained illegally, but he also knew his reputation would be destroyed if the word got out about what he'd done.

Although I played but a small role in closing this case, Stan's attitude towards me changed from that night on, and he opened up

48

his treasure trove of knowledge. It was from Stan I learned that if you make a small hole in the tail light of a vehicle you can follow it all night without getting too close. I learned how to keep a one or two-car cover on the freeway; that when you're watching a house and want to make sure someone's home, you can send them a bouquet of flowers to bring them to the door; that a person's garbage often reveals more about their life than what they choose to keep and that the truth of body language frequently contradicts the spoken lie.

Before I started with the Reese Agency, I'd considered myself a light-weight cynic. After three years of working insurance fraud cases, when I wasn't talking with hysterical mothers whose children had been kidnapped by fathers who never paid any attention to them before the divorce, my working vocabulary had degenerated into worn out wisecracks, and all the men I dated carried guns.

After earning my license, I stayed on with Stan for two years and then went out on my own. It took me ten years to build up my business, but during the fourth year, I got a lucky break and secured an exclusive claims investigation contract with Pacific Insurance. Videotape technology had just come on the market. It was a novelty then, and I was one of the first investigators to use it in the courtroom. Juries loved my pictures of disabled insurance claimants cavorting over rooftops, replacing loose tiles. One consummate faker wheeled himself into court and got the shock of his life when I played a tape of him water skiing on Lake Tahoe, just days prior to the hearing.

I met Elliot while purchasing microphones for a surveillance operation. Graceful and athletic, he got his dark good looks from his Rumanian mother. He was a much-in-demand sound engineer who sold pro audio equipment at a retail outlet during the day and worked nights at a recording studio in Encino. Seemed like everyone in Los Angeles worked at least two jobs and after Zachary's asceticism, I found Elliot's work-hard-play-hard lifestyle refreshing.

The Epstein Agency was thriving, so I moved to West Hollywood and hired two junior investigators. Elliot and I got married and were talking about having a baby. We were well on our way to the big money, when the Bingham case came along.

Amy Bingham was a petite blonde with the premature wrinkles of a devoted sun bunny. Apparently sane in other areas, she was obsessed with the belief that her lawyer husband was cheating on her and had already paid huge bills to four other detective agencies to provide the proof. The fact that not one iota of evidence had been found appeared to make her even more suspicious of Ronald.

"He's too perfect," she insisted when she came to see me. "No one looks completely innocent unless they're hiding something." She seemed a little unstable, but new clients were often nervous. If I turned away every person who exhibited a nervous tic, my active files would be cut in half. I took the case.

Ronald Bingham had a lucrative law practice, judging from the celebrity clients flitting through the doors of his penthouse offices on Wilshire Boulevard. He also taught part time at the UCLA School of Law. Borrowing a friend's student I.D., I endured several of Binghams' excruciatingly boring lectures on the subject of Corporate Bankruptcy and Reorganization. True, he was tall and well-built, with unruly, prematurely gray hair and a certain assertive charm, but I couldn't imagine a woman tolerating his company for long without the assistance of earplugs.

At the end of each lecture, when all the students had proceeded to other, presumably more interesting classes, one well-endowed female student invariably remained behind to question her handsome professor. In my case notes, I referred to her as "the nymphet" , and, although I never witnessed so much as a cuddle within those hallowed halls, I was convinced she was "the one."

Since I was sure Ronald Bingham had made at least one of the private investigators previously hired by his wife, I decided to shadow Marcy O'Reilly instead. I pegged Marcy as the type to drive a Corvette, but it was the next best thing—a baby blue Mustang—that I found myself tailing from Van Nuys to Westwood every day. On the fourth day, she broke her pattern and drove to a Hollywood hotel.

With its maze of 150 high-priced rooms, the Palace Hotel on Sunset was an ideal choice for furtive assignations. I invested some of Amy Bingham's cash in loosening the con-cierge's tongue and got a room number. Someone as astute as Ronald should have considered the ubiquitous surveillance cameras. What a lucky break for me that George Wilson, a former police officer, was working the afternoon security shift at the Palace and was only too glad to return an outstanding favor by letting me view the tapes of the 18th floor. Without this synchronicity, I might have been reduced to smoking out the lovers by setting fire to a newspaper and shoving it under their door.

Mrs. Bingham watched the tape of Marcia and Ronald ravishing each other even before they'd entered their room, and left my office without a word. In most of these cases, the client will vent some anger, blow off some steam, and I should have picked up on Amy's silence as a warning sign. The next day two things happened: She pushed Ronald over the railing of his penthouse patio, and a fifteen thousand dollar check arrived in my mailbox. Amy had planned to kill her husband all along, using me to provide her with the justification. Disgusted with myself, I decided I was in the wrong profession and called Stan to ask if he wanted to buy me out.

"A detective's job is to search for the truth," he said. "We're not responsible for the consequences. So how much do you want for the business?" I told him seventy-five thousand, and we settled on sixty.

"One hiccup and you quit?" was Elliot's reaction. The fact that I now had a hunk of cash to finance a career change, maybe write poetry full-time, made no impression on him. He'd found a flaw in my character he hadn't noticed before…I lacked backbone. He went off to work every day filled with resentment at the thought of me lounging around the house all day, even though I was taking college courses and learning how to cook in spite of being my mother's daughter. The strain grew, and we separated three months later, both glad we'd postponed parenthood.

For the next six years, I kept afloat by working two or three cases a year. The rest of the time I spent writing poetry and living the frugal life of a committed beach bum. I also learned how to date and make friends without falling in love. One morning I woke up filled with nostalgia for the changing seasons and gave in to a strong urge to return east.

51

* * *

It's 5:15 when I pull up in front of the 42ⁿᵈ Precinct. The busy Lieutenant sees me right away. Seems like there's no better recipe for friendship than bonding over a corpse. Sipping his tea after offering me a cup—this time it's jasmine, full-bodied and delicious—Saleh doesn't look happy.

"This murder in Chelsea is making people nervous," he says.

"You mean rich people."

He doesn't deny it. "The killer went to a lot of trouble to make this look like a gang execution. People who pay two million bucks for a condo with a view of Gramercy Park aren't the types who say 'there goes the neighborhood' and call the moving van. They're gonna use whatever clout they've got to pressure the Police Chief to make the bad people from uptown go away." He drains the dregs from his styrofoam cup and throws it across the room into the trash.

"They've taken this case away from you and moved it downtown, haven't they?"

"It's not official yet." He straightens the pens on his desk, lining them up in a row while he decides how much to tell me. "This morning the gang unit brought in Sonny Rodriguez. It was obvious he's bangin' it in again. I could tell he was carrying some guilt, so I told him that if he parted with some vital information, we'd try to overlook any minor infractions on his part."

"In other words, you offered him partial immunity."

The phone rings, and he takes a break from our conversation, listening intently while scribbling notes on a yellow pad. When he gets off the phone, I'm afraid he'll dismiss me and run off to the scene of a fresh crime, but he picks up right where he left off.

"Sonny told us that Dwight Davis and his two buddies knew that Gabriel was carrying cash. He confirmed Gabriel's story that they tried to rob him and he killed Dwight in self-defense."

I keep my face in neutral—Gabe's dead and this is no time to gloat. Hasim continues. "Johnson knew how it would look if the police found him standing over a dead body with four thousand in cash in his pocket. He gave the money to Rodriguez and told him to get lost."

I take it to the logical conclusion. "Sonny shot the four grand up his arm."

Hasim nods. "The gang unit thinks the two of them tan-gled over the money when Gabriel got out of Rikers and Sonny killed him."

"What do *you* think?"

He smiles at this. "You're right. It doesn't fit his MO. On the other hand, junkies can surprise you. Sonny's in and out of Sun-flower House on a regular basis."

While we've been talking, about a dozen people have popped their heads into the office, trying to get the Lieutenant's attention. Now one of them limps in, a middle-aged male wearing an unusually crisp uniform, and drops an impressive stack of files on the Lieutenant's desk. Hasim ignores him and continues at a lei-surely pace.

"According to Sonny, Gabriel refused to flee the scene after killing Dwight Daniels because he wanted to tell the police his side of the story." He pauses, and it takes a few seconds for me to realize that he's asking for my opinion. I come up with a question instead.

"Why didn't he make a deal *before* he was indicted?"

"Maybe he was biding his time, collecting enough evi-dence to implicate someone."

"That doesn't make sense to me. He was in jail for crissake. How could he collect evidence?"

"Enter Leslie Corning."

"If she's still alive, she's in way over her head." I get out the bank statement he asked me for on the phone. "Can you find out who owns the account that Gabriel was feeding?"

"Only if the account is on FINCen's list of illegal activity suspects." He's referring to the Financial Crimes Enforcement Network database, the Who's Who of money-laundering.

Hasim takes the bank statement from me and then picks up an evidence bag from a shelf in the bookcase. "A box of these turned up in Leslie's apartment." He opens the bag and hands me an Empire State Building key chain identical to the one I found on Leslie's fire escape, but minus the key. "Maybe she's doing some wholesaling on the side."

It's my turn to trade. I hesitate for a heartbeat and then pull a plastic bag containing the key chain out of my purse. "I found this on the fire escape. The key fits the padlock on Leslie's window gate."

The Lieutenant is silent. His hand falls briefly on my shoulder, and I know he's vacillating between charging me with obstruction and taking full advantage of what I know. He pulls one of the key chains from the evidence bag. "Tell you what. I'll trade you for this one and have yours dusted for prints."

I can't help commenting, "I thought you were off the case."

He examines the wall behind me with an angry stare. "This is a complex case, but as usual the people downtown want a simple solution. It's likely that the heat will come down on some kids in the Bronx while the people responsible get away with murder. I need your help to make sure that doesn't happen."

Before I leave, Saleh gives me copies of pictures taken at the crime scene as well as his home telephone number and address. Having a buddy on the police force is an advantage I've never had before. His doubtful look suggests that this may be his first time, too.

* * *

If Lieutenant Saleh thinks I'm reluctant to cooperate with the police now, he should have known me when I was thirteen. Growing up in a neighborhood where the boys in blue auto-matically assume everybody is on the wrong side of the law doesn't inspire confidence at the sight of a badge. It wasn't until after Mom and I moved from the East to the West Bronx, that I discovered I could welcome the presence of peace officers. Up until then, I saw them as hostile occupiers, arriving in our war-torn neighborhood hours, if not days, after a crime had occurred.

On the day our apartment was burglarized, two officers did show up on our doorstep, shortly before Mom arrived from her daily commute from lower Manhattan. They didn't conduct any of the crime scene tests I was later trained to perform in criminology school. They did, however, ask us for a list of what had been stolen.

My mother rushed from room to room, opening drawers and closets, rummaging through her embroidered jewelry box. Then she collapsed into the Danish modern chair she'd scraped up enough money to buy the previous week and burst into tears.

"Nothing's missing. Nothing," she sobbed.

"That's *good* news, ma'am, isn't it?" one of the cops asked. It would never occur to him that she was crying because we owned nothing valuable enough to steal.

* * *

Before going to work, I stop by the apartment to pick up my messages. "Jo, it's 3:30, and I'm with Leslie's parents at the Park Plaza, room 312. They flew in from the west coast this morning." Gloria's normally throaty voice is a high-pitched flute. "The Cornings want to talk with you as soon as possible. They're completely puzzled about the bail money—Leslie never consulted them, and they can't imagine how she got hold of such a large amount."

I call the room at the Plaza, and when Eleanor Corning comes on the line, introduce myself.

"Gloria just left," she says. "When can you get here?"

It's more of an order than a question, but I let it pass, knowing her stress level must be sky high. "I'm supposed to work until eleven, but I'll try to leave early. Let's say I'll be there by 10:30."

Reluctantly, she agrees. I have enough time to take a quick shower and grab a burrito from a street vendor to eat in the car. I'm careful not to spill any hot sauce on Ted's precious leather seats.

I see your fierce face
peering out from
behind an African mask in the window
of a 5ᵗʰ Avenue gallery
but I barely pause
intent on stalking the urban prey
we call pleasure

Chapter Six

At 6:45, I park the Protegé in front of the newsstand. Ted usually makes a point of walking around the car twice to check it out, but tonight he skips the ritual. "Thanks," I say, handing him the keys. "That's okay," he replies. "It's good that you gave the engine a workout on the highway." I'm puzzled by his new attitude until I see the latest *Post* headline—*P.I. Finds Body in Missing Social Worker's Apt.* The story mentions me by name and is artfully designed to arouse both fear and voyeuristic anticipation of violent gang incursions into Manhattan's wealthier neighborhoods.

"You've got yourself a serious case here, Jo. Maybe you should take some time off so you can give it your full attention." I'm amazed and grateful when he hands back the keys. "When you take the car out again, make sure to let me know so I won't think it's been chopped up for parts."

* * *

Taking stock of my reflection in the subway train window, I see jeans that are less than clean but a *Poetry Rules* T-shirt that's burrito-free. My frizzy hair is hopeless, as always.

I walk into the immense lobby of the Plaza, overflowing with enough overstuffed furniture to billet an army of the homeless. On my way to the elevator, I encounter an elegant, color-coordinated couple, matching each other stride-for-stride—he in forest green shorts and a beige polo shirt, she wearing a silk skirt and blouse to match. They stare off into space, eye contact with a non-important person like me being out of the question. In California, the well-to-do dress down, but in New York they take no prisoners.

Upstairs, the aroma of wealth seeps from beneath the passing doors as I search for room 312. A woman with lush dark hair and hollows where cheeks ought to be opens the door.

"I'm Jo Epstein," I say. She gives me a questioning look, and I straighten my shoulders. "I'm tougher than I look." This brings a small smile to her bloodless lips. She moves slowly, floating through a bad dream. Her speech is hesitant, sedated. "I'm Eleanor Corning. Thanks for showing up early. We were going crazy with nothing to do but imagine the worst."

The room is done in Louis XIV white and gold, with brocade curtains and high ceilings—an awkward setting for discussing murder and other gruesome possibilities. An African-American mountain of a man rises from his seat at the antique table by the window, exhibiting the heavy build of an ex-jock tackling middle age, but still fit enough to go a few rounds.

"Michael," says Eleanor, "this is Jo Epstein, the private investigator Gloria told us about." He pulls out a chair and takes my outstretched hand as I sit down. "When was the last time you spoke with Leslie?" I ask.

He doesn't hesitate. "She called me a week ago Monday, said she was going to stay with her friend Alicia for a few days."

"Did she say why?"

He thinks this over. "Leslie said Alicia was feeling depressed and needed some company. I assumed it was girl stuff—Leslie's always been a giving person." Tears fill his eyes, and I wait for him to regain control. "When she didn't call on Sunday like she usually does, we tried calling her at Alicia's and that's when we learned that she never showed up. We called Sal, since he's a friend of the family, and he said not to worry, that Leslie had lots of friends and was probably out having fun. Then, on Tuesday, Gloria called and told us they found a body in our daughter's apartment."

He falls silent, watching me absorb this information, waiting for me to ask the right questions.

"Did Leslie ever talk with you about her friendship with Gabriel Johnson?"

"No, she didn't." Corning shifts in the frail chair, and I wonder if it will continue to hold his weight. "I think she was trying to carve out a new identity for herself. She stayed in touch but tried to keep us on the periphery."

"She didn't talk about her work because she knew Michael didn't approve," adds Eleanor, who has been pacing agitated trails around the room.

"Maybe if I'd been more supportive she would have confided in us." Michael Corning's voice has taken on an anguished intensity, and from the way Eleanor comes over and grips his shoulder, I gather this admission is hard for him.

"Why did Leslie take a job in New York? There must be lots of social agencies in California that need interns."

Eleanor comes closer and sits on the edge of the bed, placing her feet flat on the floor, as if to ground herself before speaking. "Everyone thought she was well adjusted in spite of having to flip back and forth between worlds. You know, one black and one white. It can be a terrific strain on a bi-racial person. I don't think it got to her until after college, when most of her friends left town. She started complaining about our lifestyle, comparing it with the living conditions she saw when she visited black relatives in Watts. I guess she woke up to some stark realities. Moving to New York was a natural progression, given how uncomfortable she was in Beverly Hills."

Michael takes his wife's hand. "Be honest with us, Ms. Epstein. What do you think has happened to Leslie?"

"Maybe she witnessed the murder and is hiding some-place, trying to figure out what to do. She may know who the murderer is and be afraid to come forward." I decide not to mention the more worrisome details.

Eleanor starts pacing again. "There's been no activity in her bank account or on her credit cards," she says. "Do you think that's a bad sign?"

"Not necessarily. She may not want to be traced and is using whatever cash she has or can get."

Her husband gets out his checkbook. "We'd like to hire you, Ms. Epstein."

We work out a simple contract covering my daily rate and expenses, and Michael gives me their cell number. When he finds out I'm minus this crucial means of communication, he offers to cover that expense as well.

"Gloria told us you're good at what you do," says Eleanor.

"I'll do my best to find your daughter."

My feet sink into the plush hall carpet on the way out, but my spirits are high. I now have two paying clients. This violates the New York State "one case at a time" rule for non-licensed investigators, but who's gonna know? And if I can keep my incessant guilt at profiting from the misfortunes of others at bay, I just might pay off that irksome Visa card.

Outside, an elderly couple rides by the Plaza in a hansom cab, drawn by a powerfully built chestnut horse with red ribbons braided into his mane. The old man has his arm around his wife, and her eyes are shining in the yellow streetlight. Zach and I took a ride like this, just a few months after I stole him from Gloria.

That night, the horse pulling our carriage had a white blaze on its nose that looked like a lightning bolt; his hot breath tickled when he nuzzled the carrot pieces in my palm. I was feeling flush with success, having published a poem in a new underground magazine. Zach congratulated me as we clip-clopped through the Park. Then, leafing through the magazine, he couldn't resist saying, "I'm not sure what it means—'the construction crew is saving it for Lou.' Sounds like another working class stereotype."

I hardly knew what to say. My poems were stimulated by the sights and smells of the city, with its sweet and sour breath and urine-stained sidewalks. I rode the buses late at night listening for whispered conversations hinting at metaphysical destinations. "I write about what is, or what might be," I said. "You prefer what should be."

He let it go. After all, it was my birthday.

* * *

I get off the bus at 96th and Broadway, stopping at a drug store to pick up a cheap cell phone. While I'm at it, I treat myself to a sleek digital recorder, handy for dictating case notes. The salesman explains how the slim pocket-sized machine is sound activated, designed to pause when there's no noise in the room and prevent unnecessary recording.

This seems like a good night for my weekly attempt at home-cooking, so I walk across the street to shop for groceries at the Food Emporium, where the seafood looks fresh and so does the broccoli. I already have the white wine at home. By ten o'clock, I'm chewing on the last piece of teriyaki-basted salmon, pondering the key chain on the napkin next to my plate.

It takes me half an hour to figure out how to activate the cell phone and make sure the battery is charging. Then I use the land line to call Mrs. Johnson, apologizing for the late hour. "Can you tell me where Gabriel sold his photographs?"

"It was someplace close to Washington Square Park. He didn't have a vending license. They're almost impossible to get. But he told me that the street artists are in a fight with City Hall to get a group exemption."

"Thanks, Mrs. Johnson. I'll be in touch."

After dictating the day's events into my new recorder, I'm considering whether to rent a DVD or go out to a late movie when Daniel Rose calls. Says he's working late at New Beginnings and has thought of some things to discuss that might be important. Would I like to join him for a late dinner?

"Sorry, I've already eaten." There's a pause as he shifts gears. "How about coming over to my place for a drink?"

"Can it wait 'til tomorrow?"

"Tomorrow I'm running an all-day workshop at Sunflower House. I know it's getting late. I could swing by and pick you up, show off my Porsche." Blatant materialism can have its good points. At least he's not the type to berate me for buying a new sweater in the dead of winter instead of shopping at the local thrift store.

An hour later, I'm sipping my favorite Chablis in the kitchen of Daniel's West Village apartment, enjoying the view of the Hudson River and listening to Eddie Palmieri's salsa beats keeping time with pin pricks of lights blinking on the New Jersey side. Daniel's art collection of scenes from the jazz world is impressive and fills every wall of his 3-room railroad flat, open from end to end so that I can see out the front windows while standing with him in the kitchen at the back. Gabriel's photograph of the bicyclist, the same one I saw hanging in Leslie's cubicle, is lying on the butcher block table next to the spice rack.

"So what's so important you can't discuss it at the office?"

I'm about to seat myself at the white-topped table, but he cuts me off, backing me up against the stove. "I'm very attracted to you, Jo."

With me it's all about the case, and I forget that some men perceive this as indifference, and that's what turns them on.

"You're not my type, Daniel."

"Why not?" He takes a step back, and I maneuver around him, sliding into a chair. "For starters, one of your clients was murdered, and you're too busy to pay your respects to his mother."

Daniel takes another step back. "Guilty as charged. I'll send her flowers in the morning." He's playing the part of a man who'd like to be putty in my hands, but there's no mistaking the undertone of entitlement.

"You should send me a bouquet, too, after luring me here under false pretenses." He looks stung. "I *do* have information, Jo, but I thought you'd be disappointed if I didn't put on the moves."

The guy is making me uneasy, but I've been managing types like him since I was a teen, thanks to my early dating experiences with over-sexed graduate students from Columbia. "What's on your mind, Daniel?"

He puts his hands on the butcher block table, a press secretary making a revelation from the podium. "Gabriel's photography business was a front for selling drugs."

"Do you have proof?"

Daniel picks up Gabe's print from the table and pops it out of the frame. Between the photograph and the cardboard backing is a small cellophane baggie filled with white powder.

"Heroin or cocaine?"

"That's something I'm hoping *you'll* tell *me*." He holds out the open bag, and I moisten my pinky before dipping it in to take a taste. "It's cut with quinine, but it's genuine smack." If he knew me

61

at all he'd know I was lying. It's pure bunk…way too bitter.

Daniel stuffs the baggie deep into the freezer. "Hasn't it occurred to you that Gabriel and Leslie were partners in crime? Maybe they had a falling out, and she killed him. She's probably sipping tropical punch in a bar in St. Thomas right now, having a good laugh at our expense."

He's got a picture he wants to paint in my head, but I'm not seeing it. "If you're so sure of this, why did you call me instead of the police?"

"Maybe I'm more sensitive than you think. I'm telling you first so you can prepare Gabriel's mother for the bad news."

I make a show of thinking this over. "Are you willing to sit on this for a while? It might not be what it looks like."

"Alright. But only because it's you." No hints about payback, but we both know he'll try to collect when he thinks the time is right.

Daniel disappears into the bathroom—he's drunk two beers for each of my three small glasses of wine. When he returns, there's a slight stagger in his walk. I turn down his offer of a ride home and call a taxi.

* * *

Back at my apartment, I try out some new honeysuckle bubble bath and run my thoughts past Ellie. I've decided to keep calling her that, instead of Beverly, because we met when her life was already over. Besides, I don't think we keep our names after death.

Why would Daniel Rose try to misdirect my investigation unless he's got something to hide? He's a complicated person, it seems. I sense the ruthlessness of the perpetual do-gooder combined with something else less obvious.

I'm about to doze off in the tepid water when an image pops into my head: two small cardboard boxes in the basement storage area that I noticed when I moved in. In a heartbeat I'm dried, dressed, and on my way to the elevator, vaguely conscious that it's 4 a.m. and not a great time to be wandering around the basement.

The two boxes have migrated behind an old ironing board and a bag of golf clubs that my friend, Steve, who lives in a studio the size of an upscale closet, keeps here. I pry the first one open and find a bunch of battered Penguin classics mixing it up with cookbooks and romance novels. The second box contains an appointment calendar and a composition book, the pages filled with short entries written in a round, child-like hand.

Upstairs, I curl up on the couch with the diary—brimming with dreams, personal reflections and notes about Ellie's students—a testament to how she loved their quirks and peculiar way of seeing the world. Certain entries stand out, and I underline them in pencil, feeling like an intruder, but one with a mission.

October 5—

Out of all the poems, I like Elzie's the best... "someday I'll be taller than the abominable snowman, someday I'll have fuzz on my chin and no one will tease me or say I'm too thin."

They're still on the other side of that invisible line we cross, some of us at ten, some of us earlier, when we accept the impossibility of perfection.

October 7—

Took them on a field trip to the Central Park Zoo. Letitia's been acting up again. I wonder what's going on at home. Her sexual antics and flirtatious behavior are way beyond her years, and I don't know why I didn't catch on sooner that this is her way of asking for help.

Tomorrow I'll talk to Doreen about reporting to the Child Abuse Register in Albany. As the principal it's her responsibility.

October 25—

Paul hasn't called in three days. They really keep him busy at the hospital. Our first date was so promising. I don't remember whose idea the Ferry ride was. I can still feel the lightness of his arm around my shoulder at the railing as we watched the white caps and the skyline.

I was sure he'd have called by now. Maybe he's working one of those 48-hour shifts.

After all of our one-way conversations in the bathroom, Ellie's making up for lost time. She's got a voice of her own and plenty to say.

* * *

By 9 a.m., the sun has already wilted the pink geranium in the kitchen window, and I make the first phone call of the day.

"Hello, Chloe Sterling? My name is Jo Epstein, and I live at 829 West End Avenue."

"Yes?" The voice is soft, with a hint of authority.

"This is a bit awkward. I'm in apartment 9G."

"Is this a prank call?"

"Please, Ms. Sterling, don't hang up. I don't want to invade your privacy, but I've found something in the storage area that was left behind by your sister, something I think you might want to have. It's a diary."

I hear her quick inhale. "Oh. Perhaps you could put it in the mail. I'll reimburse you for the postage." She's polite, but the frost has set in.

"If you don't mind, I'd rather bring it by in person. I took the liberty of reading some of the entries, and there are some questions that came up."

"Such as?" Her voice has sharpened.

"Ms. Sterling, I don't think this is the…I mean I'm uncomfortable talking about this on the telephone."

Expecting another push back, I'm surprised when she caves. "I'm very busy with my daughter's wedding plans, but I've got a few minutes free between three and three-thirty."

"I'll be there."

Over breakfast, burnt toast with English marmalade, I sample a few more entries. It's strange there's no mention of a sister. There is a pattern, however, taking shape.

November 6—

Doreen has refused to consider my evidence as sufficient grounds for reporting, so I called the hotline myself, as required by the regulations. I had a few moments of hesitation, but then I remembered the mantra of my college philosophy teacher: "Fear not the path of truth for the lack of people walking on it."

November 11—

Paul asked me to go away for the weekend and stay at his family cabin in the Adirondacks. I wanted to accept right away,

*but I said I'd think about it. We've only been dating for a
month and I don't want him to think I'm easy.*

November 29—

*A caseworker from Children's Services interviewed me
today. She wouldn't say much about their findings after inter-
viewing Letitia, but I could tell she took my concerns seriously.
If they question Letitia's father, I'm sure he'll have lots of
excuses and say she's indulging in normal, exploratory behavior, perhaps imitating the way her mother acts with him. I
hope the investigator is astute enough to see through his
charade.*

* * *

It's late morning, but the downtown Q express is packed solid
all the way to West 4th, where I battle my way out and climb the
stairs to the street. Sanyo is setting up his stand in anticipation of the
lunch crowd. "Hey, Jo! Give me a hand," he says, and I help him
unload some produce and cans of beans from his pickup, a modi-
fied VW bus with enough chrome and iron added to be worthy of
Monster Truck.

Sanyo makes the best chili hotdogs on the east coast and
owes me one for steering his little sister away from a bogus
marketing scam. Although we grew up three blocks from each
other in the Bronx, we never met until I became a fan of his
cooking in Manhattan. He used to run with a gang, but those
days are long over. He's got the thickest black eyebrows you've
ever seen and talks in a stage whisper I find sexy. Sanyo's the only
man I know who can turn me on by inquiring if I want extra onions.
I ask him about Gabriel.

"You mean that black photographer who used to sell his
prints a couple of blocks south of here? He used to have lunch
here once or twice a week, along with some skinny blonde kid
who made me nervous."

"Do you remember when you last saw him?"

Sanyo dishes out a hotdog and a Pepsi. He knows my ways.

"Not for a month or so. Heard he tried to rape some girl in
Gramercy Park and she killed him."

Before I can take a bite he's made me lose my appetite.

"Where the hell did you hear that, Sanyo?!"

"Making chili dogs all day, a man needs some distraction. I read the tabloids. So what they said about Gabriel isn't true?"

"Not one single word. Thanks for the grub." I hand him a five. "Keep the change."

"Grub is an insect. You insulting me?"

"You know better than that, Sanyo. Your food is great; wish I could say the same about your reading habits."

Two blocks down, several artists are mounting their displays, a few already seated at their easels, hoping to attract over-the-shoulder crowds to watch them sketch. A purple-haired, waif-like young woman, surrounded by some pretty decent pastel portraits, sees my interest and makes her pitch. "You should put a frame around that face. Only twelve dollars to star in your own portrait." I plant myself in the canvas chair opposite her, and, about half way into the sitting, I ask if she knew the African-American photographer who used to sell his work on Fifth.

"Sure. Everybody's talking trash about Gabriel. The less they knew him the more they have to say, but none of it makes any sense. The only thing I know for sure is that he had a good eye for what shows character. And he was the bomb at capturing a moving target. It was like he could predict what was going to happen and be right there with his camera."

She's sketching fast, the pastel gliding over the paper, and I'm discovering how hard it is to ask questions and look interested in the answers when you're supposed to keep your face perfectly still. "What was he like?"

"He was generous, that's what he was. The last time we spoke, he was putting together a show at a bar uptown, and he said he was going to speak to the manager about saving some space for my oil paintings." She turns the chalk sideways, rubbing it with a fast rhythm, adding some shading.

"Did Gabriel sell many photos?

"He moved more knick knacks and T-shirts than prints. It seems like people either spend a fortune on art or nothing at all."

I show her the Empire State Building key chain and she chuckles. "Yeah, that's just the thing to make them reach for their wallets. Gabriel sold tons of stuff like that."

"Do you know where he got it?" I ask.

"Some novelty company delivered his stock every Wednesday morning. I thought it was weird, because it's impossible to get those outfits to make deliveries to street vendors. Who can blame them, when we never know ourselves where the city's gonna move us next? They shove us around like checkers, but we don't get to be kings when we reach the other side of the board."

She unclips the paper from her easel and I slip in one last question. "Do you remember the name of the distributor?"

"All I can tell you is they haul their stuff around in a big plywood box mounted on a flatbed truck, no name, no logo, no nothing."

The portrait she hands me isn't half bad. She's made the most of my high cheek bones and added some much needed fullness to the thin lips I've always hated. No touch up on the black roots beginning to show beneath my frizzy red hair—a stab at realism I suppose, as is the hint of a double chin and the crease in my forehead. She's nailed the green-brown mix in my eyes and added some irony I must be carrying around. In the lower right corner a signature, *Marilyn Searl.*

Marilyn takes my twelve bucks and stands up, stretching her neck like an curious swan, scanning the passing faces for her next customer. A young man wearing more earrings than I'll ever own slips into the canvas chair when I vacate. With a wave of thanks I'm off, walking south towards Washington Square.

It troubles me how the word's out on the street that Leslie is suspected of killing Gabriel. I'm sure Hasim wouldn't leak this kind of speculation to the press, even if he believed it himself. Maybe one of the Gramercy Park cops is on tap for tabloid reporters looking for juicy gossip. If Leslie's alive and breathing, she'll be good and pissed off when she sees the *Daily News.*

you covered
the scorched earth of Manhattan
with thousands of tons
thinking new soil
would provide
the illusion of history

Chapter Seven

There's something sublime about sitting in Washington Square, even when a dog pees on your bench or the remnants of an ice cream cone splatter on the ground in front of you. This is a place where, if you stay alert, you just might see the meaning of life unfold before your eyes, one of the few places I know where it seems that nothing is left to chance. If someone speaks to me in the park, no matter how unsavory or vacuous they may seem, I'll answer. And inevitably they'll say something I need to hear, just as surely as my words will carry weight with them.

Today it's two young women on roller skates, hair flying. I catch one phrase, "It's all about the money," as they glide by. Not an original thought, but to me it's the affirmation I need.

Keeping a wary eye on some Frisbee players with aim just lousy enough to clip my ear, I call Hasim.

"The bad news," he says, "is that the lab can't find a match for the fingerprint we found on the key chain you gave me. It probably belongs to someone with no criminal record."

"And the good news?"

"I heard from FINCen. The account number you gave me belongs to an offshore business account on the island of St. Dominic. Twenty thousand a month doesn't come from selling key chains and photographs. It looks like Gabriel was washing money for someone."

A teenage boy with a backpack and a brown bag lunch, probably a freshman at NYU, sits down on the bench next to mine. I turn the volume down. "Maybe Gabe was planning to name some names in the laundry business. It would explain why he seemed so confident about making a deal with the D.A."

Hasim's voice is unusually animated. "I've done the math, Jo, and this could be a big operation. If there are other smurfs involved, and you multiply the numbers, they could be cleaning millions."

"Smurfs? Aren't they hyperactive cartoon characters?"

"It's what they call couriers who scurry from bank to bank." If there's impatience with my ignorance in his tone, it's too subtle for me to pick up. "As long as their deposits are less than $10,000, they can side-step the reporting limit the Feds require and get paid a healthy percentage."

He's being open with me, and, to return the favor, I tell him about the delivery truck that Marilyn Searl described. "Could be that's how they deliver the cash," he says. "If you can come up with some hard evidence, I'll make sure the charges stick."

It's not as if he doesn't know what he's asking. "I'll keep your generous offer in mind while I'm out here on my own without any resources."

"What do you expect, a police escort?" Then his tone softens. "Jo, I appreciate all you've done. We need to put our heads together, but we can't meet at the station without tipping off the Borough Commander that I'm still working the case. Why don't you come up to my house tomorrow night around six. We can talk over dinner."

I accept the invitation and take down his address. Looks like I'm going to find out whether or not the handsome lieutenant is married.

* * *

On the D train, some high school Eminem clones stage a freestyle battle, with the passengers as a captive audience, some enthusiastic, others like me patiently sitting it out. These kids may think their show is the bomb, but insults minus poetry are just obscenities. Ask any comedian.

I call Ted from home to let him know I'll be borrowing the car again. I'd love to take a nap before driving to Queens, but instead I get out the stovetop espresso maker and cook up a strong cup of Medalia d'oro. This kick-starts my heartbeat and gives me the gumption to look through the photographs spread out on the coffee table, gory depictions of the crime scene that Hasim has entrusted to me. I wonder if he's right and the graffiti *is* phony. New gangs are coming up all the time, and it's hard for even an expert to keep track of their signatures. I make a note to find someone who can decipher the meaning of the eagle head, the upside down fist and the 8-pointed star.

* * *

On the way to pick up the car I stop at the Kinkos to make copies of Ellie's diary, since I'll be giving her sister the original. As they're spewed from the copy machine I read the last few pages.

December 5—

The weekend with Paul was heavenly. Didn't think he could be so romantic. Take a person out of the city and their normal routine and wonderful things can happen. The knotty pine cabin was right out of a Bing Crosby movie, with bay windows, cedar shingles and tinkling wind chimes that kept me up all night. There's a pot belly stove and everything you need for a cozy getaway—except indoor plumbing—but I decided not to complain. When I said the smelly outhouse was rustic he rewarded me with a kiss. Then he sat down beside me on the red leather couch and said he loved me!

January 8—

The hearing went much better than I expected. Allen Trieste was so shook up by my statement and everyone seemed surprised at my willingness to testify. Most teachers want to hide from the parents they accuse but I'm not one to do things half way. I told them I'd spoken with Letitia and that she told me what her daddy did to her. They listened, and for her sake I hope they believed me!

January 15—

Paul was out of touch for an entire week. It seemed like an eternity, but then he showed up on my doorstep with a dozen long stem roses and tickets to the opera. I've never been to Lincoln Center, except on field trips with my students. What am I going to wear???

January 20—

Letitia is not in my class any more, but at least I know

she's safe. I hear she'll be going to another school, closer to where her foster parents live. I didn't think they'd remove her from both parents. You would think they'd ask Kenneth to move out instead, but evidently that's not how it works. Maybe her mother will decide to divorce him and get custody.

February 3—

The apartment's never been so full of life! Letitia and Claire are staying here while they get ready to move to Harrisburg. I told them they could trust me—that I wouldn't tell anyone they're here. The foster parents must be frantic with worry, but as soon as I can I'll let them know Letitia is safe, and, more importantly, living with her mother.

Crawling with thousands of other drivers in slow motion towards the Queens Midtown Tunnel, I ask myself, why dig up the past? Let sleeping kindergarten teachers lie. But let's face it—in an argument with yourself, no one wins.

I'm running late but pick up a few minutes on 21st Street, heading into Astoria. Chloe Sterling lives in a high rise condominium on Shore Boulevard, a triangular building resembling a squished beehive, its hexagonal cells flattened into narrow rectangular windows. I get my thoughts in order on the ride up to the 19th floor.

Chloe answers the door dressed in an olive pants suit that only a person who takes air conditioning for granted would wear in this heat. The view of Manhattan from her apartment is enviable, but I doubt if she spends much time gazing out the window. She's brisk and efficient as a subway turnstile. Her long and narrow face, just this side of horsy, is softened by a full head of teased light brown hair.

"Come in, Jo. I appreciate your coming all this way. I hope the subway wasn't too crowded."

"Actually, it was a pleasant drive. I don't get out here very often." *And I don't like the way you tried to peg me as a loser without a car.*

She waves me to a puffy corduroy chair and seats herself on the green leather couch. "You said something about my sister keeping a diary?"

"I'm a private investigator, and there are some events that

Beverly wrote about in her diary that raise red flags. In particular, I'm referring to the child abuse charges against the father of one of her students." I hand her Beverly's journal, open to the page in question.

After a cursory glance, she closes the book and places it on the coffee table, careful not to disturb a crystal vase holding yellow silk flowers. "Beverly had an overactive imagination. It was part of her illness and frequently got her into trouble."

"According to the diary, she was housing the little girl and her mother until they could arrange to leave the city. Did you meet Letitia and her mom when they were staying with her?"

"Of course not, because they were never there. It was part of her pathology, the lies and the secrecy." She crosses her legs, hands tight across her chest, all doubt held at bay.

I try another angle. "The school authorities took your sister's accusations seriously enough to remove Letitia from her parents' custody."

It's as if she hasn't heard a word I've said. "My sister had bipolar disorder. She could have functioned well, but she frequently neglected to take her pills. If you can find a true word in her diary, then you're a cinch to win at three card Monte."

Seems to me she's protesting too much, but I decide to play along. "I may not be as gullible as you think, Mrs. Sterling. I did find some discrepancies in Beverly's journal. For example, she refers to Letitia's father as Allen, but later on she calls him Kenneth."

Chloe Sterling flinches, as if struck across the face by an invisible hand. She's not a likable person, but I have to admire how quickly she manages to pull herself together.

"Letitia's father was named Allen."

"Then who is Kenneth?"

"Can't you see how painful it is for me to talk about my sister's delusions?"

She's clearly on the verge of asking me to leave, but I can't do that just yet. "Beverly wrote about a boyfriend named Paul."

She regains her composure with the change in subject. "I don't believe Paul was really her boyfriend, but they did belong to the same book club. I attended one of their discussion groups. It was profoundly boring. Paul was a musician of some kind—I remember because he gave me his business card and said his band was available to play private parties."

"I'd like to talk with him."

"I'll pass your number on to him, and then it'll be his choice whether to contact you or not." This is a careful woman, someone who would never turn off the spell checker in her word processing program. "Why are you're dredging all this up?"

"I'm not sure myself. I just have a feeling that things may not have been what they seemed."

Chloe Sterling rises from the couch so smoothly that the leather cushions fail to squeak. "My sister committed suicide. That's a painful reality I was forced to accept four years ago and I don't want to go through it all over again. I'm sure you understand." She holds the door open, and, before I can slip in another question, closes it none too gently in my face.

The elevator takes a long time to come, giving me plenty of time to wonder why Chloe is so angry with her dead sister. I'm an only child, but even I can tell there's more at work here than sibling rivalry. I'm intrigued and plan to pursue this inquiry, in spite of Ted's voice in my head saying, *"Isn't it bad enough having clients that stiff you? Now you're setting yourself up to be stiffed by a stiff."*

* * *

The only writing teacher to get under my creative skin did so through a simple exercise. Cut out each word of a poem and toss it in a hat. Paste the words one by one on a fresh piece of paper in random order and then, and this is the tricky part, write a new poem that combines the original version with the jum-bled up one. *All is quiet in the blue room* becomes *in the quiet room blue is all*—a new way of seeing.

Although detective work focuses on events rather than words, the usefulness of the scrambling technique still applies. *Money launderers murdered Gabriel, but it looks like gang revenge* could just as easily be *gang murdered Gabriel, but it looks like money launderers' revenge*. Getting the correct take on this is going to take some time. And since my thinking processes work best undisturbed, I stop off and rent a DVD special edition of *Big Deal on Madonna Street* on my way home from Queens. At times like this it's best to microwave some popcorn and leave the back of the mind to its own devices.

* * *

Traffic is light at 5 a.m., with the calm, glassy Hudson on my left and the rising sun flickering on and off like a searchlight behind the passing trees to my right. An hour and a half later, I stop for gas and a candy bar in Peekskill before taking the country roads, where the air smells like hay mixed with jasmine and there are more cows than people. The charm of this place makes it hard to keep in mind that I'm on the trail of something ugly.

A few minutes later, the Protegé is once again kicking up rocks on the rough road leading to Sunflower House. Fifty yards past the gate, I turn around and park in the deep shadow of a weeping willow tree. With luck I won't be spotted. I'm tempted to put on my headphones and listen to the latest from the Afro Celtic Sound System, but I know better. This wisdom pays off because, with my ears free, I now hear the crunch of footsteps approaching on the gravel road. I crouch down on the floorboards, listening. The footsteps stop briefly and then continue, gradually fading away. When I sit up, the gates to Sunflower House are still closed. I presume what I heard was a neighbor out for an early morning walk.

In a few minutes, the gate opens and out drives the truck I noticed on my first visit. The flatbed is packed with bushel baskets of what I assume to be late summer fruits and vegetables. I wait until the Ford disappears around a curve in the road before starting my engine and pulling out to follow.

On the highway, the truck's top speed is well below 40, making it almost impossible to tail without being detected. Every time I think I have a one car cover, the vehicle in between takes the next exit, leaving the Protegé exposed behind the Ford. I'm in despair until a shiny new Lexus merges in front of me and keeps it's position all the way to the Peekskill Farmer's Market.

I'm beginning to wonder how I can justify this waste of time and gas to Shondrea, when Sonny Rodriguez emerges from the truck cab, no Hawaiian shirt this time, just jeans and a solid black t-shirt. He greets an elderly woman in bib overalls and together they unload the produce and place the overflowing boxes around her stand. I'm too far away to see his eyes, but Sonny's body language says he's clean. Maybe the cops put a scare in him and drove him back into treatment.

When Rodriguez gets back on the road, he doesn't head back to Sunflower House as I expect. Instead, he drives south on Route 9 and takes the Sawmill. I'm prepared to follow him all the way to Manhattan, so it's a jolt when he turns off on the Bronx River Parkway and follows the Hutchinson to I-95. When he takes the East Tremont Avenue exit, I know we're headed for his home turf. I give him plenty of room, which is a good thing, because when he hangs a quick right on Bryant Avenue and pulls into the driveway of what appears to be a glorified storage shed, I'm a full city block behind.

The low slung building, surrounded by a chain link fence, advertises it's dingy self to the world in day-glow orange. Sonny gets out to open the gate and then backs up the truck to a loading dock. A tall white man in army fatigues comes out and together they wheel a large plywood box onto the flatbed. When they're done, the two men talk for a few minutes. Through my binoculars I see Sonny's friend hand him a briefcase. They shake hands and then Mr. Two-Tone, who's wearing a brown and green hat that completes his camouflage outfit, gets into a Chevy Suburban with Georgia plates. I jot down the license number and follow Sonny when he drives out.

The truck takes an unusual route south, passing through Port Morris to Randall's Island and then taking the Triborough Bridge from Randall's Island into Manhattan. I'm still tagging along when Sonny heads west on 125th Street and then downtown.

The neighborhood in the '40s between Eighth Avenue and the waterfront was once a stomping ground for gangsters, as well as home to writers like Thomas Wolfe and O. Henry. The busy streets still exude the scent of oregano and olives but have now become a battleground between the developers who want to rename it Midtown West and the loyal inhabitants who proudly refer to it as

Hell's Kitchen.

Sonny double-parks the truck on Ninth Avenue, and I drive past just in time to see him disappear into a QuikMart. When I pick him up again in the rear view mirror, he's carrying a large soda bottle and a bag of chips. He starts up the truck, and I wait for him to pass before following him down Ninth Avenue. He makes two short stops. Although it's hard to see what he's up to from a block away and using my binoculars would invite too much attention, the presence of so many street vendors tells me that he's doing business.

Continuing south, traffic jams up and here I sit, spewing pollution with the best of them. Even the taxis, capable of passing so close they threaten to peel the paint off your fenders, can't seem to get through. There's no room to maneuver and in spite of the Protegé's air conditioning, I'm sweating the possibility that Sonny will discover he has company. I could ditch the car and take a taxi, but I'd probably lose him in the process. In spite of these worries, Sonny seems oblivious to being tailed. An hour later, we've made four stops, each of them involving transactions that I can't get close enough to witness.

As we approach Gabriel's old territory in Greenwich Village, the truck slows and puts on its one working flasher. I double park two blocks away, cross over, and then fast walk to a falafel joint directly across from where Sonny has parked the truck. He's delivering a box overflowing with T-shirts to a bare-armed, stringy-haired vendor in a chartreuse vest. Along with the merchandise, Sonny hands the peddler a large brown envelope. It's too thick for an invoice and not having x-ray vision, I have to content myself with speculating that a large sum of cash has changed hands.

Hasim's money laundering theory seems to be holding water, but if I don't find a bathroom soon, I'm in danger of losing my own. This isn't the first time that my bladder has dictated a decision, but for dignity's sake, I consider my choices. Either continue tailing the truck and possibly suffer a humiliating accident, or use the bathroom in the restaurant, chow down on a delicious falafel topped with out-of-this-world yogurt sauce, and follow the vendor to see where he takes the money. It's a no brainer.

The falafel is dryer than Letterman, and the sauce is thinner than a super model. Through the window I see the T-shirt peddler packing up his wares. It's noon, an odd time to quit, so I figure he's got important business to attend to. From the way he's stacking his stuff at the edge of the sidewalk, it looks like he's expecting a ride, so I hotfoot it back to the car and get in position to tag along. Sure enough, a dark blue van pulls up, and when the vendor starts loading his boxes, the driver gets out to help. She's pale as the inside of a radish, with silky black hair and lots of flashy jewelry. Gloria.

The van makes two more stops, picking up peddlers around Greenwich Village and taking them to three Chase Manhattan branches in lower Manhattan, where I assume they're making deposits. Afterwards, Gloria drops her passengers, with their folding tables and boxes of goods, at the Union Square station on 14th Street. One of the peddlers looks familiar, tall and skinny, carrying a black velvet display covered with gleaming silver watches and gold bracelets.

Gloria heads north, presumably to ferry more small time merchants to banks in northern Manhattan and the Bronx. All this time, I've been giving the telephoto lens on my Nikon a workout, and I think I've caught enough. Part of me is elated to have collected solid evidence to show Hasim. But I'm also troubled to see how much trouble Gloria's gotten herself into. I know it's irrational to feel protective of someone who cares more about the world than about the individuals who live in it. But my relationship with Gloria has never been simple, which is probably why we became friends in the first place.

* * *

"You're too short to be an anarchist, " popped out of my mouth, the first time we met.

"So is my fuse," Gloria shot back. Her reputation as a trouble-maker was spreading on the City College campus.

"I thought anarchists didn't approve of repressive institutions like college."

"Where else could I find undergraduates with droopy

mustaches so eager to learn how to make bombs? Actually I prefer plastique—it's so much lighter," she quipped, flinging her black leather shoulder bag over her shoulder to illustrate her point, causing me to flinch and giggle at the same time. Then she smiled, revealing a missing tooth, and I decided I liked her, a little.

Gloria styled herself as a utopian anarchist. She maintained that violence wasn't necessary, since all corrupt governments were going to self-destruct anyway. She saw it as her job to "live in the future and embody the values that will someday be universal." Like stealing food from the college cafeteria to give to street kids or, more dangerously, stealing dope from the small time dealers on campus and using the "proceeds" for the cause.

I was impressed by how she wore silk slacks and tailored shirts, spurning the dingy denim sported by her radical peers, and flattered when she invited me to her parent's apartment on Central Park West. It took only one evening at the Kelly townhouse to disabuse me of the notion that the wealthy tend to be quiet and refined. If you were in the same room, her father yelled; if you were down the hall, he screamed.

The more I saw of him the more it became obvious that nothing Gloria could do would ever repay him for the hassle of raising such a difficult child. The miles of pristine white carpet suggested the possibility of blood-soaked floorboards beneath, and, by my second visit, I began to see an equation between Gloria's war against repressive government and her battles with her father. She had invited me home because she was afraid to be there alone.

Midway through my first year as a literature major, I woke up to the fact that all my favorite poets had one thing in common—they didn't know where their next meal was coming from. So against the advice of my artsy friends, I enrolled in criminology school. My decision was largely influenced by my Uncle Jake's stories about his stint with Air Force Intelligence in the '50s, at the height of the Cold War. His infrequent visits kept Mom and I on the edge of our seats as we followed his adventures, flying missions from Greenland to Siberia, trying to jam the Moscow Molly short-wave broadcasts that were demoralizing our troops.

I was usually one or two steps ahead of the narration, anticipating Jake's next move, and once, when my mother was out of the room, he voiced his opinion that I had what it took to become an ace private investigator. Jake tried to hide his disappointment when I enrolled in City College, but he couldn't resist slipping a brochure for the Smith Criminology Institute into one of my text books.

When I made the switch, I expected Gloria to dump me faster than burgers and fries disappeared from the college cafeteria, since I was working for the "man" and couldn't be trusted. She surprised me. "What's the difference between you scrutinizing bloodstains and me analyzing minds?" Still, she scoffed at my idea that a private investigator could be an effective advocate for gun control or go undercover to expose right wing conspiracies in government. "Your clients will all be John Birchers," she predicted. "And your patients will be their unhappy wives," I shot back. We were both right.

A year before I got my criminology degree, Gloria introduced me to the new man in her life. Zachary Barnes was a rabid leftist who seemed more in love with Gloria's ideology than with her. Maybe that's why, when he asked me out a month later, I didn't turn him down. Our first date should have raised more red flags than May Day. The evening started out innocuously enough, with chicken soup and gargantuan corned beef sandwiches at Katz's on Houston. We gulped down warm cream sodas and dove into huge portions of food, worthy of hungry immigrants just off the boat. When a cockroach skulked across the table, I quipped, "Does he come with the meal or did you pay extra?" but Zach didn't crack a smile. He collared the waiter, demanding a refund for our sandwiches and then, to cover his embarrassment, subjected me to a long lecture on how miserable working conditions are in non-union restaurants. I actually think that's why I went to bed with him that night—to get him to stop yammering.

That Zach was a little mad I knew, but I was attracted like the proverbial moth to the laser-like intensity of his political views. He was the only man I'd ever met who could keep track of all the socialist factions within the United States and what they stood for, which ones were "revisionist" and which ones followed Trotsky, or Stalin, or whatever the red flavor of the month was. All I can say in my defense is that in those days I admired obsession for its own sake.

I soon discovered that underneath the fountain of Zach's rhetoric flowed a hidden reservoir of tenderness. It was as if sex opened a portal to a remote and pleasant land of timeless enjoyment where we could stay for an afternoon or an entire day, as long as no words were uttered. Because as soon as speech intruded, the spell was broken. Even a phrase as banal as "let's cook dinner," had the power to throw the switch that turned the projector off and lit the house lights, revealing two strangers sharing a lumpy mattress surrounded by stacks of polemics demanding to be read.

Zachary's mother, Dorothy, a well-preserved school teacher with shellacked blue hair and a remote manner, was the only member of his family to attend our wedding at City Hall. "You know his father committed suicide," she confided, as if she were informing me that he preferred salami to roast beef. Later, I deciphered what she was trying to say. The distorted lens through which Zach saw the world was shaped by his father, a proud man who was blacklisted during McCarthyism and lost his job as a high school chemistry teacher.

"Leo was denounced because he went to a rally against the House Un-American Activities Committee," Zachary told me one night, after consuming three bottles of Danish beer. "The FBI photographed him, and three weeks later he lost his job. Dorothy went to work in an office, and he sat home all day feeling sorry for himself."

"You must have been devastated when you lost him."

"At first I was, but now I look at it differently. I'm grateful that I learned at an early age how a man can destroy himself if he's not fully committed to his beliefs." To Zach, doubting was a sin; proof was useful, but secondary.

I was still in criminology school when we got married. To my relief, Zachary had no problem with my future career in law enforcement. He knew plenty of defense attorneys with clients who couldn't afford to hire an investigator, and he expected me to devote myself to freeing penniless activists by exposing trumped up charges. As it turned out, we weren't married long enough for me to disappoint him.

Ask the Dead

When Zach and I merged households, we also combined our meager bank accounts. When I asked him about a large deposit that appeared on our statement, almost $15,000, he said he'd inherited the money from a relative. The money disappeared a few days later, only to reappear in the account a week after that, and he continued to evade my questions. Since he was working as a union organizer, bringing home no more than $150 a week, I knew something was up, and it drove me crazy. Was he on the take? Was he robbing banks?

The answer came in the form of two bruisers who busted the safety chain when I opened the door. The tall Cro-Magnon one searched the apartment none too carefully, while the short Neanderthal explained that they were doing us a favor by looking for valuables instead of breaking Zach's legs for failure to pay his gambling debts. "Don't take this personally, ma'am. We're just doin' our job."

We had a blow out, and after that Zach kept his promise to stop playing the horses. But my husband had fallen off a pedestal of his own making, and I was the sole witness. He didn't want me around as a reminder of his imperfection. Adultery was just his way of making sure I'd ask him to leave, which I did…one year, almost to the day, after we were married.

* * *

Walking towards the Riverside Library on Amsterdam, I pass two people engaged in the popular New York pastime of solo conversation. One of them is talking into a cell phone, but the other is a battle-scarred street veteran, a large, filthy woman who in this neighborhood is free to share her sobs, loud hiccups and gravel-voiced expletives without fear of attracting undue attention. Gazes will not divert in her direction and social services will not run to the rescue, unless she has the effrontery to fall down and block the sidewalk.

Entering the library, I wish for the umpteenth time that I had an Internet connection at home. Luckily there's no waiting list for the PC's. On Chase Manhattan's Web site, there are five branches listed for the Bronx. One of them is at the intersection of University and Tremont, close to where Gabriel was attacked.

Maybe he was on his way to make a deposit after he sold the photograph.

Next I connect to Licenseplate.net and order a trace on the license plate of the Suburban from Georgia that Sonny's pal at the warehouse was driving, results in 24 hours, a bargain at $39.95. I'd ask Lieutenant Saleh to do this, but I'm not ready to unleash his pointed questions or tell him that Gloria's been ferrying smurfs around Manhattan.

After dropping off the film at One Hour photo, I head home. I didn't get much sleep last night and it's been a long day, so by seven o'clock I'm in dreamland on the couch. I wake up with a start, just as Amy Bingham is about to push me out the window instead of her husband. I down two cups of yerba matte to get the bad taste out of my mind before heading out to pick up the day's photographs and bring them back to the apartment.

In one shot Gloria faces the camera, holding one end of a table she's loading into the van. She's a study in quiet intensity, her mouth held in a tight smile of concentration—the same dedicated expression she wore in the days when she organized the minimum wage workers at the summer resort where she was a lifeguard and got herself fired. Only this time the stakes are higher, and she may have gotten someone killed.

entombed in musty pages
resurrected under hot stage lights
by heart thumping voices
poetry!

Chapter Eight

This is one of those evenings when I break down and nuke a pot pie in the microwave. Afterwards, full but unsatisfied, I give my new sound-activated recorder a workout. I know I could type my case notes on the NEC laptop Stan gave me as a parting gift, but it wouldn't be the same. I like dictating, because speech comes out relatively unprocessed and sometimes new ideas about a case emerge as I talk.

With business taken care of, I take some time to hunt through my poetry notebooks and read through a handful of new pieces I've managed to crank out during the past month. On impulse, I decide to make one of my infrequent visits to Scandals, a poetry venue in Chelsea. It's Slam night—who knows—maybe I'll get up the courage to compete. If not, others will no doubt be spouting words worth hearing.

The phone rings as I'm locking the door, and I slip back inside to answer it. "Ms. Epstein, this is Paul Boudreau." His voice is resonant, pleasing, with a slight twang, not southern, maybe Midwestern. "Chloe Sterling told me you came to see her. She was very upset. She took Beverly's death very hard—collapsed at the funeral and was hospitalized for several months."

If only I'd known. I was so busy probing for answers I didn't notice the open wound. "Are you still there?" Paul ventures into the silence.

I tug on the telephone cord, moving backwards until I can kick the door closed behind me. "Is it true that Beverly was dating you just before she died?"

"No, not really." He sounds uncomfortable, his baritone raised a notch towards tenor. "We went out once or twice for coffee after a book club meeting. We were becoming friends, but I was seeing someone else."

"Did Beverly know this?"

"I remember telling her, but Bev wasn't much of a listener—more the type who fit people into her own reality, whether it suited them or not."

There's vehemence in his tone. Something must have happened between them. I make a snap decision. "Would you be willing to get together and talk about this?"

"You mean, in person?"

I wait out his decision, stretching my neck and wiggling my shoulders to get the tension out.

"Sure," he says. "I was thinking of asking you the same thing."

We arrange to meet at Scandals at ten-thirty. Around nine, I take a cab to West 23rd Street, where there's already a small crowd lounging around outside the club, some of them mumbling pieces of poems that it's a little late to be memorizing. All of them are considerably younger than me—the women self-conscious in the kind of stylishly tight shoes that would cripple me in one day, the men uniformed in black tank tops, their arms pale in defiance of summer.

Upstairs, the walls are throbbing to the beat that accompanies the singsong rhetoric poets fall into when they come out of their caves and get to share their feelings with actual people. I pay my four dollars at the door and add my name to the sign-up sheet. I can always change my mind later. Scandals has an old-fashioned tin ceiling and a wood plank floor that make it perfect for dancing, but an acoustic disaster. Cyrus is on stage, one of my favorites—doesn't overdo it, lets the words do their magic, using his liquid, husky voice to toss his lines. "The name of this poem is *Possession*," he says, his words washing up gently on the shores of our ears.

You need to be called
you don't just sneak into my psyche
(unless it's an emergency)

Ask the Dead

you need to be called
by that invisible part of myself
that knows that a wave
is more than water
that thought is more
than electricity

you need a space to come into
so that when you see through my eyes
our vision pierces the curtain
and when you move my body
our steps are taken with careful
abandon, feeling our way
along the unseen road between your
place and mine

After Cyrus mesmerizes the audience, Marty Elias, the energetic pixie who hosts the Slam, leaps onto the stage and wakes us up with a stream of inane patter that will continue until the end of the final bout. Given the intensity of the poetry, her zany witticisms are always a pleasant relief. For the last half hour she's been circulating through the crowd, recruiting the judges for tonight's event. Marty once told me, "I look for the unopinionated, suburban faces, folks from Connecticut who haven't read a poem since college and are gonna be knocked over when they hear something great." Off stage she's a bookish-looking woman, heavy set and deceptively serene. On stage, she's a whirlwind of enthusiasm who can make the most obnoxious heckler yearn to be safe at home, yelling at the TV.

"Okay people, you all know the rules but let's go over them anyway. Each poem must be of the poet's own construction. Each poet will perform for a maximum of three minutes and points will be deducted for each second past the ten second grace period. No props, costumes, or musical instruments. Five people in our audience have agreed to act as judges this evening—let's hear some applause for these foolishly brave individuals. They will rate each

85

poem from one to ten. We then drop the high and low scores, and add up the remaining three scores for a total ranging from zero to thirty.

"Tonight we have eight poets signed up, which means that after the first round there will be four poets left and after the second round we'll narrow it down to two finalists, one of whom will win the grand prize of no less than twenty-five dollars!"

Once writing poetry was an internal journey, a way to excavate fossils from the strata of one's past, filled with subtle nuances that only the printed word could convey. The spoken word revival that swept the country during the '80s changed all that—American poetry became more political and confessional when the low and high brow categories blended into the democratic soup called the Slam.

Marty pulls the names of the contestants out of a hat to determine the order in which we'll read, and my name comes up third. Among the slammers, I recognize a few regulars who compete every week in the hopes of making the New York team. They're all good, but given that judges are chosen at random, with preference given to new faces, even a first timer has a good chance of winning.

Following a soap opera satire and a lesbian rights poem that both bring the house down, the judges' score cards add up to 27 and 26 respectively, and it's my turn. Some poets look for receptive faces in the audience with which to make contact while performing, but I've learned that Slam attendees generally want to witness, rather than participate in, the catharsis. On stage, I try to hold back the emotion 'til my belly is rock hard and focus inwards until the release. The piece I wrote last year, on how my best friend Daria and I survived the street violence in the Bronx by escaping into our fantasy world, usually gets me past the first round, and it doesn't fail me tonight. I leave the stage with an encouraging 29.

With five more poets left to perform in the round, I head for the bar and order a beer to calm my late-reacting nerves.

"Beverly would have liked this place," says a slim, boyish-looking man with large hands, introducing himself as Paul Boudreau. He's found my Dodgers cap in the crowd. I'd counted on it being the only one.

Paul's face has an ethereal quality that's not entirely due to the strobe lighting and a buzz cut that accentuates the angularity of his cheekbones and aquiline nose. He glances at the notebook under my arm. "Are you going to read?"

"Yeah, I'm slamming tonight. Already made it to the second round."

"Sorry I missed you." He turns his head towards the stage, where a performance artist I've seen before is writhing in self-induced agony, spastic movements accompanying each wrenching word.

"Where does he go from here—the U.S. Congress?"

I could like this guy. He collects his drink, and we find an open table, no small feat, with a good view of a support column.

"So tell me about Beverly."

Paul looks upward, as many of us do when talking of the dead. "We were in a book group together, and by the second meeting I could see she had a gift for cutting through pretense. Once she interrupted an erudite discussion about archetypes to propose that we examine the belly button of the person next to us to see if it was a inny or an outy." He sits back in his chair for a moment, as if surprised at himself for warming to the subject.

"Beverly had a gift for finding the child in each of us. She was the only one in the group who could call you an idiot and you wouldn't mind, because she was contrasting your foolishness with the wisdom within that you never listen to."

"Sometimes we romanticize the dead."

"I wouldn't say sometimes—I'd say always." He holds eye contact when he speaks, which I like, but there's a precision about his speech that strikes me as unnatural. "When she wanted to, she could dig in, get under a person's skin."

"But not yours."

"I've thought a lot about that. I think she frightened me." The way he strolled in tonight and made himself at home, he doesn't strike me as easily intimidated. He seems to catch my thought. "Maybe it was fear of my own emotions, and not Beverly's, that made me feel ill at ease." Either he's amazingly comfortable with himself or a complete phony.

"In her diary, Beverly refers to your work at the hospital. Are you a doctor?"

"Hell no, I'm an orderly. I also play bass when I can, mostly studio work, some classical gigs." He squints at me in the dim light. "Chloe told me you're a private eye."

"Private investigator. Retired, but not now."

"That's unusual—a poet-detective." He seems genuinely interested. Or maybe he's trying to distract me from the subject at hand.

"Did Ellie ever talk to you about a student named Letitia?"

"Ellie?"

"Sorry, I mean Beverly." I'd better not let that slip again. Who's gonna trust a gum-shoe who talks to ghosts and doesn't even get their names right? I try again. "Letitia's father was suspected of molesting her. Beverly filed the report that got the case started."

"This is the first I've heard about it."

"Beverly let the mother and daughter stay at her place before they left town. You didn't know?"

Paul chugs his beer. Whether he's dealing with his feelings or his thirst, it's hard to say. "Come to think of it, there was one time when the book group was scheduled to meet at Beverly's, but she insisted they use my place instead. She said she was backed up on housecleaning and was embarrassed."

"She was probably sworn to secrecy about Letitia and her mother's location."

"I thought she was too concerned with appearances to let us see her messy apartment." The frown lines above his eyes deepen. "Obviously I didn't know her very well. There were a lot of things about the way Beverly acted during the last months of her life that puzzled me, but after she died, I didn't think there was much point in dwelling on her problems."

Our conversation has been holding its own above the buzz of the crowd, but now Joan Tavares takes the stage, a local favorite, impossible to ignore. Paul and I turn our chairs towards the compelling sound of her singsong contralto and for three minutes experience what it's like to run a marathon while recovering from cancer.

It's not an easy act to follow, but I try to get us back on track. "Beverly wrote about spending the weekend with you, at a cabin."

"Like a lot of people, Beverly was lonely. Diaries aren't meant to be taken literally—they're usually a blend of truth and fiction."

"Like what you've told me so far?" We both laugh, but I know I've stepped over the line. Damn my uncouth mouth.

While the judges are making up their minds about Joan's performance, Paul gets up and reaches for the coat on the back of his chair. "You've given me a lot to think about. I'll stay in touch."

Not likely, given the way I've driven him off. But there's no time for making amends. I've got to get myself together for round two.

No one's more surprised than me when I score high enough to qualify for the one-on-one face off. I give it all I have, but when the crucial moment comes, my delivery wanders off—either because I'm distracted by the awkward end to my conversation with Paul Boudreau, or because my playful words are no match for Reggie Pinero's non-stop hip hop dialog with himself as his cheating ex-girlfriend, so vile that the entire audience is ready to crucify her before he's done. Either way, I come in second. Not shabby.

* * *

My cluttered writing den is also my favorite place to relax with a glass of wine. The intensity of the slam has got my juices flowing and images are popping from mind to page as fast as I can write. Tomorrow I'll prune, but tonight I write with no inhibitions, locking the editor out of the private garden and allowing myself to cherish weeds and cultivated plants alike. Having big plans for the morning, I turn in at midnight. After tossing and turning for an hour, I try watching the TV news, which does nothing to relax me. I end up on the couch with an Allen Furst novel and lose myself in the travails of the French Resistance. Waking at 2 a.m., I wish I'd brushed my teeth, but it turns out to be more than bad breath that's pulled me out of the depths of slumber.

Dimly back lit against the window shade, there's someone occupying the armchair facing the couch. His face is covered by a stocking mask, and in the dimness I make out an ugly revolver pointed straight at my head. The gun follows me as I sit up slowly.

The voice is muffled but the words are plain. "You're off the case or you're dead. Take your pick." Does he have a slight Southern accent, or is it my imagination? He takes his time getting to the door—is that walk familiar? I sit perfectly still until I hear the elevator take him away.

How the hell did he get in here? The deadbolt is unpick-able. Maybe the super provides keys for an honorarium. I'm up the rest of the night pondering that very question and rummaging around the apartment to make sure nothing's missing. First thing in the morning, I dial up a locksmith who shows up an hour later and, for a hefty fee, installs a new dead bolt, restoring the illusion of privacy.

Ask the Dead

Garden dirt
traveling under fingernails
to explore foreign soil
someday spaceships will take you

Chapter Nine

The open fire hydrant on East 6th is generously drenching bathers aged six to sixty—some traditions never die. I cross the street, hoping to stay dry, and narrowly dodge a soccer ball bouncing off the bumper of the red Camaro parked in front of New Beginnings. Once it would have outclassed the neighborhood; now it's just another sign of gentrification. Gloria leans in to kiss the driver. Out of context, it takes me a moment to place him as Larry Tollway, the CO who was so accommodating at Rikers Island. Today he doesn't look half as happy to see me, but manages a weak smile as he maneuvers the car back and forth, trying to wiggle out of an impossibly narrow space.

"Well, if it isn't the book lady. Looks like your visit to Gabriel didn't do him much good, eh?" Larry turns back to Gloria. "See you tonight, doll." Did I really hear him say that? Gloria's been called a lot of things, but I'm sure *doll* isn't one she'd take lying down. Unless lying down is a hobby they share.

"An interesting man, Larry." I remember that tone of false confidentiality from our college days. We walk inside and Gloria elaborates on the way to her office. "As a white boy growing up in Bedford Stuy, you'd expect him to be tough, which he is, but he's also surprisingly compassionate. Larry's our spy at Rikers. He helps us find the most promising candidates for the re-entry and drug rehabilitation programs." I could ask her what else he helps her find, but I've come here on more serious business.

This is a woman who's not easily flustered, so I'm truly gratified by the scarlet flush that creeps up her neck to her face as she examines the photographs I've spread out on her desk. "The Cornings won't be happy that you're wasting their money this way."

91

By now her voice has regained its usual stridency. She picks up a photo from the pile, holding it by the corner as if it were contaminated. "So what if I choose to use my car to run errands for my friends? Peddlers are a persecuted minority in this city and deserve whatever help they can get."

"FINCen doesn't see it that way," I say, handing her a copy of Gabriel's bank statement. "How much do you have stashed away off shore? A million? Two?"

Her shoulders sag, and I feel a twinge of regret. Against my better judgment, I tell her that I gave the bank statement to Lieutenant Saleh before I knew she was implicated. Seeming to take this as a sign that I'll at least consider her version of the story, Gloria brightens. "Jo, have you ever known me to be involved in something that didn't benefit the greater good?" I've observed that all politicos have the same delusions, but there's no sense telling that to Gloria. "Let's go for a walk," she says, "there's something you should see."

At 11 a.m., the heat is approaching shoe-baking intensity and, for every step I take, it feels like the humidity is pushing me back two. We stop on East 8th Street, at a spot I remember as a trash-strewn lot infested with giant rats. It's now a lush, well- cared for garden, adorned with delicate wrought-iron sculptures and filled with fruit trees and shrubs that I admire no less for not knowing their names. For me it's enough that this patch of green, reclaimed from a garbage dump sandwiched between two decrepit brick buildings, can make the sky above it appear more clear and blue than it really is.

Gloria opens the gate and we pass under a grape arbor, following a flagstone path that winds around a Koi pond and ends in front of a toolshed, locked up tight. She pulls a set of keys from the side pocket of her bright yellow bib overalls. "I'm sure you've heard about the Green Guerillas and the fight to preserve the community gardens. We managed to save more than a hundred empty lots from the developers, but that was only because celebrities got involved and bought the land."

She pulls out two trowels, but, when I shake my head, she puts one of them back on the shelf. I'm not into weeding other peoples' gardens, even if they're sponsored by movie stars. I do, however, let her talk me into pushing the wheelbarrow into the main garden, which is safeguarded by miles of chicken wire. "There are gardens all over the city now. Isn't that enough of a victory for the forces of greendom?"

She looks at me like I'm a retard. "Not by a long shot. Most of the greens have been lulled to sleep by their success. They don't see how this movement is a sham, a meaningless symbol, unless we use the gardens to teach people how to be self-sufficient." Working her way down a row of gone-to-seed lettuce, Gloria punctuates her words with stabs of the trowel, pulling out dandelions and other broad-leafed weeds that she tosses into the wheel barrel. "People are complacent and self- satisfied. Most of them want to be left alone to grow their flowers and vegetables in peace."

"Why not? It's a free country."

"Oh, I love it when people say that." She stretches to ease a crick in her neck. "What kind of freedom do you mean? Freedom to send the children of the lower classes to fight and die so we can stabilize fossil fuel prices? Freedom to anesthetize our existential pain by turning on the TV and beaming cathode rays directly into what's left of our brains?" While she talks, Gloria scans the garden as if addressing a crowd, but there's only me and a one-eyed squirrel.

"I know! Maybe you're talking about freedom to absorb distorted newscasts delivered by insincere actors and filtered by corporate interests whose goal is to ignite fear in hearts around the world that otherwise might beat to the same drum? Or freedom to watch reality shows that glorify greed and the obsession to conform? Freedom to…"

Tempting as it is to see how long her batteries will last, I put my hand on her arm. "I get the point Gloria, but aren't we also free *not* to do these things?"

She waves the trowel dangerously close to my face. "Tell that to the brainwashed mall rats who terrorize their peers for not wearing designer clothes."

"Isn't that a matter of education? Of social evolution?"

"In your dreams. We need to scrap the old system and rebuild society on an ethical foundation." By now she's left enough piles of dug up earth in her wake to aptly illustrate her words.

"Who determines what these new ethics will be?"

"The people do—once they're given the information they need to make good decisions."

"Sounds like brainwashing to me."

"So, according to you, we should all just wait around for the greedy to share and the power hungry to release their strangle-hold on the earth's resources? That's not gonna happen all by itself and that's why Sal and I want to take the green movement to another level." A few kale plants have gone missing from the row, and Gloria kicks at the empty spaces. "Damn those kids. I don't mind them helping themselves, but do they have to pull the plants out by the roots?!" She applies herself to moving some seedlings into new homes in the rich earth.

"We need homesteads that are more than temporary squats that 'make a statement.' Sal and I already own the land we need, and we're *this* close," she holds up two fingers close together, "to having the resources we need to build a self-sustaining community."

I should know better, but I can't help asking. "Who will have the privilege of living there?"

Gloria stands up and brushes herself off. "Take a look around. Who wouldn't want to exchange these grim streets for clean, affordable housing and fertile soil? This is no utopian vision—it's reality in the making, thanks to Sal's business partners from California."

"It's not a business, Gloria, it's a felony."

Peeling off her gardening gloves, Gloria puts away her tools, and we head back towards New Beginnings. Her work in the garden may be finished, but the stream of words goes on, unabated.

"Money laundering happens to be the third largest business in the world, Jo. It's practically a national institution, although the term didn't appear in print until some journalist coined it during the Watergate scandal."

"That's your benchmark?"

She stops me in the middle of a crosswalk, yelling above the horns blaring their objection to our presence in the middle of the street. "Let me ask you something. Do you think marijuana should be legalized?"

"You know I do."

"Then you have to agree that we're reinvesting profits from a morally legitimate enterprise. There's no harm done and the smurfs are well paid."

"Gabriel was paid somewhat differently."

"His death had nothing to do with this."

Miraculously, we reach the curb alive. Now it's my turn to get excited. "Gabriel was a client of yours, he was bailed out by one of your colleagues, then murdered before he could make a deal with the District Attorney. How could there *not* be a connection?" This puts a kink in her stride, and she stumbles perilously close to an open cellar door that's flush with the sidewalk. "From what I've read in the newspapers, it was a gang execution."

"Or maybe one of your associates decided he was a threat to your operation."

In angry silence, Gloria wipes her mud-encrusted boots on the New Beginnings welcome mat. Inside her office, she gathers up the pictures and shoves them at me. "We're not some kind of crime syndicate. We're just a handful of people, all of whom I trust. If you knew them like I do, you'd feel the same way."

"What does Daniel Rose think about this?"

"He writes his little grants and doesn't ask questions about the large donations Sal drops in his lap. The man's too steeped in theory to stoop to practice. He's such a stiff shirt that if he knew what Sal and I were doing, he'd shut the place down and throw our clients out on the street. You won't say anything, will you?"

"What if I'm next on the hit list, Gloria? I had a visitor last night who promised me a very short future if I stayed on the case."

The puzzled look in her eyes seems as authentic as the Kandinsky watercolor on the wall of her office, but I wouldn't bet on either one. "Here's what I propose, Jo. I'm willing to help you find out who killed Gabriel. All you have to do is promise not to turn anyone in, except the murderer."

"No matter who it turns out to be?"

"I've got nothing to fear on that score. None of our partners are killers. You can check us out, collect alibis, the whole deal." She knows it's a tempting offer.

"First, tell me, where does the money come from?"

"There's a big grow operation in Mexico. Sal flies the money in from California in his private jet, and we distribute the cash to the smurfs. They make the deposits, we get our share—very simple."

"Maybe Sal is freelancing for someone else, someone who didn't want Gabriel to talk."

"Have it your way, Jo. Go ahead and chase shadows if you want to. What you should do is track down the gang members who killed Gabriel."

A few more minutes of this circular conversation and I've had enough. I decide to leave Gloria up in the air about my decision on whether or not to bust her and Sal. Needing a good think, I mosey over to Tompkins Square Park, where a few kids are playing roller hockey, their goals marked by tipped over garbage cans. In our college days, Gloria and I came to the Village looking for people who knew more about life than we did. Now those people are us, and we still don't have any answers.

* * *

Ellie, you must be getting curious about my relationship with your ex-boyfriend. It's entirely innocent, I assure you. I intend to find out if your death really was a suicide. If you're watching, maybe this amuses you. Perhaps you're pleased to see how Paul regrets missing his chance with you. Stay tuned, Ellie. You're not a paying client but that doesn't mean you're any less important.

It's the first time I've spoken with Ellie outside of the bathroom, having abandoned this restriction on our relationship under stress. And stress is what I feel as I pack up the photographs I just showed to Gloria. I'm sending the pictures to my mom for safekeeping. No instructions are included on what to do in case anything happens to me. Losing me would be hard enough on her without the added hassle of having to clean up my mess.

I make a long overdue call to Leslie's parents at the Plaza.

Michael skips the greetings and spits it out. "Why aren't you answering our calls? Where have you been?"

"Trying to locate your daughter and find some hard evidence that will get her off the hook for murder." That quiets him down, and he agrees to meet with me tomorrow.

I'm usually inclined to ignore the doorbell. People who enter the building unannounced on the intercom are frequently up to no good. But when "Police! Open up!" resounds in the hallway there's not much choice. I take a quick look through the peephole and comply.

Fresh-faced detective number one, his NYPD shield clipped to the pocket of a cheap Armani knockoff, darts his frenetic eyes around the room like a lizard hunting for crickets. His partner is more sedate, a tall, reed-like woman with fluffy blonde hair and a sharp nose. "I'm Detective Leisel," she says, "and this is Detective Marsh. May we come in?"

"What's this about?"

Marsh's voice is a surprising basso profundo. "Josephine Epstein, we have a warrant for your arrest, on charges you violated Penal Code 220.39—Criminal sale of a controlled substance in the third degree."

"And where was this sale supposed to have taken place?"

"Lady, if you want to be the one who asks the questions, then get yourself a badge. You have the right to remain silent. Anything you say can and will be used against you in a court of law. You have the right to speak to an attorney, and to have an attorney present during any questioning. If you cannot afford a lawyer, one will be provided for you at government expense."

"This is crazy. Are you sure you have the name right?" Neither of the pair is willing to dignify this question with an answer. "Fine. Have it your way, but I'm going to call my lawyer first."

Sheila Blondt isn't in, but I know that she'll respond to my message requesting the honor of her company at the 24th Precinct, just as soon as she gets around to checking her voice mail.

some
take what they want
others
want to be taken

Chapter Ten

My first ride in the back seat of a police car is less than two minutes long. My first night in a cramped precinct holding cell approaches eternity. Sheila's words, so much less than reassuring, replay in my sleepless mind. "When they unpacked the box of books you brought to Rikers, they found a quarter ounce of heroin packed into a hollow space inside one of the paperbacks. You'll be taken downtown for arraignment, probably tomorrow morning. I think I can get you ROR, given your employment and standing in the community, so you'll be able to go home, but there's no question they'll get an indictment from the Grand Jury and take this to trial."

"All this over a quarter of an ounce?" I had naively inquired.

"Believe me, one ounce and a quarter more and you'd be facing an A1 felony, instead of a B, and have as much chance of making bail as an ax murderer. You say you were set up?"

"I *know* that I was. You don't spend much time with the innocent, do you?"

"Who knew you were delivering the books?"

"A CO at Rikers, my employer at the newsstand, my client and her attorney, Silas Harding."

"So how come you didn't call Silas when they arrested you?"

"I wanted you."

Sheila grilled me for an hour. She's a tough lady, makes no promises, and lets not one strand of her thick gray mane escape her elegant hair-do, in spite of the grueling days she spends navigating the Manhattan legal system in a wheelchair. By the time she left, I felt I knew where I stood. No wonder I'm a wreck.

I have an entire cell to myself, something I should be thankful for, but between the glaring lights, the loud coughs and louder complaints transmitting through the cement walls, sleep is no refuge.

Being confined in this coffin-like space has me struggling to control my claustrophobia, which at 3 a.m. threatens to escalate into panic. I try retreating into thoughts of who might be responsible for my being here and what I'd like to do to them when I get out.

I intend to ask Hasim to run a background check on Larry Tollway. No harm in that, although I'm not sure I was deliberately framed. Maybe someone saw the books being delivered and seized a convenient opportunity to move some contraband around the jail. From what I've heard, buying drugs on Rikers can be easier than scoring on the street. We're talking about the jail where an assistant deputy warden and three correction officers stole a Salvador Dali original right off the lobby wall.

At 9 a.m., they load five of us into what used to be called a paddy wagon, but has now, according to Nikolai, been re-christened a lunakhod (Moonwalker) by his witty compatriots. Upon arrival at the mammoth Manhattan Criminal Court building on Center Street, me and my new smelly friends are herded into the "pens" behind the courtroom. An hour later I'm facing Judge Rohmer, known for tapping her long purple nails instead of a gavel when she's displeased. Sheila makes a strong case for ROR, using terms like reliable and gainfully employed to paint me as an upstanding citizen who is not a flight risk. Luckily for me, Judge Rohmer waives bail, and I'm out on the street faster than a politician can shake your hand and size up your bank account at the same time.

* * *

On my way home in a cab, I call Hasim. If he's amused at my recent discomfort, his voice doesn't show it. "I'll run some background on Tollway, but I doubt if he set you up. DOCS doesn't hire people without checking them out."

As soon as I put the cell phone back in my pocket, it rings again. I'm beginning to feel like the character in a Ray Bradbury story who craves privacy so much that he dares to take off his wrist communicator and in the end is hunted down for the crime of being unreachable.

Eleanor Corning's voice conveys equal measures of relief and panic. "Leslie called and she says she's okay but she won't tell us where she is. She knows she's wanted for questioning but she doesn't want to turn herself in. How can they suspect her? Leslie wouldn't hurt anyone. She's a vegetarian!"

"The caller ID was turned off," says Mr. Corning, who's been listening in, "but I could hear some music in the background. It sounded Latin."

"I may know where she's staying, Mr. Corning, but right now it's probably best if she stays put until I'm able to find some evidence to clear her."

He thinks this over. "I guess being charged with obstruction beats facing a murder rap." I tell them both to hang tight and that I hope to have some news for them soon.

My apartment has never looked so good—nothing like a night in jail to bring out the gratitude. By the time I scour the grime from my body and the paranoia from my soul, it's close to four o'clock. I need to get a move on if I'm going to stop at the library and still get to *The House of Art* before it closes.

At the library, I sign up for computer access. I have to wait ten minutes and stop two people who are not on the list from cutting me before I can log on. According to Licenseplate.net, the Chevy Suburban with the Georgia plates belongs to the Budget Rent-a-Car in Macon. This will take some follow up, but there's something about the driver in the camouflage outfit that doesn't jibe with Gloria's operation, and I want to know what it is.

One more stop at the post office on Columbus and I'm feeling infinitesimally lighter, having mailed the photographs. Now I'm ready for the main event of the day.

Taking a taxi to Lexington and 63rd, I commandeer the doorway of an out-of-business boutique, populated by nude mannequins, their modesty protected by brown paper sarongs that in this trendy neighborhood might become a fashion statement. I appreciate their quiet company and together we keep watch on the entrance to Alicia's workplace. At five sharp, out she comes, heading north at a nice clip. She stops off at D'Agostinos, and I corner her in the produce department, where she's adding a large bunch of bananas and some turnips to her cart.

"Shopping for a vegetarian isn't easy," I remark. Alicia jumps sky high, which isn't far, given the low ceiling.

"I've got dinner guests coming," she improvises.

"If I'm going to help Leslie you've got to let me talk to her."

Alicia's attention is claimed by a fascinating bunch of rhubarb. "I don't know where she is."

"Then you won't mind if I walk you home. I can help you carry the groceries upstairs."

She turns to face me. "You're violating my privacy."

"If you don't cooperate it's your freedom that will get violated, and by folks who are a lot less forgiving than me."

She bows her head in mock submission. "Alright then, you might as well help with the shopping. I need some peas and carrots from the freezer. It's at the back of the store." High marks for quick thinking—she's angling for a chance to use her cell phone.

"Sorry, I'm staying here with you. That way Leslie won't leave your apartment before we get there."

"How did you know?"

"I like Brazilian music as much as you do, but you should have turned it off when Leslie called her parents."

* * *

Sitting on the gleaming white sofa, her appearance only hints at the way she looks in the photo pinned to her cubicle wall. She's replaced her micro braids with a short natural cut that makes her eyes seem larger and her cheekbones more elegant. But this new mature look is cancelled by the nervous brown hands busy tearing a tissue to shreds in her lap.

"My parents told me they hired you, but it won't do any good." Her voice is rough silk. "The press has already convicted me."

I pull up a chair, so that we're sitting knee to knee. "Tell me what happened."

"When I got back, Gabriel was dead."

"Back from where? Please, start at the beginning."

Leslie takes a deep breath. "That would be when I went to see him at Rikers after he was arrested for killing that gang banger. I remember how guilty I felt—knowing that I'd been at a fancy

101

breakfast meeting at Sunflower House while he was on the street fighting for his life. When I offered to help, Gabriel asked me to look up a friend of his in the Bronx who saw the attack."

"You mean Sonny Rodriguez?"

She's looking into space like a tired child. "I didn't have much luck with Sonny. He's not what you'd call altruistic."

Alicia plays hostess, bringing in some cookies and chai, looking relieved that things have come out in the open. Leslie ignores the food, but I can't resist the almond crunch. When she continues her voice is stronger.

"A few days later Sonny showed up at my house. He said he needed a place to store some boxes for a few hours. This weird kid was with him, and it was clear that turning them down wasn't an option. They came back a few hours later to pick up the boxes, and right after they left, I got the shakes. It was awful, not feeling safe in my own apartment, so I moved in with Alcia." Leslie looks up and smiles at her friend, who comes and sits down beside her, giving me a look that says *this is a fragile person; go easy.*

"Did you tell anyone where you were?" I ask Leslie.

"No, not a soul, except my parents and Sal. And the only reason I called Sal was because I was worried about Gabriel. Sal told me that we had to bail Gabriel out right away, that his life was in danger. He said he was going to put up the money—two hundred thousand in cash. On Saturday, he picked me up and drove me to Rikers so I could post the bail." From her matter-of-fact tone she could be talking about buying a pair of shoes for a hundred dollars, rather than a man's freedom for two hundred thousand. If I ever get that blasé about money, maybe I'll hire someone to write my poems.

"Did you ask him why he didn't want to post the bail himself?"

She hesitates here. Sal is her friend. "Yeah. He said it was something to do with your investigation and the money and what he called 'footprints'."

"So you went to Rikers…and…" I'm starting to feel like a prompter rehearsing a reluctant actress.

"We waited for hours and finally Gabriel came out of the

holding area. When he saw us…there were tears in his eyes. The three of us went to my apartment, and Sal gave Gabriel new identity papers—a driver's license with a fake name and a matching social security card. He also gave us two plane tickets for a flight to Los Angeles."

Alicia's eyes are now glued to Leslie's face, like she's seeing her friend for the first time. I wonder how much Leslie has told her.

"Why did you think Sal was doing all this?"

"I thought he was incredibly generous. He must have known that as soon as we left the state he'd lose the bail money."

Now we're getting to the hard part—getting from their arrival at the apartment to Gabriel ending up dead. While I'm thinking up the next question, Leslie surprises me by continuing on her own. Her nerves seem steady now, as if telling the story has given her some distance from it.

"Sal and I left the apartment while Gabriel was taking a bath. I went to Macy's to buy some carry-on bags so we wouldn't have to check our luggage." The obvious question occurs to both of us and she adds, "I paid with cash, and I didn't bother to save the receipt."

I've seen it before. How the promise of an alibi can appear and disappear in an instant of unwelcome magic. "What time was this?"

"Around five-thirty." She pauses to gather herself for what comes next. The room is totally quiet, no traffic noise from the street, no ticking clock. "When I got back to the apartment I found Gabriel in the bedroom. I couldn't believe he was dead. I sat there, in shock, holding his hand. Then the panic set in. I know I should have called the police, but I ran."

"Did you use the fire escape on your way out?"

"No, I went out the front door. I was afraid that the person who did this would come after me! I took a taxi to Alicia's. I told her if anyone calls, even my parents, you don't know where I am." She looks down at the pieces of tissue littering her skirt. I should give her a break, but there are a few more things I need to know.

"When I came here the other day, did you tell Alicia to give me the key to your apartment?"

"It was my idea," says Alicia. "Leslie was listening in the other room. Later we agreed it was a good thing."

"To let me find Gabriel's body."

Alicia flinches, but her eyes hold steady. "Someone had to find him and since you were working for his mother…"

"Please think carefully, Leslie. Do you think Sal is capable of murder?"

She gets up and wanders over to the window, standing in front of the air conditioner, the cold air filling the pleats in her skirt to create a pale green fan. "You don't know him like I do."

"I don't know him at all. But what a killer needs is a good motive and Sal has two—the bail money he stood to lose when Gabriel left town and his own prosecution for money-laundering if Gabriel talked to the District Attorney."

Alicia puts down the tea cup that was on its way to her lips. "What do you mean, money-laundering?"

I fill them in on what I've uncovered so far. This makes me the bearer of bad news, and Leslie looks like she wants to slap me. Instead she picks up the phone and punches in a long distance call. "Hi, it's Leslie, is Sal there?" There's a pause, and then, "Sal, I need to see you. No, it can't wait. There are some things that need explaining."

She listens for a while. "Alright, I'll ask Jo Epstein to give me a ride." She hangs up and gives me a defiant look. "He'll meet us at Sunflower House after his shift, at ten."

"You're telling me the Chairman of the Board of Directors babysits the residents?"

She shoots me a look filled with resentment. "Sal's not like…what you think."

"So I've heard. I'll handle this myself, Leslie. You'll be safer here."

"Don't patronize me! I feel responsible for what happened to Gabriel, and I'm going with you. If Sal agrees to back up my story, I'll turn myself in."

She's made of stronger stuff than her parents give her credit for. I arrange to pick her up at nine.

Riding the bus back to the West Side, I puzzle over why the

104

fake identity papers didn't turn up at the crime scene. There's no getting around the fact that if Sal came back to the apartment to kill Gabe, he'd have had good reason to take back the papers.

* * *

After I collect Ted's car, it takes me forty-five minutes to reach Hasim's address on Pelham Parkway, long enough to follow a few play by plays on the radio—the Yankees vs. the Seattle Mariners—and decide I'd better not tell him where Leslie is until we get her alibi confirmed by Sal.

Hasim's tidy brick house with its leaded windows and well-kept lawn looks like the perfect refuge for a cop who spends his days in the war zone. The woman who answers the door has soft brown eyes set wide in a round face. She laughs at my confusion as I try to shake her hand and take off my shoes at the same time. Her short black hair is stylishly cut above a dark blue cotton dress that's loose and comfortable. A woman who's not out to impress anyone with her beauty, but doesn't feel compelled to hide it.

"You must be Jo. I'm Samarah . My husband tells me you're a pretty sharp cookie." So he *is* married.

"He's no slouch himself." I pause to admire an embroidered wall-hanging in the foyer, covered with Arabic letters. "You'll find these in most Muslim homes," she tells me. "It translates as God is Great." I can tell she's made this explanation before and enjoys playing the ambassador.

The furniture in the living room has weight and substance, as does the large wooden dining room table, set for three. The eating utensils are solid silver and the legs of the armchairs are intricately carved in walnut, yet this feels like a house where possessions are valued for their use rather than their style. On the mantle a bust of Queen Nefertiti presides.

"Tonight's my turn in the kitchen," says Hasim, proceeding to bring a parade of dishes to the table. I stuff myself with creamy hummus dipped in flat bread, and then dig into the main course of stewed meat, Kebab Halla, served with rice pilaf. We make small talk and Samarah, who works at the United Nations as a translator, tells me about a colleague of hers who mistook the Vietnamese word for "enough" for a universally understood expletive causing an

105

uproar in the General Assembly. Hasim laughs heartily, although I'm sure he's heard the story before. I feel a small pang of jealousy at the easy give and take and the telepathic looks they exchange whenever one of them needs something.

After the chocolate cake, Samarah leaves us and Hasim gets down to business.

"According to FINCen, the money trail from the St. Dominic bank account leads to one of the biggest marijuana distributors on the west coast."

"How do they know this?"

Hasim takes a sip of Samarah's delicious coffee—he's no tea drinker at home. "Here in New York the average cop has to search three or four databases before he can piece together the information he needs. Because I know a few people in Washington, I was able to get access to the FINCen Gateway System. As soon as I entered the information you gave me, a query alert came up."

He looks pleased with himself, pauses for effect, then continues, "That's what happens when more than one agency does a search about the same subject. From that one New York City bank account number, the database came up with two leads. One of them points to a bank in the Caribbean, and the other red flags a bank account in California that's already of interest to investigators in Los Angeles. Gabriel's friends are cleaning money for a major player."

"I thought you said you didn't have any hard evidence," I say, failing to mention that I've recently found some of my own.

Hasim leans forward in his chair and locks his brown eyes on mine, proposing a partnership. "We need to find out who the New York smurfs are and how they receive the money they deposit in those bank accounts."

Here's my chance to break my word to Gloria and win lots of points with the police. Instead I don my ingenuous face and say, "I thought we were investigating a murder."

He sits back, puzzled by my attitude. "It's likely this murder was committed to cover up a money-laundering operation. If we cast a wide enough net, we can catch them all."

This neat and tidy scenario doesn't appeal to me, and I say so. "But what if you're wrong? Can't you hold off the Feds just for a few days? Tell them we're close to identifying the smurfs and don't want them to muddy the waters."

Hasim's manner becomes as formal as the day we first met in his office. "You're forgetting who I am, Jo. One lie can destroy a thousand truths. I thought better of you. Please leave my house." His deeply rooted sense of hospitality is probably the only thing that keeps him from telling me off.

Samarah looks puzzled at her husband's coldness when I bid them goodnight. She walks me to the door and then steps outside, something on her mind. "Can I have a word with you, Jo?" I steal a glance at my watch—Leslie is waiting—but Samarah chooses not to notice. "Hasim has told me a lot about you. He would never say so, but he does admire your perseverance on this case."

A rueful chuckle escapes from my throat. "Right now your husband is not my biggest fan."

Oddly, this news seems to please her. "I know a way you can get back in his good graces." She pauses for effect before plunging on. "You could help us find Khurram." Samarah's brown eyes, appealing and flecked with gold, keep me rooted to the spot.

"Hasim's sister, Halima, came with him to America in the '70s. When she married, she went back to Egypt to have the baby. Khurram was born in Cairo. In January of 2001, Halima sent Khurram to live with us so he could go to graduate school at Columbia. After 9/11, they rounded up all the Muslim men from foreign countries, but Khurram had a student visa and all his papers were in order. Silas Harding went to the INS hearing with Khurram and made sure that he wasn't detained. Naturally, we were relieved, but what we didn't know was that two of Khurram's Pakistani friends at NYU were under surveillance. Two months ago they were arrested."

"I read the story in the Times, Samarah. What happened to them?" Some unspoken signal gets us both walking towards my car, and she continues her story.

"Nothing was proven, but it made no difference. On the day the Pakistanis were deported, the tabloids put Khurram's picture in the paper, as if he too were involved. Then Khurram vanished— disappeared into thin air. Hasim did everything he could to find him, but his hands were tied."

She didn't have to tell me why. As a naturalized citizen—and a relative of Khurram's—any move he made would probably do more harm than good. We're at the car now, and I pull out my keys, thinking hard.

Samarah fidgets with her shawl. "Halima is trying to get permission to come here from Cairo to look for him. She's going out of her mind with worry."

I tell her that I have no friends in the Justice Department, that she'd be better off talking to a civil liberties attorney. She hunches her shoulders, arms crossed across her chest, and turns to walk back to the house. I've demolished her hopes and now I'm leaving. I reach for her elbow. "I'll do what I can."

Samarah's relieved smile makes her look ten years young-er. She pulls a snapshot out from under her shawl. "This is Khurram with his mother, taken the day before he left for the United States."

The young man in the picture is dressed in white, standing against a white background so at first it's hard to distinguish his features. His charcoal-shaped eyes are glancing sideways at the woman in black seated next to him, and his mouth curves slightly at the corners, as if tugged upward by both pride and humor. There's a stillness about Halima in the picture, as if she sensed that even a small movement could break the tenderness of the moment. Samarah turns over the picture. An overseas phone number is written on the flip side.

"Please, call her. Khurram telephoned her almost every day. She'll convince you he's done nothing wrong."

Samarah's smile keeps me warm all the way to the East River; then the quarrel with Hasim starts to replay in my head. I switch on the radio to drown him out, and Mose Alison takes over. *Your mind is on vacation and your mouth is workin' overtime.* How right he is. Why didn't I learn about tact, instead of Trotsky, from my mother?

* * *

Parking spots on the Upper East Side are harder to find than a native New Yorker at the Statue of Liberty. Five blocks from Alicia's, I squeak into a space behind a bus stop, barely legal. The front wheels of the Protegé will have to fend for themselves.

Leslie meets me in front of Alicia's brownstone and we walk down 85th Street, where store owners are already sweeping the sidewalk and closing their shutters for the night. Pleased to see that my favorite papaya stand is still open, I treat her to a creamy drink. We sit down at a fluorescent yellow table by the window and watch the commuters swarming out of the subway exit across the street. The bright lights and colors act like a stimulant, and Leslie's thoughts and feelings spill out like warm soda from a shook up bottle.

"It used to be that the worst thing in my life was being called an oreo by my black friends and a social climber by the whites. I came to New York to put that all behind me, and now I find that everything I valued about working at New Beginnings— the dedicated people, the fresh ideas—it was all a front for selfishness and greed."

I can offer small comfort. "Your illusions are nothing compared to Gloria's. She's planning to use her cut from the money-laundering operation to start a community of utopian anarchists. She wants to take over where the Paris Commune left off."

"The Paris Commune. Sounds like a '70s rock band," she says, dabbing at her papaya moustache with a napkin.

"Yeah, well it was the '70s alright—the 1870s. The workers took over Paris and held it for two months before being massacred by the French army."

"This is Gloria's blueprint for success?"

The kid's sharp. We throw our paper cups in the trash and walk the remaining block to the car. Leslie tosses her travel bag on the back seat, and we drive through the park, towards the West Side Highway.

"I've known Gloria for a long time. Anarchists think that if you get out in front and set an example, the rest of the world will follow."

Leslie surprises me by coming to Gloria's defense. "At least she's been helping the street peddlers fight the City Council."

We're running late. When we hit the Thruway, I push the Protegé up to 85 and turn on the cruise control. I turn on the stereo

109

and the CD player launches into *You Got No Right*. It's hard to picture Ted cruising to Nirvana, but living for three quarters of a century gives him dibs on any damn generation's music.

On a deserted stretch of the Sawmill River Parkway, a dark blue Subaru is flashing its hazard lights, parked perilously close to the white line. I slow down. The roof light is on, revealing the driver slumped over the wheel, either asleep or unconscious. "That looks like Sal's car," says Leslie. "We should stop."

I'm reluctant to do this, but also anxious to earn Leslie's trust. Pulling over, I stop a few yards in front of the vehicle. I intend to handle this myself, but Leslie is out of the car before I can stop her. By the time I get my door open and step out, she's leaning in the driver side window of the other car.

"Hey!" she yells and jumps back, as the Subaru's door flies open and a gun emerges, followed by a man, definitely shorter than Sal, wearing a ski mask. He grabs hold of Leslie's arm, pushing her towards me with the gun an inch from her ear, and shoves her into the Protegé. It looks like he's going to leave me by the side of the road, but then he bellows at me, "You! Get in and drive!"

Why didn't I see this coming? Too many nights counting magazines at the newsstand. With our captor covering us from the back seat, I have no choice but to follow his directions. We turn south on the two-lane highway, and then head west near White Plains. Leslie stares straight ahead. Out of the corner of my eye, I watch her chest laboring. She seems to be trying to control her panic with deep breathing. When we pass the sign for the airport, I give her an encouraging smile. She probably thinks I'm crazy, but I figure that with luck we may soon be 30,000 feet over, instead of 6 feet under, the ground.

We're passing the 8-foot barbed wire fence that surrounds the airfield, when a muffled order comes from behind, "Turn here." I cut the speed to 10 miles per hour and keep driving straight ahead, seeing no driveway to turn into. "Back up and turn, you idiot!" he screams through the mask, poking me with the butt of his gun for emphasis. I slam the Protegé into reverse, then carefully examine the fence as we move backwards. I still don't see an opening. "Stop! Turn right now!" This time I obey, expecting to crash into unmoving, wire mesh. The Protegé breaks through the fence, encountering no resistance. The pre-cut hole, invisible until the moment of impact, drapes itself over the front of the car like a modern sculpture. Directly in front of us, a sleek Citation business jet is warming its engines on the runway, a ramp in place in front of the cabin door.

Someone opens the airplane's hatch from the inside and at that moment the airfield is flooded with a dazzling white light. A tinny, amplified voice booms out from behind the fir trees lining the runway. "This is the F.B.I. You're under arrest. Come out with your hands behind your heads."

Hasim, you've gotten us killed, is my first thought. Our captor scrambles out of the car, opens the passenger door and grabs Leslie's arm, pulling her onto the runway. I start to follow. "Stay here!" he commands, the flash of gun metal backing up his words. Using Leslie as a shield, he walks backwards up the ramp. The last thing I see, before the airlock closes, is Leslie's terrified face in the floodlights. Seconds later, the jet screams down the runway.

most of the kids
never leave the neighborhood
I think they're afraid of wandering
into some strange gang's territory
and never coming back

Chapter Eleven

Everything done by the federal agents who descend on me with guns drawn is calculated to make me feel instantly guilty and humiliated. I'm handcuffed without a word and shoved into the back of a van, where they obviously expect me to cower in fear as I imagine what it will be like to be held in a basement indefinitely, finally cracking under the pressure of sensory deprivation and incessant questioning.

They do succeed in making me feel I've entered a foreign country where civil rights are suspended. Which is why the sight of Hasim through the window, deep in conversation with one of the gray-suited pack, is so welcome. There may be a storm gathering on his face as he approaches the van, but it's powered by the flesh and blood anger of a frustrated cop, not the mechanical sadism of a well-machined bureaucracy. He slides the door open but remains outside, frowning in at me.

"I had my doubts about you, but at the very least I thought I was dealing with a sane person, not a professional screw up. This is my reward for giving you an inside track—you're not content with messing up a major mone- laundering bust, you have to facilitate the kidnapping of a witness to a homicide as well. You knew we had an APB out for Leslie Corning, but you didn't have the courtesy, the common sense, to call me when you found her." He steps into the van and reaches beneath his coat at the same time. For a crazy second I think he's going to shoot me. Instead, he pulls out a key and unlocks the handcuffs. I follow him outside.

The floodlights are still on and Saleh rubs his eyes, red from lack of sleep and irritated by the glare. "God help me, I told the FBI that you're assisting me on this case. What happened?"

I owe him an honest answer. "Leslie and I were supposed to meet with Sal Salvatore, to ask him to come forward and confirm her alibi. She claims that Sal gave her the cash for Gabriel's bail and that he was with her when she left the apartment while Gabe was still alive."

His face is a picture of suspended judgment. "Was it Salvatore who abducted her?" he asks.

"I don't know. The kidnapper wore a mask."

Hasim takes a brief call on his cell phone, turning his back to me and listening intently. Then he motions for me to walk with him towards his car.

"They filed a flight plan for Miami, and we'll be tracking them through the regional control centers in Washington and Atlanta. If they don't land in Miami, we can ask Air Defense to intercept them, but with the girl on board there's not much they can do."

"Gloria told me that Sal owns the plane and usually flies it."

An angry twitch visits the muscles around his mouth, but he gets it under control. "We already know that, no thanks to you. After 9/11, all pilots of private planes have to confirm a confidential ID with the tower before filing a flight plan. As far as we know, Salvatore's flying that plane, but we might as well make sure. Why don't we go to this meeting that you and Leslie were so anxious to attend?"

Hasim opens the door to his cruiser and gestures for me to get in. He grips the steering wheel as if he'd like to strangle it and jerks the car into gear. "That was a vital piece of information you withheld. We could have picked up Sal, grounded the plane, and prevented a kidnapping."

When the odometer tops ninety, I risk a question, hoping to slow him down and keep us both alive. "How did you know about the jet?"

No change in speed, but he does answer. "Something called good police work. We already knew the money was stashed in an account on St. Dominic, where banking restrictions are not what they could be. I requested a list of airplanes registered to American owners in St. Dominic. Then I contacted the New York Regional Control Center for a list of small aircraft with flights booked from

St. Dominic to New York suburban airports. Sal Salvatore's Citation came up as a match in both cases, and it always flies out of Westchester. This particular Citation has a maximum takeoff weight of less than 12,000 pounds, which makes it exempt from the new security check regulations. We told the air controller in Westchester to let us know when Sal filed his next flight plan and tonight we got lucky."

"Leslie didn't."

"And whose fault is that?"

My silence tells him he's hit the mark, and he relents a little, slowing the cruiser to a speed less than life-endangering as we drive through Peekskill. "They filed a flight plan for San Juan, but I'm sure that's not their final destination. The FBI is monitoring the regional control centers between here and Miami—Washington, Atlanta, and Jacksonville. Air Defense could send up a fighter and try to force a landing, but these desperados know they won't be shot down as long as they're flying over a populated area and the girl's on board. Once they've flown a hundred miles off the coast, the Citation will drop off the radar, and if they're smart enough to turn off the transponder, even the satellites won't be able to keep track of them."

At Sunflower House the windows are dark, except for a light on the ground floor where the library is. It takes ten minutes for a slim dark figure in a bathrobe and floppy slippers to respond to the buzzer on the security gate. He squints at us through the bars as Hasim flashes his badge. "I'm James, the night supervisor. What's going on?"

"We're looking for Mr. Salvatore."

James stares at us, making no move to open the gate. "Sal's not here. He left around eight. I remember, because he told me he was catching a ride because his car wouldn't start. It might have been Ms. Kelly who took him home—she came by in the late afternoon." He looks over his shoulder, towards the tennis court. "That's strange. The Subaru was parked near the tennis court but I don't see it now. Maybe he came back for it later."

"Where does he live?" asks Hasim.

"On Red Wing Road. Go back to the highway, turn left and

then left again at the Red Rooster Market. It's the first driveway on the right."

Sal's house is a modest A-frame, so simply constructed he might have built it himself. The porch light is off, and there's no moon. Hasim takes a flashlight from the cruiser. He knocks, and when no one answers, opens the door. "Lots of people in the country don't bother to lock up," I say, but I know what we're both thinking.

We find Sal on the kitchen floor. The knife embedded in his chest has a grooved black handle, one that's commonly used for switchblades. I wonder if the same weapon took Gab-riel's life. At first glance, the graffiti on the wall above the sink looks similar to the markings left at the murder scene in Gramercy Park. Hasim calls the state troopers right away. He's not the type to trespass on another agency's territory. I wait as unobtrusively as possible while he briefs the local authorities, and then we leave.

In his car, driving back to the Protegé, the Lieutenant surprises me by sharing his thoughts. "Looks like we'll have to question Ms. Kelly."

It's the first time that Gloria's name has come up between us. I've got a feeling it won't be the last.

"You should talk with Sonny Rodriguez, too." I tell him about the boxes that Sonny stored at Leslie's apartment. "I think Sonny was using the truck from Sunflower House to make some money on the side. Maybe Sal found out."

"Thanks for the lead, we'll follow up." Hasim's tone is cold. He knows I'm not telling him the half of it. He stops behind Ted's car, still parked near the airport runway. I'm sure by now the police have gone over every inch of the Protegé with a fine tooth comb.

"I know it's my fault that Leslie was taken."

"Don't blame yourself—at least not entirely," Hasim grudgingly advises me. "This happened because those lowlifes found out how broke they are. The Feds have frozen all assets linked to the off shore account."

Hasim waits until I'm behind the wheel, and then leans in the window. "Next time I won't cover for you. I should have known better. As we say back home, 'Trust that man in nothing who has not a conscience in everything.'"

"Do they say that about women, too?"

There's no reply. I promise to come to the precinct in the morning for what he calls an honest talk.

On the drive back to the city, I try to think of what I might have done to avoid this mess. Short of refusing to take the case in the first place, nothing comes to mind.

* * *

It's 3 a.m., and if the elevator operator at the Plaza had x-ray vision he'd be able to see the ton of guilt weighing heavily in the pit of my stomach. I've made a present of my client's daughter to some kidnappers. The only thing missing was a ribbon tied around her neck.

Lights blaze in the Corning's room. Michael opens the door and as soon as I enter, he slams it shut. We stand facing each other in the hallway next to the bathroom, since he's too angry to invite me further inside. "We've had a phone call from Lieutenant Saleh." His voice is an enraged whisper, and his eyes bore into mine. "Do you think there'll be a ransom demand?"

"Yes. I think they know how wealthy you are." He recoils from this bald truth, but it's me who is on trial here.

"Can you give me any reason not to fire you, Ms. Ep-stein?"

"No, I can't. I had your daughter in my car, and instead of returning her safely to you, I drove her into harm's way. I let her talk me into taking her to Peekskill because she said it would help her to establish an alibi for the time of Gabriel's death."

Eleanor Corning comes out of her trance and pulls us both into the room. "You know how persuasive Leslie can be," she says to her husband. "Jo was smart enough to find her once. Maybe she can do it again. We can't waste time bickering." She turns to me, in her mind the matter seems already settled. "What do we do now?"

"Try to get some sleep. I'm going to meet with Lieutenant Saleh." Eleanor sees me out, while Michael sits by the window, eyes inward, watching a horror movie projected by his fears. "I'll get Leslie back," I tell him. He doesn't look up.

* * *

"We lifted Sonny's prints off the box of souvenirs we found in Leslie's apartment, and the gang unit has tied him to the Scorpions. It's enough to bring him in for questioning on both murders. There's an APB out, but my hunch is he's on board that airplane with Leslie and well out of U.S. airspace by now." I'm sitting in Hasim's office, barely awake after three hours sleep and minus the usual cup of tea because I'm in the dog house.

He's put his desk between us and the words come out well rehearsed, and, I admit to myself, well-deserved. "Now that you know how dangerous these people are, surely you're willing to help us stop them. If you're covering for someone, it's only a matter of days, maybe hours, before we catch up with them. Everyone involved with Sunflower House will be questioned, and we're also looking at that agency on the Lower East Side."

A private investigator often has conflicting allegiances, and this is one of those times when I have no choice but to sit back and watch as the interests of my client and the demands of the law duke it out. Yes, I should tell Hasim about Gloria's involvement with the smurfs and her possible complicity, however unintentional, in murder. But if she's arrested or held for questioning, she won't be available to help me locate and rescue Leslie. And on top of that, Gloria and I have a long-standing, albeit tumultuous, friendship.

"I've got enough to hold you as a material witness. Is there any reason I shouldn't?"

"Lieutenant, I wouldn't be much use to you in jail. You've got to give me more time. I promise I'll cooperate fully when I've got the evidence you'll need to make the case."

Hasim stands up, indicating the meeting is over. He's questioned hundreds, if not thousands of people during his career, and he knows he's not getting anywhere with me.

"I don't think you have any idea of the ruthlessness you're dealing with. You're playing with a snake and calling it a worm."

I get to the doorway before it comes to me. "David knew how big Goliath was but he also knew that sometimes a sling shot works better than a cannon. " Two can play at this proverb game.

*a city
is only as green
as its money*

Chapter Twelve

Walking down Canal Street, I zigzag around the piles of garbage that insist on belying Tribeca's veneer of gentrification. The dilapidated building where Gloria lives once housed a garment sweat shop, in the days when these dismal streets were trudged by immigrants instead of art collectors and tourists. She still inhabits the same drafty loft where she hosted hundreds of passionate political gatherings and equally intense all-night parties. Student sit-ins, peace marches and civil rights demonstrations were all organized around the massive library table, usually over tart glasses of cheap Chianti.

Gloria was always well-connected in progressive circles, and one night I dropped by to find several members of the Bolshoi Ballet troupe doing stretch exercises while waiting for her to drive them to the theatre. She liked to hang out with Marxists, and few of them were aware that she was a dyed-in-the-wool anarchist. Paradoxically, it was me she saw as a safe repository for this knowledge. As far as I know, she saved her late night tirades about Emma Goldman's fate for my ears alone.

The freight elevator creeps up to the second floor, where Gloria waits on the other side of the rusty wire mesh. Her brown skirt and dark red blouse make her look more subdued than usual, unless you take into account the purple hoops dangling from her ears and the pink headband.

She's replaced the mimeograph machine and typewriter with a Xerox copier and a computer, and candles of every size and scent fill the windowsills in the spacious living room. I follow Gloria into the kitchen, where she resumes eating her late breakfast of yogurt and bananas. When I suggest she pour us a couple of brandies, she knows it's going to be bad and chooses the large snifters.

"Has something happened?"

118

Seated at the gray-with-white-speckle Formica table, she listens with closed eyes to my description of the disastrous events of last night. "Sal's been murdered and Leslie was kidnapped." She repeats the words slowly, as if they're in a foreign tongue. "It doesn't make any sense. There's no reason." It sounds like she might approve if the rationale was strong enough, but I don't go there. It's time for some shock therapy.

"I need you to help me find Leslie, and if you do, maybe I can keep you out of jail."

Her green eyes pop open. "Are you threatening me, Jo?"

I sip my brandy, trying to keep my voice casual. "Just a simple horse trade."

She pauses for some internal calculations. In spite of the rhetoric, Gloria's always been a stone-cold realist. "What do you want to know?"

"Who you've been dealing with."

"I don't know the names. Sal said it was for my own protection. They're friends from his California days. Pot heads making pots of money, Jo, not killers. They give money anonymously to UNICEF and to a shelter for the homeless outside San Francisco. They do good works, like Sal did. These people aren't criminals; they're pacifists, dedicated to peaceful social change. They're into helping people, not kidnapping or murdering them."

"Well, it appears that your flower power friends have sprouted thorns. Do they grow the weed themselves?"

She gets up to refill our glasses, playing for time, I'd say, figuring out how specific she can be without giving away the store. "They've got connections with a farmer in Mexico. They sell what they bring across the border, fly the cash to Westchester, and we take it from there. After the money's clean, we get a ten percent cut."

"One thing for sure. Last night Sal wasn't flying the plane."

"If I knew who the pilot was, I'd tell you." She's added an edge to her voice, a sign that we've arrived at the perimeter of what she's willing to say, and she's about to shut down. I step back into safer territory. "How much did Gabriel know about your operation?"

She opens the tap part way. "Only as much as a smurf needs to be told. Deposit the money, withdraw your cut and the rest will be automatically transferred. If you get busted, keep your mouth shut, and we'll find you a lawyer."

"Could Sal have been working with some new people, maybe expanding into territory you didn't know about?" I'm betting on her vanity, her need to prove she's always in the know, and she takes the bait. "We weren't expanding, we were contracting!" she insists. "In a few months we'd have shut down the business and bought enough land upstate to sustain a community—an alternative to corporate wage slavery, even if just for a hundred people."

The phone rings and Gloria leaves the kitchen to take the call in her bedroom. This is my chance to migrate to the front room and reacquaint myself with her living space. Not many changes are evident since I was last here more than twenty years ago. The two beige upholstered armchairs are new, but the bright blue futon has been here forever.

A picture of the New Beginning's staff posing in front of their office on East 6th Street is prominently displayed on the mantle of the fake fireplace, Daniel Rose and Leslie standing in the center next to Gloria, other employees arranged for the camera on either side. I have a closer look at the copy machine I noticed when I came in. The power light is on and the tray holds fifty copies of a flyer printed on pale pink paper, advertising a work party at the community garden we visited a few days ago.

I sit down on the futon and browse the books and politically correct magazines covering the coffee table. Next to a gilt-edged invitation to a dinner party at the Chinese Embassy, I notice the *Alive!* guide to the Caribbean. An airline ticket is serving as a bookmark and the guide falls open to the section on St. Dominic. It takes just a few seconds to Xerox the ticket stub, as well as a double-fold map from the guidebook, stained with red ink. In a trice, I'm back in position at the coffee table, innocently awaiting Gloria's return.

She's put together her *I must be strong in spite of my grief* face. "That was Sal's sister, Rachel. She wants me to help with the funeral arrangements." I make some commiserating noises and let her see me to the door, but I'm unmoved by Gloria's red eyes when she bids me goodbye. She leans forward for the comforting hug she expects, but instead I pull back and let loose. "Maybe it's just as well you didn't mention you were at Sal's house last night. Much better for the police to investigate your involvement than me, given that we were once friends. That's right, Gloria, James told me you drove Sal home around eight o'clock."

I'm out the door and halfway down the hall before she calls out. "You're not serious, Jo. I can't believe what you just said!" The noise from the closing elevator doors drown out the rest of her protestations. Upon closer examination the ticket stub reveals that Gloria Kelly traveled from San Juan, Puerto Rico to St. Dominic on July 16th.

* * *

A few blocks east of the Canal Street subway station, I stop in at the Cyberion Internet Café and log on to one of the iMacs lining the wall, recalling the days, not so long ago, when the only mice found in restaurants were bona fide rodents. On Expedia, I select a morning flight to San Juan on JetBlue—with a connection to St. Dominic—scheduled for 8 a.m. I use my Visa to reserve a seat, wondering, as I always do, if this time a disgruntled, online worker-bee will get up the nerve to steal the number.

The taxi driver who drives me home emigrated from Somalia three years ago and hasn't seen his wife and kids since. We talk about the insanity of war and how good people never seem to get into politics. I surprise him with a tip I hope is big enough to pay for an overseas call.

The new locks on my door are stiff and a neighbor watches curiously as I struggle to open them. I sip some Chablis while listening to a day old voice message from Shondrea, her soft voice competing with the noise of the running bath. "Jo, I'm calling to let you know that the memorial service for Gabriel is at 2 o'clock tomorrow, at the Baptist Church on 138th near Lenox. I hope you can come."

In the bathtub, I crack open the jar of bath salts that Mom gave me for Chanukah two years ago. I lean back and close my eyes, rinsing my hair underwater, and imagine Ellie slipping below the surface, heavy sleep carrying her away on waves of blackness. *I wonder if your family held a memorial service. There was no mention of one in the newspaper article. Strange to think of your spirit leaving your body right here in this yellowish porcelain tub, weightless, massless, a wraithlike wisp of smoke floating out of the tiny window next to the sink, up through the airshaft into the dispassionate sky. Was there a bright light beckoning at the end of the tunnel? I like to think so.*

I haven't worn my one black dress since my grandmother died ten years ago. Luckily, there's a pair of dark blue shoes in the back of my closet to go with it.

The pews of the Abyssinian Baptist Church are full, and the service is almost over. Not wanting to disturb anyone with my arrival, I take a seat in the back. At the far end of the row, I'm surprised to see Sonny Rodriguez sitting by himself, keeping a low profile.

When the mourners rise to sing *Amazing Grace*, I move forward and slip into the pew across the aisle from Shondrea. She smiles when she sees me, but her eyes have a faraway look, and I know she's with Gabriel.

Outside she embraces each friend in turn, saying "I'm so glad you came." There are a lot of friends. When my turn comes she hugs me tight and whispers in my ear. "I found this hidden under Gabriel's mattress." I take the envelope she gives me and put it in my purse. Then I re-enter the church and find Sonny, standing in the shadows, waiting for the coast to clear. He almost looks like a citizen in his dark brown suit.

"The police are looking for you, Sonny. They found your fingerprints all over a box in Leslie's apartment. You know, where Gabriel was murdered."

He pulls out a comb and swipes it through his two-tone hair—not exactly a flight response. "I was hoping you'd be here. We need to talk. Come on, there's a coffee shop down the street."

It's more like a chicken 'n ribs place, and it's still open for lunch. The linoleum has seen better days, but the place is jammed, with only one booth open, the one with beige fluff peeking out of holes in the red vinyl. Fortunately, the spicy red Manhattan clam chowder is more than adequate compensation for the dingy décor. I concentrate on my soup while Sonny works out what he wants to say.

"Gabriel never knew I set him up to get jacked."

"You're talking about the four thousand?"

He nods, picks up his spoon, puts it down again. When he looks up, unbelievably there are tears in his eyes.

"So your conscience is bothering you. How touching."

He straightens in his seat and looks me in the eye. "Hey, I'm not proud of what I done. I was using, but I'm clean now and tryin' to stay that way." Sonny picks up the bowl of chowder and gulps it down, then carefully wipes his mouth with a napkin.

"Before the Feds froze the bank accounts, Sal was paying me and some of the others at Sunflower House good money to run his deposits. But Sal wasn't our only customer. A few months ago, we started working for this heavy-hitter goes by the name of Spike."

"Is he from Georgia and wears army duds?"

"Yeah," says Sonny, making a show of looking around to check for eavesdroppers, as if the folks in this establishment haven't heard it all before. "Spike showed up at the warehouse with ten thousand he wanted to clean—said a friend sent him. It was too sweet a deal to pass up."

"A sweet deal that somehow turned sour."

He purses his lips in agreement. "Stupid Gabriel took a picture of one of Spike's pals who didn't want his face in circulation. Spike asked me to arrange for him to buy back the negative."

"And you got the bright idea of having your Scorpion friends jump Gabriel after the sale. No wonder the police have got you on the suspect list for two murders." I let the words hang in the air for a bit, and Sonny takes his time buttering his roll.

"My miserable junkie ass will rot in hell for selling out Gabriel and cheating Sal, but they were my friends. I would never pop them. I came to the funeral to find you so I could offer my help."

Maybe he's on the level, but it's more likely he's shoveling shit. If addicts went to work selling swamp land, they'd have us catching crawfish from our porches in no time. So much wasted talent. "How do I know you're not running drag?"

The waitress brings the check, and Sonny picks it up, with a sad grin at my incredulous face. "Because if you're willin' to believe your own eyes, I've got something to show you."

We walk to the subway and seated next to him on a plastic seat molded for two, listening to the uptown express rumble through the darkness, I consider why it is that paying heed to his conscience isn't something I'd expect from Sonny. With all the friends I've watched rotating through the revolving door, in and out of treatment, you'd think I'd be accustomed to dual personalities, one straight, one stoned. But in Sonny's case, it's like the entire surface of a painting has peeled away to reveal a brand new landscape beneath.

An hour later, we're walking down Bryant Avenue, Sonny running his hand along the side of a chain link fence, making it rattle and giving me a bad case of the jitters. He stops at the gate to the warehouse and digs into the inner pocket of his jacket, pulling out a card key that he swipes through the black box scanner. We're in.

Sonny guides me through a maze of stacked cardboard boxes packed with T-shirts, key chains and other cheap trinkets typical of a novelty company's inventory. "Looks like Sal put a lot of trust in you," I say.

"Best damn gig I ever had, specially after he started paying me extra to drive the truck." The concrete floor and the metal roof have created a natural oven that only a scorpion could appreciate. Sonny sheds his suit jacket and shirt, revealing a remarkably clean undershirt and a tiny dragon tattoo on his left arm. A minute more of searching and he finds what he's looking for—a solid-looking crate, all by itself in the corner. He uses a knife blade to pry off the hinges, grunting as he works.

"It's way too hot in here," I complain.

"Not as hot as these babies," he says, removing the heavy lid and tossing it with a crash to the floor. He pulls out what looks to me like a sawed off shotgun with a telescopic sight and hands it over. "That's an M79 grenade launcher, the real McCoy; that's what Spike called it. He said that when the Army replaced them with M203's, it created a flood on the market."

I open the barrel by rotating the locking lever to the right, and inspect the breech. It's empty and so is my bag of firearm tricks. Sonny smirks. "Not bad. There was a butt-load of these crates here last month—military surplus—machine guns, helicopter parts, electronics. According to Spike, if you know what to look for, you can assemble an entire missile guidance system from spare parts."

I hand Sonny the grenade launcher, and he re-packs it in the crate. "Aren't these weapons supposed to be demilled by the Army before they're sold?"

He replaces the lid, tapping on the edges to secure it in place. "That's a big joke. Anyone with a screw driver and a manual can make a fortune."

He walks towards the back of the warehouse, and I follow. "Wasn't it taking a big chance, storing weapons here. What if Sal found out?"

"It was a one time deal. This trafficker in Florida was so hot he had to move his inventory to the Bronx. Spike asked me to make a pickup in New Jersey, at Jameson Field." Sonny unlocks a dull orange door, and we enter a small, airless office. Under the black dress, my antiperspirant gives up the ghost and sweat trickles down from my armpits, heading south.

"This gun dealer from Florida—was he the guy who didn't want his picture taken?"

"More camera shy than that crazy millionaire in the movie. I never met him, but I heard Spike talking to him on the phone. It was the day I drove to Jersey. He called him Miroslav."

"Let me guess. You had to empty the truck before driving to the airport, so you stored some boxes at Leslie's apartment. You put a good scare into her."

"That was Mokie. He was very nervous about what would happen if Sal found out we were doing some business on the side. He worshipped Sal."

"But not to the point where he'd turn down some extra cash."

Sonny retrieves a gray metal box from the bottom drawer of a scratched up gray metal desk that Hasim would love. "Spike's money was in here. I picked it up every Wednesday, along with the regular stock of T-shirts and junk that I used as a cover, and made my deliveries. Simple."

"Why are you telling me all this?"

Sonny walks back into the storage area to retrieve his suit jacket and shirt. "You may not think much of me, but I don't like seeing my friends get killed."

"Maybe you just don't like the idea of joining them. Okay, Sonny. I'm leaving town for a few days, but when I get back, I'll report what you've told me to the police. Maybe they can trace Spike. Do you know his last name?" He rolls his eyes. In his world even first names are largely fictitious.

Sonny walks me to the subway and, with a conspiratorial wink, disappears down the street to continue his quest for survival.

* * *

On the D train headed downtown from the Bronx, I open the envelope that Shondrea gave me and remove a single frame of film, holding it up to the sputtering fluorescent light. A figure stares back at me, dark skin and white hair, a negative white man.

The rotund proprietor of the one-hour photo booth on West 89th has a deep southern drawl and generosity to match. When I offer to pay for an entire roll, he holds up his hand. "Tell you what. I'll just print this negative while I'm waiting for that other batch to dry, no charge."

Five minutes later I'm looking at a picture of a heavyset man in a navy blue jacket, his fleshy face supported by broad cheekbones and featuring a soul patch that fails to compensate for his receding hairline. This must be Spike's secretive friend, Miroslav. He's looking directly at the camera with a sour expression and his arm is extended to shake hands with someone standing outside the frame, someone who is wearing a pinky ring. It's a good likeness, so good that Miroslav went to a lot of trouble to obtain what he thought was the only negative. How tricky of Gabriel to snap twice.

* * *

I call my cell phone carrier and add international service to my plan. No questions asked, although I know it will be no bargain. While packing, I share the latest with Ellie. *I'd never have pegged Sonny as a genius, but he's totally on the ball when he's not completely baked. Should I believe him when he says he didn't kill Gabriel or Sal? And even if Sal and Gloria weren't laundering gun money for Spike, how could they have failed to notice the extra money accumulating in their account? Somebody must have withdrawn the excess as soon as it was deposited in St. Dominic. Somebody with a password.*

I know what you're thinking. I should call Hasim before I leave, but all I have to offer are a bunch of loose ends. And if I tell him my plans and they backfire, I'll have more egg on my face than da Vinci used in the tempera for the Annunciation.

Yes, I know I'm leaving Hasim in the dark, but I haven't forgotten my promise to Samarah.

I feel Ellie looking over my shoulder as I call Jordan Nash. "What are you doing at your desk?" I ask, because Jordan spends so much time in the field that his editor once accused him of being too busy to write his own stories. Jordan and I had a brief fling when I met him, fresh from my California days and still in mourning for my wrecked marriage to Elliot.

"I'm on deadline, Jo. Can I call you back?"

"Only if you're not interested in the Khurram Saleh story."

"Just a second. I'll get this to the copy editor and then we can talk." He puts me on hold. I turn on the speaker and pull my one sleeveless dress out of the closet to pack. In a few minutes, he comes back on the line and, while I'm stuffing my suitcase, we have a short chat about long detentions and where Khurram might be hiding. Jordan says he'll try to pave the way for me to see some people. "Are you sure you want to do this?" he asks.

"Why not?"

"Because they're not…how can I put this…they're not used to talking to Jews."

"Then maybe it's time they had some practice."

Jordan never laughs, he snorts in derision. No use my trying to mimic him; my nose is too small.

* * *

Before take off, the JetBlue flight attendant informs us that our aircraft has been christened the *Wild Blue Yonder*. Judging from the amount of turbulence we experience, the name fits. I fall asleep and dream about a calypso singer serenading a Wall Street crowd from a hot air balloon. He hits a high note, transmutes into an ancient Egyptian priest spouting proverbs, and I wake up in time to gulp a cup of coffee before we begin our descent into San Juan Airport.

During the short layover, I sample some fried plantains and then find a copy machine that spews out an excellent enlargement of the map from Gloria's guidebook. Someone has drawn a route from the airport, winding into the hills and ending with a clumsily drawn five point star marking a destination. I assume this treasure map will lead me to Gloria's utopian homestead, where a few select members of the urban masses are expected to live on rice and beans while they build windmills and cultivate shade grown coffee.

At the departure gate, several of the more swarthy men are pulled into another room to undergo strip searches, while the rest of us are directed to board a small Beachcraft, manic propellers on the whirl. The flight is rough, and I bury my head in a magazine. The irony isn't lost on me that if we crash my last thoughts in this life will be about "how to find out what your man really wants."

When things calm down, I glance out the window and am spellbound by the Caribbean, sparkling with reflected sunlight, an endless blue green expanse sprinkled by some giant hand with tiny specks of land. As one of these dark anthills grows closer, the pilot's mellifluous voice fills the small cabin.

"We're due to touch down at Melville Airport at 3:18, ten minutes ahead of schedule. It's 85 degrees Fahrenheit on St. Dominic, with the wind picking up from the west, and if you rent a car, don't forget to drive on the left side of the road."

The plane banks steeply as we approach the island, and I get an eyeful of surf breaking on white coral reefs, tall mountains in the interior and the intense green of jungle foliage. The landing is so smooth, they must have buttered the runway.

at the top of an undersea mountain
sunbaked descendants
of runaway slaves
prosper

Chapter Thirteen

The yellow rental jeep, with its light metal frame and canvas top, seems more appropriate for Disneyland than this rugged country-side. Heading south from the airport on the coastal road, the cliffs are on my left—the same side I'd better not forget to drive on—and the proximity of empty space is both terrifying and exhilarating. When the road curves, I'm so close to the edge that I can see the roots of the palm trees growing out of the rocky cliffs. Down below, the waves of the Atlantic crash onto black sand beaches, while up here the salt spray gently stings my face. I'm entranced by the sounds of *cadence-lypso* on the jeep's radio, a heady mixture of calypso, rhythms from Haiti, and down home funk from the U.S. If only this were a vacation.

Turning inland, the curvy red line drawn on Gloria's map becomes a bumpy reality, filled with steep turns and sharp rocks that slow the jeep to a crawl. The driving may be diffi-cult, but after the exhaust fumes and overall stink of the city, I luxuriate in the fresh smells of sage and lemon that rise from the earth to meet me. This pleasure is short-lived, because as the jeep zigzags up the mountain switchbacks, I get so dizzy I almost lose my San Juan lunch.

Carved out of a giant piece of driftwood, the *Welcome to Anarchy* sign blends into the scenery so well that I almost miss the turn off. The jeep skids into the narrow driveway carved through the thick brush. On the right side, piles of discarded construction materials, bricks and chunky cinderblocks, have been left to scorch in the sun. I pull behind the largest mound of debris, hoping this will hide the bright yellow jeep from view, and continue on foot. The driveway ends at a sturdy, wrought-iron gate, secured from the inside and connected on both sides to a high barbed wire fence. If

129

this is a utopian freehold, then Thomas Moore has some explaining to do.

Through the burnished wire, apparently newly strung, all that's visible of the house is a clay chimney. The blazing red flowers of a poinciana tree block the rest of the estate from view. There are no parked cars, and the place has a deserted feel. I trek back to the junk pile, looking for a crowbar or a shovel.

The sight of a long bamboo pole brings back images of awkward athletic endeavors at summer camp better forgotten. My one successful vault took place on an athletic field equipped with safety gear and cushioned landing pad. It still required all the skill and daring I could muster. Today's flying leap over unforgiving barbed wire requires utter insanity.

I search through the junk pile for something sharp to dig with. All I can find is a rusty iron rod. It'll have to do. In front of the fence, I scoop out enough dry earth to form a shallow trench, a primitive version of a vault box. I walk back twelve paces and pick up the bamboo pole, knowing what I'm about to do, but still not believing it.

I focus on turning my legs into high-speed windmills and struggle to hold the pole straight and steady as I run. Swinging the pole into the trench at the last possible moment, I hoist myself up and fly through the air, twisting my torso to gain height. My cotton blouse snags on the barbed wire, causing me to fall perilously close to the fence on the other side and land with a sickening thud. It's a miracle that my legs respond when commanded to stand. I shake the dirt from my clothes and, idiot that I am, briefly regret that no one was here to witness my accomplishment. I should be grateful for the lack of response; it means I'm alone in the enemy camp.

The stucco house has a corrugated tin roof with a shady veranda that might look inviting under other circumstances. The front door is unlocked, a sign of overconfidence that I'm afraid may be justified by superior fire power. Unarmed, and some might say unhinged, I walk inside. It's a split level, with two stairways in the foyer—one going up to the living room and the other down to the basement (a must for any house on a hurricane prone island). I check out the living room first, thanking the hand-made bamboo furniture for the sturdy pole that lifted me over the fence. Four doors line the hallway off the large country kitchen, set up to feed a multitude. Each door leads to a small bedroom with a set of double-decker bunks and a large dresser. The rooms have an unused look, and I wonder who the lucky inhabitants will be.

Downstairs the bare concrete is covered with wood shavings. Someone has dug out a large tree in the middle of the room to create a primitive canoe. The other half of the basement is walled off and secured by a heavy padlock attached to a green metal door. A tray containing a half-eaten sandwich and an empty juice glass sits on a chair nearby.

"Leslie! Are you in there? It's Jo!"

Her reply is barely audible, "Please! Get me out of here!"

I search the woodshop and, embedded in the log, find a hatchet. Taking aim at the padlock, I'm interrupted, mid-swing, by the sound of car tires on gravel. "I'll be back. I promise!" I call to Leslie, already in a dead heat to return the hatchet to the canoe and get upstairs.

The sparse furnishings in the living room offer little in the way of cover, and the best I can do is to open one of the floor-to-ceiling hurricane shutters on the veranda and squeeze in behind. I thought I'd lost more weight on last year's diet. Through the wooden slats there's a limited view of the front yard. The gate opens and a white Mercedes pulls in, followed by a red Land Rover. Long legs in khaki pants, supporting a lean man wearing a camouflage shirt with hat to match, climb out of the Mercedes.

Spike.

The door of the other car slams shut, but my view of the second driver is blocked. Looking tense as a cat sniffing a new kitty litter, Spike walks towards the porch. They mount the steps together, his companion showing me the side of his face, puffy and bruised. Mystery man stops just inches from my hiding place to scratch the back of his neck, and I say a prayer of invisibility. Once inside, the argument begins.

"Remote is good, but did you and Gloria have to choose an island with roads worse than Chechnya?"

"It's a great spot, Spike, and you know it. Where else puts you in spitting distance of both Colombia and Florida?" The voice is nasal and unrecognizable, as if the speaker has a broken nose.

Spike sounds unimpressed. "Miroslav's coming in two days to collect the coins. Let's just hope he can find this place."

"Two days doesn't give us much wiggle room."

"You're an idjit," Spike informs his accomplice, "if you think Miroslav will give us even an inch. He doesn't care if the bank account is frozen, and he'll kill us if we tell him the ransom money is late. What he wants is payment in full and no excuses."

"No worries," says the hoarse voice. "I told you—Leslie's daddy is as loaded with money as his films are loaded with blood and gore. He'll probably think this whole thing has been cooked up by one of his screenwriters."

"So you're saying the girl's father is a sure thing?" Spike's beginning to relent, and I can taste the relief in his friend's voice when he replies. "Sure as there's an "h" in Hollywood."

The wind has been picking up steadily, and now it whooshes through the open windows. One of the men has turned on the radio, because the next thing I hear is a woman with a French accent, probably broadcasting from Monserrat, calmly announcing that a force three hurricane is expected to land by nightfall.

"I better close the shutters," says Spike's buddy. *Damn, I should have hidden behind the couch.*

"I hope you've got a backup generator."

"It's in the basement."

The sound of their footsteps going down the stairs provides a glimmer of hope that my life will not end as abruptly as expected. Slipping off my shoes, I take the steps two at a time, pass through the unlocked gate—this time with no need for gymnastics—and make a run for the jeep. I release the brake, let out the clutch and start rolling downhill, amazed at how much noise the tires make on the rough road.

As soon as I'm sure the jeep is out of earshot, I start the engine. The wind competes with me for the steering wheel, pushing the vehicle towards the edge of the narrow road. The rain, beating ever harder on the flimsy roof of the jeep, reminds me of how thirsty

Ask the Dead

I am. One thing is clear, parched and dry as my mouth may be, I'm up to my neck in water far deeper than the lagoons encompassing this lovely island.

does solving small mysteries
make it easier to live
with the big one?

Chapter Fourteen

Though a few hours remain before sunset, the dark clouds are engrossed in creating a night of their own. On the coast road the rain falls in sheets and visibility is zero. As soon as I leave the jeep, I get soaked to the skin, running in slow motion against the wind towards the shelter of a battered roadside café. The crooked roof looks like it has stood up to storms like this for centuries. "Bon jour," says the elderly proprietor, coming out from the kitchen. I must look like hell because his slightly bloodshot eyes look concerned, peering out at me from beneath his floppy, canary yellow hat.

"Bon jour," I reply in my terrible high school French, raising my voice to compete with the noise of the storm outside.

"Wéla ou ka alé?" He continues in Creole, just to be polite. I shrug and he laughs. I point to my wet clothes and to the carryall slung over my shoulder. He points to a door marked "Femme."

When I return, wearing a fresh oversized blouse over dry jeans, he seats me at a table close to the lunch bar and offers me a menu. Like his face, his hands are dark and weathered. "I suggest you try the spiny crabs. They're marinated in rum and will warm you up faster than a bonfire."

He moves slowly, probably from arthritis, but the food appears on the table within minutes. After I've taken a few bites and told him the cuisine is "tres bien," he asks, 'Where are you staying?"

"I need to find a hotel with international telephone service and email."

"Take your pick. And don't be deceived by appearances. We may prefer five star rain forests to five star hotels, but our telecommunications are state of the art."

When asked if he knows the Americans who live in the hills above us, he responds with a grunt of disapproval. "They seemed nice enough at first, and people were pleased to see them purchase most of their supplies on the island."

"And after that?"

"On St. Dominic we take care not to spy on our neighbors, but trucks filled with barbed wire call attention to themselves. Are these friends of yours?"

"I'm looking for someone who may be visiting them," I reply, embarrassed to be associated with the kind of people who import their troubles to paradise.

"I hope your friend is okay." The offhand remark hits home. Does he suspect something? Although there's something about him that invites confidence, there's also something that keeps a healthy distance from stressed out foreigners. That's why, when I pay the check, I'm surprised to hear him say, "I live in Calibishie. Come for a visit if you like. Just ask for Marcel."

"Pleased to meet you, Marcel. I'm Josephine." I haven't used the long version of my name since fifth grade, but with Marcel it seems appropriate. He opens the storm shutter on the window facing the highway. "The wind is dying down. It looks like the storm is passing over, but you'd better drive slowly. There are a lot of turnouts on the road in case you need to take cover."

Leaving this kindly man makes me feel oddly incomplete, an unusual reaction considering we've just met. I'm beginning to understand why Gloria chose this place for her community.

In Rosetown, I find the hotel Marcel recommended, a white-washed two-story building covered with flowering vines. The ferocious wind is shredding the woven baskets hanging from the balconies, but the amused porter reassures. "We're in no danger, miss. They changed the forecast and Lady Marcia will be out to sea in just a few hours."

Even with the shutters closed, it's hard to hear myself speak when I put in a call to Leslie's parents. Eleanor answers. "Where the hell are you, Jo, and what's that roaring noise?"

"I'm on St. Dominic, there's a hurricane, and I know where they're holding Leslie."

"Please, Jo, don't do anything hasty. The ransom call came this morning. It sounded like a female robot, and Michael says it was probably generated by one of those anonymous Internet phone services. The voice said they want two million dollars in gold coins, to be purchased with a cashier's check from a dealer in Manhattan."

"Where's the drop?"

"Michael's flying to St. Dominic in the morning—a friend of ours with a private plane is taking him. I'm to stay here at the Plaza, in case they call and change the plan while Michael's en route. After Michael goes through customs, he's to wait in the bar at the air strip until they contact him on his cell phone."

"I can help, Eleanor."

"I don't think so. Once he's on St. Dominic, Michael's forbidden to make any calls or talk with anyone. They'll be watching him."

"That's what they want you to think—there are only two of them."

"And only one bullet would be enough to kill our daughter." She doesn't have to add that I've done little so far to give her confidence in my abilities.

"Tell Michael that I'll be watching for them to drive Leslie out of the compound. He won't be alone when the time comes to make the exchange." Eleanor reluctantly agrees to pass on my message.

That went pretty well. The next phone call may not be so pretty.

"Lieutenant Saleh speaking."

"Hi. It's Jo. I'm calling from St. Dominic."

"What the hell are you up to now?" I knew he wouldn't like this, but I plunge on, hoping to redeem myself by deluging him with information.

"Leslie's on the island. She's being held by two people. One of them is named Spike. I don't know his last name. He cleans cash for illegal sales of military surplus overseas. Spike was running a large amount of cash through the smurfs in New York when the funds in their accounts were frozen. The cash belonged to an arms dealer named Miroslav, and Spike plans to use the ransom money to pay him off. Miroslav is on his way to St. Dominic right now."

"If Miroslav has entered the country recently, the FBI should be keeping track of him," Hasim says, smart enough to put aside his resentment and get on with it. "Can you tell me anything else about Spike?"

"He's tall, white, has a muscular build, and wears military camouflage."

"Him and all the other militia types in the country."

"If you call the Budget Rent-a-Car in Macon, Georgia, you may be able to get his last name. He was driving a rental Chevy Suburban in New York two days ago."

"Nice of you to tell me now."

"You're right, Hasim. I should have called sooner, but since Leslie was taken it's all been a blur. Her father will be here in the morning with the ransom—two million dollars in gold coins."

"Jo, listen to me. Trying to handle this by yourself is crazy. If you can wait a few days, I'll send you some backup."

"The ransom deadline is tomorrow. Michael Corning and I don't have a choice. We'll have to go it alone. Don't worry, I've got a plan."

"Does this plan of yours involve apprehending any of these criminals, or are you still in the business of making excuses and giving out second chances?"

I let that one pass. "You might also have a look at all the flights filed last month with the Flight Service Station connected to Jameson Field in New Jersey. According to Sonny Rodriguez, they flew some red hot stuff in and out of that airport."

"I should have had you arrested for withholding evidence when I had the chance, Jo. It wouldn't have been a bad idea to put you away for your own protection either."

"I'm not worried. These people are in a panic already—all I have to do is capitalize on it."

"True. But keep in mind that when you defy an enemy by doubting his courage you run the danger of doubling it."

All in all our conversation went a lot better than I thought it would.

* * *

It's two-thirty. An hour ago Michael Corning called from Barbardos to say they were refueling the plane and his ETA at the tiny airstrip three miles from here would be about four o'clock . The jeep is hidden by the same thick brush I'm relying on to cover any pee breaks, and the road leading up to *Anarchy* is fixed in my unblinking sights. When I roll down the window, the wind still threatens to blow the skin off my nose, but the worst Marcia had to offer is already meteorological history. To stay alert I listen to DBS radio. I'm able to decipher one Creole word out of a hundred and use my imagination for the rest.

At three o'clock, out comes the Land Rover, the driver wearing a hat and sunglasses, unrecognizable, at least to me. I make a tough call to stay put, hoping it won't haunt me later.

A long half hour goes by before the white Mercedes speeds down the hill with Spike at the wheel and takes off down the highway. If Leslie's in the car, I can't see her. I let a milk truck pass so I can use it for cover and then edge out on the road. Five minutes later, the Mercedes turns off the main highway. The cloud of dust Spike is creating suggests I'd better hang back so he won't see mine. He turns left and I follow, until a Dead End sign stops me cold. The last thing I want is a showdown on a narrow road with no way out. I'm turning the car around when my cell phone rings, causing a narrow miss with a tree while I'm trying to dig the damn thing out of my purse.

"Jo, something terrible has happened. I'm afraid they're going to kill Leslie!"

"Michael, don't panic. That's what they want you to do. You've got to try and pull back as far as you can, to look at this as if it were happening to someone else."

"If only it were. I'm still trying to figure it out. On the airplane I kept the case on the seat next to me the whole time. When I went through customs, they took the coin case into another room, but then they returned it without saying anything about the coins—I think a lot of people bring their wealth here to avoid the IRS. I opened the case and checked out the coins before leaving the customs area. Then I went directly to the café, just like they told me and took a table in the corner, away from the bar. I was only there for two or three minutes when this guy comes over and tries to grab the case out of my hand. I held on to the handle until I heard him say, "Sit tight. You'll hear from us shortly," and then I let go. What else could I do? After that, things seemed to be going according to plan. My cell phone rang, just like they told me it would. The caller asked me, "Have you got the coins with you? The Liberty V nickel, the set of Walking Liberty Half Dollars?" He caught me completely off guard, but I went with my instincts and told him no problem, and he said he'd call me right back."

"Can you describe him, the man who took the case?"

"Not really. Medium height, baseball hat and sunglasses. He had a bruise on the side of his face."

"You did the right thing, Michael." I'm thinking maybe I should have followed the Rover instead of the Mercedes.

"Jo, tell me what to say when he calls." Michael's voice has deepened; he's holding steady.

"Don't say a word about the coins. If he has them, which I doubt, he'll ask you to raise more money, and you'll agree. If he's unaware that the coins were stolen, he'll give you directions to the drop and you'll follow them. You've got to stay cool and take your cues from him."

"Coolness isn't something I'm sure I can deliver."

"You can do this. Once you know where the drop is, call me. I'm only a few minutes away and I can meet you there."

Minutes later, Michael calls to say the exchange is to take place at the water tower on top of Victoria Ridge. "He kept telling me to come alone, Jo."

"Don't worry. We can still pull this off. But first you have to go to the gift shop and buy a small carrying case, something that's obviously the right size for carrying coins. After that, take a taxi to Victoria Ridge. The driver will know where it is."

* * *

Watching Michael Corning get out of the taxi and walk towards me, I marvel at how someone can look so capable, determined, and utterly beat at the same time. Trickles of sweat have drawn dusty trails on his dark brown cheeks. A small travel bag rides on his hip, attached to a strap across his chest. He takes the water bottle I offer. "What now?"

"Tell the taxi driver to wait."

Corning hesitates. "Why do we need a cab when you've got the jeep?"

"The seats will be more comfortable for Leslie. She might be in bad shape." Corning takes in this information with no visible reaction, then turns and goes back to the taxi. He has a brief conversation with the driver and the noise of the engine cuts off. He returns to the jeep and swings his bulk into the seat beside me.

"We're going up this road to get your daughter back," I say, pulling a twelve inch piece of lead pipe from under the seat.

"A formidable weapon," he comments, a bit of unexpectedly wry humor, given his anxious state.

"Sometimes less is more," I reply, turning the ignition key and stepping on the gas.

The road continues for about five hundred feet, ending at a log barrier marking a narrow footpath through the brush. We exit the car and creep upwards, walking as silently as possible, painfully aware that Spike is expecting to hear one person's footsteps on the ridge, not two.

Michael sets the pace, and I struggle to keep up. The head of the trail is well maintained, and we make good progress, the scrubby trees on either side shielding us from whoever may be watching from above. Towards the top of the steep incline, half of the water tower becomes visible above the foliage. The path divides here, one fork going straight up and the other more narrow pathway veering to the right and circling upward. I take the offshoot, motioning for him to stay on the main trail. Using sign language, I tell him to slow down at the top and wait for me.

The new trail is covered with thick, dark mud and after slipping a few times my light khaki pants have collected a heavy load of brown soil. I pull out the tiny pocket compass that has hung from my key chain since I got lost in the woods in Santa Cruz county and try to keep a steady heading of northeast as the path curls upwards. I should be seeing the water tower by now, but instead the trail disappears, trees and brush bunched together, impassable. I double back, watching for the fork that I must have missed, take the first left, and in a few minutes come out at the edge of the clearing, directly behind Spike.

Minus the camouflage hat, his sticky brown hair is pasted to the back of his scalp. Michael emerges from the trees to face us, only thirty feet away. Spike's revolver is steady in his hand. As instructed, Michael walks slowly forward, holding the travel bag out in front of him to keep the kidnapper's attention on the prize.

He stops just short of delivering the bag, forcing Spike to reach for it and putting him slightly off balance. I come from behind, tempted to knock him out with the pipe, but acutely aware that Michael is likely to be hit if the gun fires. I jab the pipe behind Spike's ear. "Drop the gun and lie face down on the ground." He complies without a word, unaware he's been intimidated by a piece of plumbing.

Michael retrieves the gun and hands it to me, a heavy Magnum. Then he grabs Spike by both arms and leans into his face. "Where's my daughter?"

Spike shakes himself free, straightening his sleeves and looks at Michael disdainfully. "Do you think I'd be stupid enough to bring her with me? For all I know, you've got a squadron of policemen waiting at the bottom of the hill."

Corning lunges at Spike. "Hold up!" I shout and reluctantly, he backs off. "You've come this far Michael, don't lose it now." Using the gun as a pointer, I wave Spike over to a nearby tree. "Get up against that tree and spread 'em. Michael, get his keys."

As Spike hugs the tree, Michael detaches a heavily laden chain from the kidnapper's belt and tosses it over to me. Spike looks over his shoulder as I examine the keys. "Which one is it?" I ask softly. He turns around, pulling down his arms and bringing his legs together into a more dignified posture. "What good will it do you if you don't know where she is?"

"Listen and learn," I say, keeping him covered with the gun while giving instructions to Michael. "Take the jeep. It can handle the back roads better than the taxi. There's a small map inside the rental agreement in the glove box."

I hand him the keys. "These will open the padlock on the front gate and the room in the basement where they've got Leslie. Take her straight to the hospital and send the police here."

It's a pleasure to see the smirk on Spike's face disappear. Michael throws the Flamingo Air bag over to me with a wink. Then he kicks Spike behind the knees and sends him sprawling, before disappearing down the trail at a dead run.

My captive sits up, brushing the leaves from his hair. It's time I had a talk with the man who's been pulling the strings. With the gun in one hand and the coin case in the other, I see no reason not to get straight to the point.

"As I see it, you have two choices. You can go back to New York and face charges or you can languish in jail here until you're extradited. Either way you face jail time for kidnapping and murder."

His voice has a faintly Midwestern twang. "I think you've got the wrong impression. I'm a businessman, not a murderer. It's my job to move product around the planet just as it's yours to move words around the page."

Much as it pains me to do it, I put some grudging admiration into my voice. "How do you know I'm a poet?"

"A friend of mine in New York is a fan and read one of your poems to me. I didn't get it."

"I don't discuss aesthetics with murderers." I take the snapshot from my pocket and show it to him. "You may not have pulled the trigger, but you had Gabriel killed because he could identify one of your business partners. Is this Miroslav?"

"Not a bad likeness. Too bad the sight of his face seems to upset certain people. I arranged to buy back the negative, not to kill the photographer. Gabriel's death though, I admit, was convenient."

A red-necked parrot swoops across the clearing, announcing that the sky has cleared. The view from the ridge is dazzling, the curve of the ocean on the horizon speckled with tiny boats. I think I can see Monserrat in the distance. Spike, from his seat on the ground, follows my glance.

"It's beautiful here, isn't it? For just a nickel, you could live comfortably for a lifetime." He's talking about the coins he thinks are in the case, offering to cut me in. I provide some silence as encouragement.

"Understand that I had no choice. It was the only way I could raise the money to pay my client the money I owed him for product delivered."

"By product you mean weapons. Why not just say so?"

He starts to stand up, but I wave him back down with the gun. My wrist is feeling the weight, so I switch the weapon to my left hand and the coin case to my right. "Heavy isn't it? Not made for a woman." I'll never admit it, but he's got a point. After holding the Magnum for just a few seconds, my left wrist begins to ache, too.

Spike pulls out a pack of Marlboros and some matches from his shirt pocket and starts to light up.

"Put those on the ground!" I yell. I'm not about to give him a potential weapon—not after seeing a bail jumper in Long Beach throw a lit cigarette down Stan's shirt.

Spike reluctantly complies. "I'm not ashamed to tell you that I was the middle man in a deal with the Revolutionary Armed Forces of Colombia. They paid Miroslav $2 million cash for surplus military equipment that I helped him purchase from the Air Force. They were especially excited about the Cobra helicopter parts. But as sometimes happens, the RAFC never received the shipment; it was intercepted by the para-militaries. On top of that, the cash that Miroslav entrusted to me—money that was supposed to be laundered and then returned to him through the banking system—was confiscated by the U.S. government. I'm a man who believes in paying his debts."

"It's understandable you'd be a man of honor." My throat almost betrays me by closing up on the carefully chosen words. "From the way you dress, I assume you've been in the military. You're a man who's paid his dues."

He bites like a bass who thinks he owns the lily pond. "I was just another underpaid private working at a surplus depot. You can't blame me for taking advantage of the fact that the U.S. armed forces sells de-commissioned military hardware to almost anyone with a resale license."

"And that anyone with two hands can rebuild these weapons

and use them," I finish for him. Spike brightens. Maybe I'm going to see things his way. "Perhaps you'd be interested in keeping the Liberty Half Eagle. It's PCGS certified and has a market value of $75,000."

"Why not offer me the Liberty V? I'm told it's worth a million and a half. But don't waste your time agonizing over the limits of your generosity. The bag is empty. Your partner took the coins from Michael at the airport."

Spike responds to this news with a classic "the fates are against me" shrug. He stands up, in defiance of my threatening gesture with the gun. "You won't shoot me," he declares, turning his back on me and walking away with a jaunty confidence I can't help but admire. I grip the giant Magnum tightly with both hands, take careful aim to the left of his left leg and pull the trigger. He whirls around, hands now high in the air. "If you knew how to handle that elephant gun, I'd have been blown apart."

I make the call, and we sit in silence until the police arrive. I can tell from his stone face there's no use explaining that I aimed to miss.

* * *

At the hospital, Leslie is resting comfortably. She's come out from under the sedatives, exhausted but unhurt. Michael tells me they're planning to take the next plane to Puerto Rico. He's beaming.

"You look like a man who's won a million dollars, not lost it."

"Physically, she's fine, but it'll take a while for her confidence to come back." His good humor evaporates when he relates how Spike's partner threatened to rape Leslie while she was in captivity. "She says he never actually touched her, but he was wearing a mask and approached her in a way that made her sure of his intentions. Luckily for her, Spike punched him out. Leslie heard him say that damaged goods were bad for business."

I send him down to the cafeteria to get us some refreshments, so I can talk with Leslie privately. There's no way I can soften the question. "Do you know who tried to rape you?"

She shakes her head no, and then has a question for me. "Will they ever find the person who killed Gabriel? He was special, not the way people talk about him. He went through hell and somehow managed to preserve his humanity, his compassion, intact. I respected him, as an artist and as a person. I don't think I'll ever have the privilege of knowing someone like Gabriel again." Leslie's question is one I know I'll be taking home with me.

On the way to the airport to see the Cornings off, I think about how close we came to being blackmailed for a higher ransom. Maybe I'm not as bad a detective as I thought. The hugs I get from Leslie and her father at the terminal seem to confirm this.

* * *

Back at the hotel, I'm surprised to see Hasim in the lobby.

"I'll bet you had fun convincing NYPD to pay your travel expenses."

"Not as much fun as I had getting through airport security. I thought my ID and shield would speak for themselves. I should have had the Borough Commander call ahead. Then they would have been expecting someone like me."

Someone like me. "I'm sure you're not the first police officer to get racially profiled since September 11th." *Shoe on the other foot and all that.*

"You're right. It's not the first time I've been searched, and I know they're just doing their job. It's the passengers—the way they avoid looking at me, and when they do, the fear in their eyes…"

Our conversation is interrupted by a seven foot giant wearing coke bottle eyeglasses that make his eyes look microscopic. Hasim introduces us. Jorge Ansonia looks like he hasn't cracked a smile since graduating the FBI Academy. I invite them up to my room, and, at the Hasim's request, Ansonia shows me the passenger list for tonight's flight from Bogotá. One name is underlined in red. Miroslav Semilian. Since it's show and tell time, I open my suitcase and share Gabriel's photograph of Miroslav.

"It's a pity he won't get a chance to cash in his frequent flyer miles," quips Ansonia. Evidently he does have a sense of humor, as long as the joke's on someone else.

The three of us make a crowd in the tiny room. Hasim plants himself in an overstuffed chair near the lumpy bed. "All we have to do is be there when Semilian takes the coins from Spike Andrews.

145

Yeah, that's the name Spike gave us during interrogation, and it checks out with the Air Force. He worked at the surplus sales office at a base in Georgia for a year. That's where he made all his sales contacts."

"Andrews doesn't have the coins." As I narrate the afternoon's events, I realize I may not have been so clever after all. "If I could have been two places at once, I'd have followed Spike's sidekick."

Ansonia cracks what I'm sure is one of his rare smiles, and I know he's figured out an angle. "We'll have Spike set up a meeting with Semilian. All we need are some gold-plated coins and a few members of the local constabulary to help us out."

"You've made this easy for us, Jo," Hasim says, putting out his hand. "Nice work securing Leslie's return. We can take it from here."

We shake, and I know it's useless to object. At least he's finally given me credit for doing something right. "Let's stay in touch," the Lieutenant says on his way out, throwing me a bone.

I have no problem leaving the cleanup to the law enforcement professionals. It's time to get back to my life in New York. Ansonia will nab Semilian for smuggling, and Hasim will put Spike away for money-laundering and kidnapping, if not murder. So why do I feel so uneasy?

there's a little bit of trance
in ev'ry romance
skepticism turned inside out
embrace s the opposite
of doubt

Chapter Fifteen

Given the chilliness of our last encounter, it was difficult convincing Gloria to meet with me, but here we are, sharing a crumb-covered table at Nemo's Café, where a generation of beat poets, now replaced by glassy-eyed tourists, once sustained itself on onion soup, served thick with bread crusts and cheese.

Today's circumstance brings to mind an episode from our college days, when Gloria's English Lit professor hit on her, implying that if she didn't do the dirty with him her grades would be less than exemplary. She hid her fury, letting him think his ploy had worked and then, when he showed up for a rendezvous at her apartment, confronted him with a group of her outraged friends. Now that I've presented her with the facts, direct from St. Dominic—including the part about Spike and his unidentified partner using *Anarchy* as a base for arms smuggling—I expect an equally enraged reaction. What I get is phony concern wrapped in mild repentance. "If Sal suspected something, he should have told me, and I would have kept a closer eye on the operation," she says.

I show her the photograph of Miroslav Semilian. "This is Spike's business associate. He's a world class thug. Do you know him?"

Gloria retreats into her shell, a turtle in denial, and I raise my voice, determined to get through her dense cranium. "I think Sal was killed because he found out that his warehouse and his airplane were being used to smuggle guns. If you know anything at all about these people, you've got to tell me. You owe it to Sal." Unshaken by this emotional blackmail, Gloria's face hardens.

She's getting on my nerves and to hide my annoyance, I bite down hard on my avocado and cheese sandwich, reworking my approach. If guilt doesn't motivate, then try revenge. "By now the Feds have Spike in custody, and it's a slam dunk that he'll make a deal and never stand trial for murder. What I need is some hard evidence that he killed Gabriel and Sal, or had them killed. Give me one solid lead I can leak to the press, and we can prevent the Feds from pleading him out."

Gloria butters her roll carefully, spreading the butter thin. "I wish I could help you Jo, but I never met this Spike or his friend, and whatever Sal knows he's taken to his grave."

"And whatever you know, you're not telling. How can you let them get away with Sal's murder?"

Gloria shifts in her chair and coolly changes the subject. "While you were playing detective in the Caribbean, Sunflower House was totally shut down. Many of the residents are homeless thanks to your mindless interference."

"What did you expect the FBI to do, give unemployment compensation to the smurfs?"

"Those kids got a lousy deal, and it's my fault."

"Spare me the crocodile tears, Gloria."

"Why don't you leave me in peace?"

There are a million reasons I could throw in her sanctimonious face, but I've got a date with a more than generous boss who is probably wondering which of ten ways I've chosen to get myself killed. I throw a ten on the table to cover my half of the bill. "I'm done making excuses for you, Gloria. You're on your own."

"You always were a sell out!" she barks, causing heads at the neighboring tables to turn. I leave the restaurant with most of my lunch still on the table, unsatisfied in more ways than one.

* * *

Flowers won't do the trick with Ted. I stop in at the Cat's Tale bookstore on 85th and pick up the collected stories of Saul Bellow as a peace offering.

"Solve the case?" he asks, giving the book a cursory but approving glance.

"Not exactly." I go with the short version, but even that takes a good while.

Ted scratches his head. "Let's see if I get the picture. One murder suspect kidnapped another so that he could use the ransom to pay off an arms supplier. Then on top of the kidnapping comes another murder, driving the count up to two unsolved homicides. And here you are, finished with detecting and ready to come back to work?"

"Not really."

"Get out of here and don't come back until I get to see some scalps hanging from that beaded belt of yours. The car's on 96th, near Columbus."

* * *

I open my mail while listening to the stacked up voice messages on the speaker phone. The one from Jordan Nash brings back the promise I made to Samarah that night at Hasim's house.

"Jo, it's taken me a while but the word around the Mosque in Washington Heights is that Khurram Saleh had a girlfriend, and she wasn't a Muslim. She drove him there for services and a few people saw her drop him off. The description is vague—a blonde driving a Jetta—but it's better than nothing. Let me know if I can help."

I call Hasim's home number, and Samarah picks up on the first ring. Turns out she's expecting him to call from the airport. I tell her what Jordan told me and ask if Khurram had a girlfriend.

"If he did, he never told us. Unless he was closer to Diane than he admitted."

"Who is Diane?"

"She was in Khurram's journalism class, and they talked on the phone almost every night. He said they were writing an article together for the *Spectator*."

I tell Samarah I'll check this out and will call her back later.

The next voice mail in the queue is from Paul, and he begins with an apology. "I was so distraught, thinking about what you said about Beverly, that it took me a few days to realize I'd like to see more of you."

Anyone who can work the word distraught into ordinary conversation deserves at least a second date. Besides, a little distraction might leave my subconscious free to work out this

149

complicated case. We agree to meet at the Angelika for the eight o'clock show.

* * *

There's a hint of September in the air as I walk a half-mile uptown to the *Spectator* offices on Broadway. I punch #11 on the keypad attached to the gray door, and with the buzzer ringing in my ear climb up to the third floor. At the top of the stairs a boyish-looking young man looks up at me from his computer keyboard. His pink cheeks and short stature suggest someone who skipped a grade or two to get here. Or maybe it's my distance from him in age that makes him seem so young.

"I'm looking for Khurram Saleh."

He continues typing feverishly with two fingers while he answers. "Khurram's not around this summer. I think he went to California with Diane." Maybe this easy break is my reward for trying to help Samarah. "What's Diane's last name?" I ask, holding my breath while he searches his brain. "Sullivan," he says with assurance. I could kiss him for saving me days of footwork. Instead I thank him and on my way out, sneak a five dollar bill into the donation jar on the table with the sputtering Mr. Coffee.

* * *

In *Adaptation*, Nicholas Cage plays a writer with a block twice as big as mine on my worst day. The movie puts me in a good mood, and afterwards I agree to accompany Paul to the Cacophony, where some friends of his are playing. In the parking lot near the club, he opens the trunk of his '79 Volvo and pulls out a bass guitar and a heavy amplifier. "Just in case they ask me to sit in. I have this obsessive need to control my own sound."

Steep cellar steps lead down to the club, and the low ceiling and bare cement walls complete its resemblance to a bomb shelter. The acoustics are almost as bad as the décor, but that doesn't keep the crowds away. The stage is so small the drummer has set up her kit on the floor in front, with the piano and sax players squeezed in on the platform behind her.

Paul leads me to a small table reserved for the band, moving the coffee cups and water bottles to one side. The trio smokes its way through a jazzed up version of *Norwegian Wood* that makes

150

me hear the Beatles in a whole new way. During the applause, the piano player notices Paul and waves him up.

By the time Paul plugs in, the band has started an Elling-ton tune I don't recognize. His first, full-throated note comes on the downbeat of the bridge, and now it comes to me—*Sophisticated Lady*. Sitting close to the speaker, I enjoy the feel of the low sound waves reverberating in my chest.

The Paul I see on stage is a different person from the one who drove me here, more confident and relaxed, in tune with his world. He rejoins me at the table when the set is over. "Next time, bring a poem, and I'll back you up."

"I just might do that."

It's 1 a.m. when he walks me from his car to my elevator, and we ride up to the apartment.

"You're sure you've never been here?" I ask. His eyes cloud over, but then he sees I'm teasing and he smiles. I'm tempted to ask him in, but too exhausted to follow up on the impulse. So our first kiss is in the hallway, a sweet good night. Later, in the bathroom, I feel like a teenager, hesitant to brush the taste of him off my teeth. *Ellie, I hope you're not too jealous.*

* * *

I sleep in the next morning. After a brunch of quesadillas washed down with beer, I call Stan in Torrance and ask him to try to locate Diane Sullivan, a Columbia University journalism major living somewhere in California. Stan agrees and gets off the phone, no questions asked. Must be his busy season. With business taken care of, I'm ready to treat myself to an afternoon of writing poetry.

At 5 o'clock, I swap my pajamas for jeans and trot over to the library to do some research on Miroslav Semilian. Both Google and Yahoo fail to bring up his name. I search the Inmate Population database at the Department of Correctional Services, but no luck there either. On a hunch, I type in Spike Andrews, and there it is: Andrews did time at Rikers in 2000.

Heading for the Bronx in the early evening, I check the bodegas on Tremont as well as the park, but there's no sign of Sonny. The address I have, courtesy of the Sunflower House files recently liberated by Hasim, is on Washington Avenue, near the library. The smell of fried bananas follows me up the stairs to number 306. More paint than not has peeled off the dull green door that Sonny, dressed in a colorless remnant of a bathrobe, opens. I can tell from the dull look in his pinprick eyes that I won't get much out of him.

"I need to know who else was working for Spike. We'll give you protection so you don't have to worry about reprisals."

Sonny's skinny friend drifts out of the shadows to stand behind him. He's pale, tall as a basketball player but short of the grace, and painfully thin, with hair as fine as corn silk dyed bright yellow and watery blue eyes to match. "You've got a lot of nerve harassing my friend Sonny. He was interrogated for two days but the cops couldn't stick the charges, so they sent him home. I'm sure you can see he's sick."

"I'm Jo Epstein," I say, wishing I could remember his name and holding out my hand. Skinny ignores this gesture. "I remember you," he says, looking me over. "You were hassling Sal, and he bounced you out of Sunflower House."

He's blocking my way into the apartment, but doesn't try to stop me when I walk around him. The living room is almost bare of furnishings. Most everything that could be sat on was probably sold a long time ago. I'm sure the shapeless orange couch where Sonny now sprawls in a semi-comatose state would be long gone if it weren't so heavy.

"Sonny is facing two possible murder charges. If he cooperates, maybe I can help."

"Yeah, I'm sure you're in his corner," sneers Skinny. The way he's twitching, either I make him extremely nervous or some illegal substance is doing the job for me. What a pair they are, one zooming on meth and the other nodding out. Gloria was right—it *is* too bad they closed Sunflower House.

"Look, you can't assume I'm the enemy just because I'm…"

"A bitch who works for the man?"

My patience is wearing thin. "Look, Sonny's got a motive for killing both Gabriel Johnson and Sal Salvatore. And the graffiti left at both murder scenes definitely puts the Scorpions in the mix."

This last statement is a reach on my part, but it pays off. As if pinpricked by an angel, Sonny sits up. "I seen the pictures and those throw ups weren't pieced by no Bronx tagger," he says. "Any banger would ID it as Elmhurst or Corona."

Skinny isn't buying. "You're off base, Sonny. That upside down fist has Scorpions all over it."

I don't like this kid. "Maybe you know your gang markers, but you don't look tough enough to be a player. What did you do, take a class?"

Skinny raises his fist, prompting Sonny to stumble between us. "Chill, Mokie, don't let her dog you. Look, I was straight with you about setting up Gabriel to be jacked, and I showed you the AK's at the warehouse. What more do you want?"

There's a long list, and I start at the top. "You can tell me who you worked with on the gun smuggling operation. It had to be someone with a pilot's license, because Spike Andrews doesn't have one."

"I'm not givin' up no dopeman so he can blow my dome in a drive by."

Mokie stands up, looming over me. "Don't you think it's time you did a ghost?"

There's a light scratch at the door. "You'd better take a pass, Jo," says Sonny. "We got some business to do."

The interview is threatening to be over before it begins. I thrust the photograph of Miroslav Semilian under Sonny's nose and he recoils before responding to the visual stimuli. "Yeah, that's Spike's friend from Florida."

I point to the hand Miroslav is shaking, its owner well out of the frame. "Know anybody with a pinky ring like this one?"

"Yeah, the social worker who runs that place in Losaida—Daniel something."

On my way out, I slide past the two junkies in the hall.

Barely managing to stay awake on the drive home, I'm grateful to find a good parking spot. The elevator is there, waiting for me in the lobby. Although I've been a fool, I'm too tired to beat myself up, which is unfortunate because the hooded man in the hallway has more than enough energy to do it for me. The last thing I hear before passing out are the words, "give it a rest, nosy bitch." It's easy to oblige.

Ask the Dead

the pulsing lights
are signals from a mind
trapped in the amber of its thoughts

Chapter Sixteen

The first thing I see with my one good eye when I wake up is Hasim, holding a bouquet of red carnations. "Thanks," I croak.

"The way you've been working this case, I should have brought you a badge and gun instead." It's not clear if this is meant as a put down or a compliment. "Good thing your neighbor decided to take out her garbage at midnight or you'd be dead. Any idea who it was?"

"No, but whatever he hit me with didn't bounce."

The Lieutenant pulls a chair up to the railing around the hospital bed. "Spike Andrews agreed to turn state's evidence and wear a wire to his meeting with Miroslav Semilian. When Semilian was arrested, he acted like he'd been invited to a black tie affair. Very smooth. They'll both be extradited in a few weeks. And my hard work has been rewarded—I'm reassigned to the Johnson homicide."

"Congratulations."

He leans over for a closer look at my face. "Anything I can do?"

"You could get me the pictures from the crime scene at Sal Salvatore's house. There's something we've been overlooking."

I give him a rundown on my visit with Sonny Rodriguez and fill him in on the smurfing operation, everything except Gloria's involvement. Why can't I let her go? As I talk Hasim looks around for a glass that he fills with water from a plastic pitcher, then carefully adds the flowers, one by one.

"Spike won't tell us who his partner was in the kidnapping."

"I'm surprised he'd protect someone who had the nerve to steal the ransom right out from under his nose."

Hasim finishes his flower arrangement. "Maybe he's saving the information to deal with when the stakes get higher."

155

As soon as Saleh leaves, the door swings open and in walks
Ted. He doesn't say much, but it means the world to me to have
him hold my hand while I fade into oblivion.

In the morning my vision clears enough for me to see that the
figure sitting in the chair by my bed isn't my boss. It's Daniel Rose,
no pinky ring in evidence. "I hope you feel better than you look."

The nurse comes to take my vitals and pronounces me well
enough to go to the cafeteria for breakfast, and in a flash I'm
dressed and grabbing my purse. There are a lot of people on
stretchers in the hallway, all of them in worse shape than me. "How
about I help you escape, and we go someplace more cheerful?"
Daniel proposes.

"I have to see the doctor before I can check out."

"We'll use the back door. Does the Chaucer Grill appeal to
you?" Immediately I'm suspicious. This is not a politically correct
destination. On the other hand, how can I pass up a chance to dine
in style while gathering information?

An hour later we're lingering over chocolate mousse, rich and
sweet enough to marry. "Your name came up last night when I was
talking with Sonny Rodriguez." I display the infamous photograph.
"Is this your ring?"

"What if it is?" The chocolate turns sour in my mouth.

"I remember that day because it was Leslie's birthday and
we had a party at the office." Daniel smiles, the fatherly employer.
"Gloria brought this gentleman with her, and Gabriel snapped a
picture of him shaking hands with me."

"Gloria claims she's never met Miroslav Semilian, that she
didn't know what he looked like until I showed her the photo." It's
pleasurable, seeing the smile flee his face, and I realize I'm still
smarting from the incident at his apartment. "It's her word against
yours, Daniel, and given your gift for fabricating evidence… You
were smart to use quinine, but too much is a dead giveaway."

"I didn't kill Gabriel." The amusement I see in his eyes doesn't
make sense, but his walking out of the restaurant in a huff does. The
food here isn't all that much better than at Nemo's, but this time I
finish my lunch. I should have known he'd stick me with the bill. I
pick up his wine glass, wrap it in a napkin, and put it in my purse.

* * *

Hasim is waiting for me in the reception area of the police lab. He hands me a thick file. "Not good bedtime reading," he says. Inside are three close ups of gang tags, each taken from a different angle, including one that shows Sal's blood splattered on his kitchen wall. I give Hasim the glass to take into the lab. While waiting for the results, I stare at the blue plastic chairs and floral prints that must have been selected by the same color- blind decorator who chose puce for the walls.

When Hasim comes out he tells me that one fingerprint on the wine glass matches the print on the key chain I found on Leslie's fire escape. "We have almost enough evidence to bring Mr. Rose in for questioning on the Johnson homicide. All we need is a motive."

"I've given this some thought, Hasim, and I doubt that Mr. Rose was involved in Gabriel's murder."

"What are you talking about? You're the one who was suspicious enough to lift his prints."

"I know. At criminology school they used to call me the human polygraph. I've always been able to tell when people are lying, but today I let my anger cloud my judgment."

"What you need is detachment, Jo. Familiarity can be like the sea that kills the fisherman."

"There are plenty of fish in the sea, Hasim. I think you're angling for the wrong one."

"A solution isn't wrong, just because it seems obvious."

"Yeah, well nothing's been obvious since my first day on this case. Please, give me a few hours before you pick up Daniel. I've got a hunch, but I need the facts to back it up."

"Who was it that said, if the facts don't fit the theory, change the facts?"

"You know very well it was Einstein. I thought all your proverbs were Egyptian."

"Einstein belongs to everyone.

"Just like Anwar Sadat?"

"Exactly."

This is probably the closest that Hasim and I will ever get to talking politics, but it reveals all I need to know.

at 15
the first death he's seen
stone cold on the sidewalk
no more back talk
no more "how 'ya doin?"

Chapter Seventeen

It's hard to believe that only a few days have gone by since I last dropped in on Sanyo. Today he's running a special, free Mexican orange soda if you buy two chili dogs. It's the dinner hour, and I'm hungry enough to go for it. After consuming one last delicious bite, I show him the gory pictures from Peekskill and ask him what he thinks of the eagle head and the upside down clenched fist next to the star. He's a straight citizen now, but I know he likes to stay in touch with the street.

"It looks like the Scorpion marker, and it's in the Bronx style, but this work is too much of a burner—it's got a dope outline, a def handstyle with block letters and wild colors and fades. It's too sophisticated to have been pieced by your average banger. This is the work of a king, he's def—a real artist—but it's still as phony as a transvestite's tits."

I wonder at Sanyo's choice of metaphor until I see his inspiration tripping across Sixth Avenue, dressed in satin and vinyl boots. "Hey, Elaine, you're looking gorgeous today," Sanyo calls to his friend, giving me a wink. "One of my best customers."

He continues his analysis of the crime scene graffiti. "You're never gonna see the symbol for the Street Kings in the same piece as the Scorpion marker, not without the star being crossed out. They're enemies with a serious beef. That's why I'm sure this piece is a bite. You're looking at a forgery, but one that approaches high art. The subway cars are clean now but stuff like this is starting to pop up in museums."

"How come you know all this?"

"I was a motion tagger myself once. Nothing beats the thrill of hitting a moving train."

"Thanks, Sanyo. This is a big help."

Further up Sixth Avenue I spot Marilyn Searl. She's adding the finishing touches to a portrait of a thin, vivacious woman who looks so much like a poodle that it's surprising how attractive Marilyn has made her appear.

"More questions about Gabriel?" she asks.

"Just one. Did you ever see him hanging out with someone named Mokie?"

"There was this white kid—I remember being surprised at how he talked like a rapper. It seemed phony to me, but Gabriel didn't seem to care. Everyone on the street called him Mokie but I think his real name was Sean."

Gulping down my free orange soda, I place a call to Shondrea. "He stayed with us for a month, until he was arrested, but I never heard Gabriel call him Mokie," she says. "His last name was Smith and I remember thinking it sounded like a phony name, Sean Smith. Do you think he had something to do with Gabriel's death?"

"That's what we need to find out. I'm going to ask Lieutenant Saleh to bring Sean in for questioning. Do you have any idea where he lives?"

"Someplace in the suburbs. He wasn't a city kid. All the tough guy mannerisms in the world couldn't hide that. Long Island, that's where he was from. Hold on a sec, I think he left some things in Gabe's room."

I wait on the phone while she hunts around. "Westbury, that's the name of the town. I found a letter addressed to him at 211 Red Fox Drive."

"Thanks, Shondrea. I'll follow this up and hopefully get some results."

My next call is to Hasim. I relate how Sean crashed at Gabriel's house until they were both arrested and how he then turned up at Sunflower House and again at a shooting gallery with Sonny Rodriguez. "I'll call you right back," he says, and when he does, it's to tell me that Sean Smith, aka Smitty, aka Mokie got out of prison three months ago and was referred to Sunflower House for a six-week stay. "He's got a sheet long enough to qualify him for three strikes," says Hasim.

"Can you pick him up?"

"You know better than that, Jo. You don't have the evidence to justify a search warrant. From what you tell me, your suspicions are based on a gut feeling, and that, along with three bucks, will buy you a latte."

"There's nothing to stop me from going out there and questioning his parents."

"No, but if you find anything incriminating, keep your hands off and let us do it by the book."

* * *

These days when you drive or take the train to Elmhurst or Glen Cove, you don't find the cookie cutter houses and homogenized culture that were once typical of Long Island. You'll see folks from New Delhi and Haiti and Taiwan who moved here so their kids could get a good education and breathe fresh air. You'll find mosques and Buddhist temples, along with churches that celebrate mass in Haitian Creole, Spanish and Indian dialects.

If you're looking for the kind of town where residents dress up in Revolutionary War costumes and spinning wheels are used to create wool instead of skid marks, you have to continue east and south until you slip through a time warp into the Hamptons. It would be difficult to find a more extreme contrast to the derelict buildings of the East Bronx.

Judging from their choice of architect, Sean Smith's parents must be avid science fiction fans. Their residence resembles a flying saucer made of glass, and is attached to a concrete boat ramp stretching out over dry land in the direction of the ocean. The see-through doors to the garage reveal a vintage Mercedes and a Mini Cooper, both of which I wouldn't mind owning.

Thirty steps lead to the entrance to the house and, by the time I reach the top, I feel as exposed to view as a subway flasher. The gleaming copper doors are decorated with an upside down number five, scrawled in black paint. Sean, the wannabe gansta', has posted a challenge to the 5-O's. In the past it's made me laugh, the way rappers insist on casting police officers as daytime TV actors, forever condemned to saying, "Book 'em Danno." But today the

161

sight of a thin, almost invisible wire rigged to the bronze door handles raises hairs on the back of my neck.

Sean sticks his head out of one of the porthole-like windows. "Go ahead. Open the door. My mom's original Jackson Pollack will be blown to hell, but I won't be around to embarrass her anymore."

"How come you weren't at Gabriel's funeral, Sean?"

"You know, I can blow us to hell and back before you make it down the steps."

Not my ideal way to die. I push the picture from my mind. "You were with Sonny when he stored some boxes in Leslie's apartment, isn't that right?"

"Yeah, that's when I lifted the key to the window gate." Whatever he's on, it's making him talkative.

"And then you came back, two days later."

"Yeah. I was gonna get me some loot. She was rich and I figured she had some jewelry."

"You saw Leslie leave the building?"

"After she came out, I was up that fire escape faster than Twista runs his motor mouth. There was some good jewelry, but it was mixed in with a lot of junk. I was leaning over the night table and somebody came from behind and put me in a choke hold. He didn't say anything—just grabbed me. I was amped out of my skull and trying to get loose. I got my knife out and twisted around to stick him. How was I supposed to know it was Gabriel?"

I'm not sure, but I think he's crying. I've got a crick in my neck from looking up at him, but I don't want to break eye contact. "You've still got some choices to make Sean. If what you say is true and killing Gabriel was an accident…"

"It doesn't matter! We both know what happens to a perp if somebody dies during a crime. It's a 187, a homicide, period."

"Sean, why don't you disarm this thing so I can come inside and we can talk. My neck is killing me." He pulls back from the window and a moment later the door opens, minus the expected explosion.

As soon as I'm inside, Sean makes sure I see him re-connect the wires to his detonator—an innocent looking kitchen timer on a table in the entranceway. It starts to tick. Looks like it's set for ten

162

minutes.

The narrow hallway is covered with priceless works of art. These people have an everyday acquaintance with Picasso and Rauschenberg. The house appears to have been designed around the paintings, with the rooms as afterthoughts.

"I can see where you get your artistic inspiration. Did you paint the graffiti on Leslie's bedroom wall to make it look like a gang killing?"

"I had my backpack with me, with all the paints and caps I needed for a throw up. And the cops fell for it. They thought it was the Scorpions getting their revenge."

Seeing me admire the masterpieces lining the walls, Sean says, "I know what you're thinking—if my folks have so much money, why do I have to steal? They cut me off, is why. When your son is a speed freak and you give him money, you might as well put a gun to his head and pull the trigger. They thought it was tough love, but all it meant to me was that scoring drugs got tough-er."

We've entered the ultra modern dining room, where chrome and steel predominate, warmed only by the thick oak beams that brace the ceiling. The long, glass-topped table is covered with electronic paraphernalia, sticks of explosives and cans of spray paint that I'm sure are the ones Sean used on the walls of Leslie's bedroom.

"So where *are* your parents?"

"Beats me. I have a PO box in the city that I check every once in a while to see if my Dad has broken down and sent me a check. There was a postcard from Denmark, so I figured I could come out here for a few days and crash. I disarmed the security system, and, while I was at it, I added some features of my own. I'm good with electronics."

We both hear it, the sound of sirens approaching. The look of betrayal on his face is unmistakable. "I swear Sean, I didn't call them. One of my friends on the force knew I was coming out here. He must have decided I needed backup.

"You'd better tell him to go away before they try to force the door. I can change that timer to zero, and they'll never know what hit them."

I stick my head out the window above the door and yell at Hasim and another officer I don't recognize, both of them taking the steps two at a time. "The front door is wired with explosives! Go back to your car, and we can talk on the phone."

Hasim and his backup retreat in a hurry and my cell phone rings a minute later. "I'm calling in the SWAT team, Jo. When you said the front door was wired, was that code for telling us it's safe to go in the back?"

"No way, Hasim, that's a recipe for disaster. I need some time to convince Sean to give himself up."

"You've got ten minutes," he growls. No use telling him that the clock has only five left.

It doesn't make sense that now that the police are here, with the big bang set to follow close behind, Sean has actually become less jumpy, holding his head as it droops over the table. He looks like he's crashing off amphetamines. He stumbles into the bathroom and now's my chance.

I run to the front door and gently pick up the timer. Sean didn't take the time to replace the back piece and the wires are still exposed. Holding my breath would be a waste of time. I close my eyes and yank the wires apart. The wobbling I feel in my knees tell me I'm still alive, and I hustle back to the dining room just in time to see Sean come out of the bathroom, totally amped, his pupils dilated, firing words in rapid bursts as his mouth tries to keep pace with the velocity of his brain.

"I bet you didn't know that piece on Sal's wall is mine, too. I done it as a tribute. I knew he fancied himself a collector of street art and that he wanted his very own authentic mural with gang colors and def shading. It was no throw-up—I painted a real burner with original designs. Sal was like a father to me. It's a shame he had to die. He was gonna turn me in for what went down with Gabriel. He said he believed me when I told him it was an accident and that the police would, too. But I knew the 5-0's don't take no kid's word, not a speed freak with my record."

"I'm trying to understand what happened, Sean. Were you working for Sal as a smurf?"

"Yeah, all us losers at Sunflower House were bank runners. It was a tight deal. Most of us were recruited at Rikers, hand-picked by Larry T."

"You mean a CO was involved in the money-laundering?"

"You wouldn't be so surprised if you'd been inside and seen him at work shaking down the inmates for their duckets in exchange for referrals to drug rehab. He's a real twisted guy."

"If we can show that you're a minor who was recruited into criminal activities by adults, it may help you get some leniency, Sean. Why don't we go outside and talk with Lieutenant Saleh?"

"You're trying to force me to give myself up. Well, here's today's headline: this is *my* day. I'm in charge of what happens, so don't fuck with me. You think I'm loco? You think after I told you all this I'm gonna give myself up and let them try me as an adult for murder? You think I'm gonna volunteer to shack up on death row so you can keep filing appeals and feel sorry for me until I fry?"

"Sean, I know you're scared, but I can help you."

His senses are keyed higher than a dog whistle. "You think I'm scared? Well, here comes hell and see if I don't blink." Sean's looking at his wristwatch, counting down the seconds to our mutual extinction. His voice starts at a crescendo and ends with a soft whisper. "Five! Four! Three! Two! One!"

Nothing.

I make a run for it, reaching the front door and getting it open before I turn to look at him. He's walking towards me, slowly, deliberately, a gun in his right hand. I could grab the timer but in that split second he could easily shoot me. I step outside and close the door behind me, hoping against hope that he doesn't re-arm the detonator. I'm at the bottom of the steps and headed for Hasim's car when I hear the explosion that knocks me off my feet.

Hasim helps me up. My eardrums are so blown I have to read his lips.

"He almost took you with him."

"I had to try, Hasim. A few less milligrams of meth and maybe he'd still be with us."

"You never give up, Jo. It's the one thing I like about you."

* * *

Stuck in heavy traffic on the West Side Highway, I have plenty of time to focus my thoughts on the way to Harlem. Shondrea deserves some clear answers.

"How exhausted you look," she comments, and I'm touched by her show of concern. She looks better today. Maybe the pain has receded into a deeper place, making it easier for her to function. As we talk through the events of the past few days, over Earl Grey tea splashed with whiskey (a first time for me and delicious), I see relief flooding her careworn face. Now she knows for a fact what she already knew in her heart—that Gabriel died while acting on behalf of a friend.

I'm reluctant to accept my fee, a new sensation. So this is what it feels like to be paid for doing what you love to do. This is what Stan was talking about.

police horses
trained to stand perfectly still
enduring the siren's blare
large eyes wide inside blinkers
obligatory blind spots
unlike my own

Chapter Eighteen

Rough lava scratches the soles of my feet, once liquid fire, now jagged mounds covered with green lichens, stretching towards the calm, empty sea. Then shock waves roll me off my feet and into a whirlpool pulling me down, a vise grip on my ankles taking me deeper, lungs filled to bursting. As Sean's face recedes from above, the buzzing in my ears turns into the ring of the doorbell, and I waken.

Paul's brought me scones and coffee. Hands full, he nods towards the newspaper carried under his arm. "You're famous today." His pale, ascetic look is heightened by a stark black turtle-neck. "Thought I'd come by and bask in your glory."

"I pushed a boy over the edge—nothing heroic in that."

"From what I've read, it sounds like he was charging full speed ahead toward destruction, and you tried to slow him down."

"Let's not talk about it. OK?"

"Better yet, let's do something to distract you from your worries."

"What do you have in mind?"

"A nice day in the country. Get your coat. We're going for a drive."

There's nothing like escaping Manhattan on a weekday morning, everyone skittering across the Washington Bridge in a panic to be on time for work and us driving at a leisurely pace towards nowhere in particular. It's a tonic, having someone else at the wheel, floating on the superb shocks of Paul's early model Volvo, the engine purring towards an unknown destination. With my head on his shoulder, my worn out psyche gradually releases control, and I slip beneath a sweet blanket of nothingness.

Bumped into consciousness by the ruts in the road, my first impression is that Beverly's journal has come to life. The cabin is exactly as she described—the cedar shingles and bay windows, the wind chimes hanging from the eaves and inside, the knotty pine walls, pot belly stove and red leather couch.

"Why the frown," asks Paul. "I thought you'd love this place."

He looks so concerned that I come right out with it. "How come Beverly described all this in her diary if, as you say, she was never here?"

He drops his duffel bag on the braided rug and scratches his chin, not the angry reaction I'd expect. "That's a reasonable question, in spite of its implications. The answer is simple. I was trying to rent this place, and I passed around some pictures at a book club meeting. Beverly must have been there."

It's my turn to be thoughtful. "Do you remember who else was at the meeting?"

"I don't remember. We met at Roberta's house. Why don't you give her a call, if that'll clear the air."

I'm tempted to drop the whole thing, but if he's bluffing I'll never know. So I go through with what turns out to be an embarrassing phone call. "Yeah, I remember those photos," says Roberta, in the over-enunciated tones of a Boston Brahmin. "Especially the one of his cat drinking from the toilet in the bathroom."

Paul's in the kitchen, unpacking our supplies. I find a corkscrew in a drawer next to the sink and open the Pinot Noir, while he slices the cheese in silence. When he looks up, he's smiling. "If you didn't have a skeptical nature, you wouldn't be a detective, would you? And if you weren't a detective, I'd never have met you. So, I guess I'll take you as you are."

And that's the end of it. We settle in with wine and magazines, luxuriating in laziness until it's time to pack a picnic lunch and trek over to the lake, where we nibble on smoked oysters (and an occasional ear) and wolf down salami sandwiches with root beer chasers.

On the walk back to the cabin, my cell phone rings, and

against my better judgment, I answer it.

"The Adirondacks? That's the trouble with cell phones—you could be in Istanbul for all I know." It's Hasim.

"I presume you've got a reason for tracking me down, Lieutenant?"

"If you're not interested in hearing the results of the background check you asked me to run on that CO from Rikers, just say so." Do I detect some irritation with me for taking some time off?

"I'm all ears, Lieutenant."

"Larry Tollway did a two year stretch in the Air Force before signing on at Rikers three years ago. He has a clean service record and no priors. He didn't qualify as a military pilot, but he attended flight school in Arizona and got his commercial license six months ago."

"Where was he posted in the service?"

"Fort Benning, Georgia. Same as Spike Andrews.

"Are you going to pick up Tollway?"

"It's all circumstantial. Unless Spike talks…"

"There's someone I know who might be able to help. I'll give him a call and, if it pans out, I'll be sure to get back to you."

Hasim sighs. "A promise is a cloud, fulfillment is rain."

* * *

Although his number is stored in my cell phone, it's not easy for me to call Uncle Jake. In all my years as a working detective, I never tapped him as a source. When things in California were going well, I did send him newspaper clippings about my high profile cases and, on alternate years, we exchanged greeting cards. When Jake's wife Andrea died, I flew to New York for the funeral. After that, my life seemed to go downhill, and I imagine his did, too. It adds up to us being out of touch much longer than in.

I try his number in Flushing, half wishing that he's moved to Florida like he always said he would. Jake picks up on the first ring.

"This is your long lost niece. How's it goin'?"

"I'll be damned! It's great to hear your voice, young lady." It's like we've been buddies all along, an unbroken chain. Jake chortles when I describe my dilemma. "I knew you'd appreciate me someday. Tell me everything you know about these guys." It isn't much, but I comply. "I need to know if there's a connection between Tollway, Spike Andrews and an arms dealer named Miroslav Semilian."

"Semilian. Sounds familiar." Jake asks for twenty-four hours, and, from his tone of voice, I can tell he intends to come through.

The rest of the day with Paul goes by in a haze of good wine and good will, with some physical pleasuring thrown in. The next morning, I find the smell of coffee made by someone else to be as delightful as the bird chatter on the patio that competes with our breakfast conversation. It's late afternoon when Paul drops me off on Broadway, where I pick up some groceries and a blouse that's been languishing at the dry cleaners before walking home.

Ellie, I can't say I blame you for falling for Paul. He's so easy to be with. I'd like to tell you more, but how can I continue to confide in you? I know it's ridiculous, but I feel like a traitor, in spite of the fact that you were never his girlfriend. It's what you wanted, and I've got it.

* * *

Jake's call comes right on schedule. "Semilian was deep into moving surplus weapons around the globe. He's a shadowy figure and busting him was a major coup. Spike Andrews was dishonorably discharged from the Air Force, under suspicion of inaccurate coding of surplus weapons systems."

"What's that in plain English?"

"Spike Andrews and Larry Tollway both worked at the same DRMO—Defense Reutilization and Marketing Office. It was like assigning two bank robbers to guard Fort Knox. According to the Defense Logistics Agency, Andrews assigned codes to weapons and electronic guidance systems that designated them as destroyed, or demilitirized, when they were actually in full working order. They suspected both of them of taking kickbacks from surplus dealers who bought the weapons and shipped them overseas, but the charges couldn't be proven."

"This information is golden, Uncle Jake. I'm only sorry I waited until I needed something to call you. I should have stayed in touch."

"Hey, you've made me feel useful, which is more than I can say on most days." We agree to see more of each other, or at least visit on the phone. He sends his regards to Mom, but being she's his favorite sister, he probably talks to her more than I do.

Larry Tollway may have a lot of things to hide, but, when I look him up in the phone book, I find that his address on East 82nd isn't one of them. I stock up on snacks at the QuikMart on West 94th and walk up to 97th, which is where I left the Protegé. The needle's close to empty. I should have gassed up in Westchester. Driving east, I cruise the cross-town streets that connect First Avenue and York, starting at 80th and working my way north, looking for Larry's red Camaro and, all the while, blessing him for choosing a conspicuous color.

Nothing doing. The best I can do is try to park near his apartment building, and I'm forced to take a spot under a street light at the west end of the block, near the corner of Second Avenue and 82nd. I settle in for what will probably be a long and uneventful vigil. There's enough chocolate in the glove box to provision a small climbing expedition and a bathroom in the Starbucks nearby.

It's several hours after nightfall, and I'm biting into my third Cadbury when I see someone who might be Larry emerge from the brown brick building down the street. I don't get a good look at him until he's close enough to see me, too, but Larry's walking fast and his attention is elsewhere. The bruises on his face have healed. Tollway walks by me, and, as soon as he's out of sight, I speed down the block, hang a right on First, another right on 83rd and zoom back to Second Avenue in time to see him crossing with the light.

I follow as slowly as I can without stalling the Protegé's engine, pissing off some drivers in the process, but the sound of honking horns is so prevalent around here that Larry doesn't even turn his head. Who would have guessed? Larry's snazzy car is hidden in a funky garage on East 79th.

At this time of night traffic is thin, forcing me to hang back more than usual to keep from being burned. I'm still in the land of the blind, but tonight I get the feeling I'm following the one-eyed king. When my subject takes the Briarcliff-Peekskill Parkway, he confirms what I suspected. It's time to get Hasim on the line. Samarah answers. He's out in the field, and she's not sure when he'll be back. She promises to get hold of the station dispatcher, and I ask her to send Hasim to Sunflower House as soon as possible.

About a half mile from my destination, I pull over, park the car, and proceed on foot. There's enough of a moon to light my way along the overgrown fence at the back of Sal's property. By climbing the fence, I'm gambling that the alarm system was deactivated when Sunflower House was officially closed. All bets are off when the sirens start to blare. Precariously balanced, I have to choose whether to jump inwards, towards the house and its alerted occupants or backwards to the road.

Tired of playing cat and mouse, I choose the direct approach and get about fifty yards towards the house before Larry grabs me from behind, using an impressive chokehold backed up by a gun in my back. He frisks me, making me wish I'd bought that piece off Sanyo six months ago. Escorting me into the library, Larry pulls a chair into the middle of the room. "Sit there, where I can keep an eye on you."

"That bruise on your face has healed up nicely. Spike's got a solid right hook."

"What kind of shit are you talking?"

"I heard you were overly fond of your captive and your partner had to stop you from damaging the goods."

"You're making this up as you go along."

"What's that I heard you say? 'Her daddy is as loaded with money as his films are loaded with blood and gore.' Not a bad analogy."

"I'm not as dumb as you think."

"Even so, I hear you left so many fingerprints in the cockpit of the Citation on Jameson Field, you might as well have taken out an ad in the New York Times." This is a calculated guess, and it appears to pay off.

Larry grabs the large portrait of the late Sal Salvatore's father off the wall and heaves it half way across the room. This action reveals a wall safe, which in turn discloses a red leatherette coin case that he takes out and puts on the table.

"I'll bet this is the first time you've cracked a safe in order to put something inside." I put a little admiration into my words. He's avoiding eye contact, and I need to get him talking. "When Leslie called Sal at Sunflower House to arrange to meet him, it was you who answered the phone, and you listened in on their conversation. You disabled the Subaru so that Gloria would have to drive him home, and then you used his car to kidnap Leslie."

He waves the Mac 10 around for a bit and then points it directly at me. "There's some duct tape in the closet. Go get it. Now!"

After I retrieve the tape from the closet, Larry shoves me down into the chair and takes up position behind me. I try to slow the beat of my heart so it doesn't drown out the sound I'm listening for. As soon as he rips the tape from the roll, I kick the chair out from under me and make a grab for the hand I hope is holding the gun. Then two things happen. The Mac 10 goes flying, and Larry dives after it. I close my eyes, expecting to be shot, but instead, he lets out a loud yelp. From my position on the floor, I can see that his hand is under the heel of a purple suede boot that can only belong to one person. Gloria retrieves the gun, holding it with two hands as she steps back and takes control.

"You wouldn't," Larry says softly, rising from the floor and walking towards her. The gun spits fire and the force of the bullet carries Larry backwards several feet before he falls to the floor and lies still. There's a raw hole in his chest, and I can see there's no use in feeling for a pulse.

Gloria's arm remains extended, the gun barrel now sighted on me. "Why are you looking at me that way? He was going to kill you."

"Maybe. But that's not why you shot him. Larry was going to keep it all, no two-way split."

She doesn't deny it. "Sal and I spent three years building up our account on St. Dominic and then, because of you, they froze our assets, and we lost it all in one day."

173

"Including the assets Sal didn't know about. The money you and Larry were laundering for Spike."

Gloria reaches down and closes Larry's eyes, whether it's a compassionate or triumphant act it's hard to say. "Larry was a hard core mercenary, but he knew how to make things happen. I know what you're thinking, Jo. We were cleaning blood money. But then I thought about all the kids from the Lower East Side and Harlem who could get a second chance on St. Dominic—how it could be the start of a whole new eco-movement."

"You make it sound like you were writing a grant application! It was money-laundering, kidnapping, and murder."

"We didn't kill anyone!" Do I detect a ring of truth here? "Yes, we were guilty of kidnapping, but that was only because Spike's supplier gave us no choice. Either we recouped his losses, or we lost our lives."

"Spike will give you up, now that he's in custody."

"I've got the payment for his silence right here. His share will be waiting in a safe deposit box until he gets out." Gloria pats the coin case. "When the Cornings told me all the details about the ransom drop, how Michael was supposed to wait at the airport bar for a phone call, I knew this was a window of opportunity that we couldn't pass up. Larry's not, or should I say he wasn't, very bright. He was afraid of Spike, and it took some convincing for him to see things my way. It went off perfectly, until my itchy-fingered partner got back to New York with the coins."

Keeping the gun level, Gloria picks up the duct tape and thrusts it at me. "I won't make the same mistake he did. Tape your hands together." I twist the tape around my wrists as loosely as I can, but she uses her free hand to jerk the strip taut, forcing a skin tight fit. Gripping the coin case, she pushes me out the door.

I want to tell her that running away isn't the answer, that a tropical paradise makes no sense to kids growing up on the streets of New York and won't change the lives of millions hypnotized in front of their TV sets. Instead, I obey orders, walking to the dark blue van parked behind Larry's Camaro and get in the front seat.

"Where are we going?"

"I'm not sure, Jo. I could take you home and ask you to think about whether or not I deserve to go to jail. I'm tired of lying to you and though you may think the worst of me, I've always thought the best of you. On the other hand..."

Before Gloria can elaborate, she's distracted by approaching headlights. The cruiser pulls alongside, and Hasim flashes his lights, signaling us to stop. Gloria punches the accelerator and, in the rear view mirror, I see him turning around. The sound of a siren splits the night air.

Gloria hangs a sharp left, and we're plunging through a field. She turns off the headlights and rows of corn race past us in the moonlight. Hasim follows, the siren now quiet, but Gloria keeps the lead. All I hear for a while is the sound of cornstalks whipping the windshield and the tires squealing.

Suddenly we're back on paved roads, zigging and zagging through the countryside, and I'm sure we've lost him. The van hits a few bumps and threatens to roll over, but Gloria's speed never slackens, which is why she fails to see the Dead End sign and has no time to prevent the van from flying through the air where the road disappears. A few interminable seconds, and we land with a loud splash in a body of water that I hope is a shallow creek. As we start to sink, so does my optimism.

on the verge,
slim threads holding us
back from the brink
don't wanna' think
just wanna' find the strength
to make beauty
living on the verge

Chapter Nineteen

"I can't unlock the windows!" As the car goes down, Gloria struggles wildly with the door handle.

"No," I say, "we have to wait for the pressure to equalize on both sides." I'm in panic mode, too, but I know the doors won't open until the car is almost full of water.

"I can't swim," she wails, blackness covering the windows, leaving us in total darkness with the water rushing up to hip level. The duct tape around my wrists won't budge. I wiggle the fingers on my left hand and free them enough to wiggle the door handle—no luck, I can't get enough leverage. I try using both hands at once and finally mange to open the passenger door and swim free. But as soon as I break contact with the van I lose all sense of direction. Which way is up? My lungs are craving air but the only option is H_2O.

I force myself to stay calm and rotate my body 360 degrees, straining my eyes for the slightest sign of moonlight. Finally, I get a fix on a faint luminescence and with a lot of kicking and praying, reach the surface, gasping for air.

I take in as deep a breath as I can before diving down to help Gloria. It's like swimming through ink and with my hands still tied in front of me, all I can do is wave my arms up and down, hoping to make contact with the car. On the second try, a vice like grip grabs my elbow, pulling me down. My feet make contact with the top of the van and I kick my legs out, pushing off of the roof with all the power I can muster. Gloria relaxes her grip. Either she senses what I'm doing, or she's lost consciousness. We break the surface, and I turn onto my back, kicking towards shore with her struggling to hold on, amidst fits of violent choking. With the last of my energy, I drag us both onto the rocky bank, scraping my back in the process.

The air temperature is a lot cooler than the water, and we're both shivering. If this was winter, we'd be dead from exposure. Still coughing, Gloria helps me loosen the tape on my wrists.

"You saved my life," she sputters.

"I'm not exactly sure why. Apparently flesh and blood has little value in your eyes compared with your grand ideals."

"Ideals have their own life, when you believe in them."

"What about the people who will be murdered and mutilated with the weapons that Spike sold?"

"Collateral damage. It happens."

Where is the Gloria who once told me that the goal of anarchism was the freest possible expression of all the latent powers of the individual?

"Gloria, you are so full of shit! It's bad enough that conflicts all over the world are being fought with weapons our own country supplies, but when people like you, who spout off about peace and utopia, are running guns…by the way, the paramilitaries intercepted the shipment. They're probably using those guns to kill innocent people right now."

"Jo, there's two million dollars worth of coins in that van. You're a good swimmer. Why don't you retrieve it before someone else does?"

"No thanks. I had my fill of murky water while saving your worthless life."

"So this is the *friend* you've been protecting?" Hasim's sarcastic voice makes us both jump.

"Don't you ladies know that sound travels over water? It looks like you've both done some traveling yourselves."

* * *

The phone rings at 8:30 a.m.. "Gloria Kelly has been charged with second degree murder and kidnapping."

"Good morning to you, too, Hasim. I'm surprised you didn't charge her with Salvatore's murder, too."

"It was tempting, since she admits she drove him home the

night he was killed. Unfortunately, she has an alibi for later in the evening. On the other hand, Sean Smith was indentified by the cashier at the Red Rooster Market—he bought some candy and cigarettes on the night of the murder—and she remembers how twitchy he was. Add the fact that the same knife was used to kill Gabriel and Sal, and we have enough evidence to support Sean's confession to you on both counts, case closed."

"So why wake me up so early?" I ask.

Hasim chuckles. "I'm the one who was up all night doing paperwork on your midnight swim. Gloria says you can verify her story that she shot Larry Tollway to keep him from shooting you."

"What she says is partially true. If Larry had managed to retrieve his gun, I'd be checked into the morgue instead of him."

"A half truth is a whole lie." He's hit me with a Jewish proverb this time, definitely below the belt. "There are lots of unanswered questions about this woman. Why do you insist on being loyal to her when she's up to her neck in it?"

I ponder this annoying question in the kitchen, over huevos rancheros and orange juice, but no reasonable answer emerges. Maybe our memories are selectively self-serving, like Elliot claimed whenever we had a fight and I'd bring up the time he forgot the sunscreen, and I got such a bad burn at Zuma Beach that my shoulders glowed like a helicopter searchlight.

Helicopter. It takes a few seconds of internal wrestling before I can bring the dreamy remembrance into focus. A rooftop on East 12th street under a full moon. Enough LSD to levitate the nearby Williamsburg Bridge and enough opium-laced marijuana to haul it back down again. *White Rabbit* blasting so loud that we don't hear the police copter until it's directly overhead, searchlight sweeping across the crowd, probably up there for some other reason— maybe a liquor store robbery—but now they've spotted us and hover over the party, waiting for their backup to arrive and block the stairs to the street.

Gloria pulls me off my blanket and hustles me over to the dark side of the roof, to the fire escape ladder. "Jo, you can do this. Take a deep breath and hold on tight. When you get near the bottom you'll have to use your weight to pull the ladder down to the street. Come on, get yourself together."

"Are you coming?"

"There's no time. They're coming up the stairs right now. When you get home, call my mom. She'll take it from there." Calm and cool, that was Gloria. The next day, when the drugs wore off, I realized that she acted as a decoy and got herself arrested so my future career in law enforcement wouldn't be endangered.

It's too bad, Gloria. Last night's events have made this debt null and void.

* * *

When you walk into Martin Luther King Elementary School in Washington Heights, it's immediately apparent that despite the danger lurking in the streets outside, these children intend to beat the odds. In the entranceway, colorful origami peace cranes dangle from the ceiling like welcoming ambassadors. Exhortations to read, succeed and excel are everywhere.

I join the sniffling crowd in the waiting room outside the Nurse's Office and try to keep my inhales to a minimum. On the wall a child's watercolor shows stick people running away from a falling skyscraper.

"Art can be the best therapy." Sarah Clark's proud smile is edged with sadness. She dispenses some kind of medicine and writes one little girl a note excusing her from class before inviting me into her office.

"You said on the phone you were with Stuyvesant Life?"

I hand her the phony business card and get straight to the lie. "Beverly Ellis' family claims they have proof that she did not commit suicide and therefore the suicide exclusion cannot be used to deny payment of the policy."

"How does this involve me?"

"Your principal told me that you were the designated reporter to Children Services when Beverly Ellis worked here. I've heard conflicting reports about what happened ."

"I was in the dark myself, until Chloe Sterling came to see me about the charges that were filed against her sister."

179

"Don't you mean the charges that were filed against Letitia's father?"

"No, it's a matter of record. Letitia's parents accused Beverly of harassing Letitia into making false statements and frightening her so badly she was having nightmares."

"Did you question the child?"

"She was examined by a Children Services caseworker who concluded that she was afraid of her teacher and would have done anything to avoid displeasing her. I had worked with Beverly for six years and couldn't believe she would do such a thing, until Chloe convinced me. What she told me is extremely sensitive, but I can reveal that Beverly's behavior was caused by a childhood trauma affecting both sisters."

"Can you be more specific? Everything will be confidential."

"In that case, I'll tell you what I know. After all that's happened, I'd hate to see this family put through a murder investigation. Chloe told me a tragic, but all too common, story. When she was eight years old, her new stepfather sexually abused her. He did this regularly for two years, but her older sister, Beverly, ignored what was happening. Maybe she was afraid that if she interfered the same thing would happen to her. The abuse only came to an end when the stepfather left the family. Chloe kept this to herself until she was fifteen, and, even then, her mother and Beverly claimed not to believe her.

"When she came to see me, Chloe was convinced that Beverly's suspicions about Letitia were created by her own feelings of guilt. After the caseworker interviewed the child and determined that Letitia feared her teacher, rather than her father, I recommended that we terminate the investigation. A few weeks later, the family brought charges against Beverly."

We're interupted by a small boy with a nasty cut on the side of his pumpin-round face. Ms. Clark calmly wipes away the blood to determine the extent of the damage. If she notices me wincing, she gives no sign, leaving me to speculate about Chloe Sterling's behavior. Was it really sisterly concern that had prompted her interference? Or had she tasted sweet revenge after all those years? There was no getting around the fact that she'd given the prosecution exactly what they needed to make a case against her own sister.

The nurse cleans and bandages in one smooth motion, while continuing her story.

"I knew she was going to lose her job, but I had no idea how unstable she was or I would have made sure that she was treated by a therapist. Beverly was in terrible emotional pain. Along with the barbiturates, the police found two empty bottles of OxyContin. It wasn't reported in the paper, but my nephew's on the force, and he told me about it."

"It sounds to me like her feelings were overpowering and there's not much you could have done."

I'm almost out the door, feeling pretty rotten at having obtained information under false pretenses, when Mrs. Clark adds, "I think what really pushed Beverly over the edge was her boyfriend Paul breaking up with her. I often saw them together, and I thought they were a lovely couple."

* * *

There's no cure for betrayal, but drinking with likeable strangers can help. And not everyone here tonight is a stranger. Scandals is filled to capacity with nervous poets filling up with liquid courage before the semi-finals. Maybe it's the gin and tonics or the fact that literary insanity is contagious, but somehow my name gets onto the sign up sheet once again.

If you asked me why I'm willing to compete in front of painfully arbitrary judges and rowdy audiences for the honor of winning infinitesimal prizes, you'd be missing the point. As oft-quoted slammer Allan Wolf puts it, "The points are not the point; the point is poetry." I'd go a step further and say that the point is the poets. Mutually supportive in a dog-eat-dog world, their receptive faces defy the city's impenetrable stare.

Marty Elias is in fine form this evening. "I'm pleased to inform those of you who were unlucky enough to miss last week's Dead Poets Slam, that Langston Hughes beat the crap out of Emily Dickinson. Now let's get to it. You know the rules, but…"

Her voice fades into the background because I've just spotted Paul near the stage, which means I have to walk by him to get to the microphone. "Good luck," he whispers.

"You're the one who needs it. You lied to me," I drain my glass and then I'm in the spotlight and had better choose a poem before I open my mouth and the 3-minute clock starts ticking. I'm too drunk to care, so the poem goes over beautifully—a little story about imaginary horses that protected me on my walk to school every morning. I qualify for the second round, and score a perfect 30.

Once again Reggie Pinero and I are picked for the one-on-one face off. I know how much he wants to compete in the nationals, but for me the Slam has always been a relatively safe way to challenge myself without taking the outcome too seriously. Tonight's different. Something clicks during my three-minute version of the twenty-page poem I wrote after my second divorce. When I'm done, tears are streaming down my face, and Marty is dancing around the stage, waving a handful of crisp five dollar bills. "Come back next week! You've made the tryouts for the team!"

After the excitement dies down, I look around for Paul, but he's gone. I can understand that the lie he told me was probably a continuation of what he told the police four years ago, when he didn't want to be involved in the investigation of Beverly's suicide. But for now, I'm going to continue to ignore his calls. Why do these masters of deception keep showing up in my life? I should guard my heart more carefully, but then again, who wants to run background checks on all their lovers?

* * *

I call Ted and ask him if it's okay for me to take a few days vacation on the West Coast. "Why not a month," he says, "and while you're at it you can take my ATM card. Maybe you'd like to take a few of my first editions to read on the plane."

"I get it, Ted. If you give my job to someone else, I'll understand."

"Why would I do that? Just wait until you see all the work I'm saving up for you."

the bombs have been made to wait
zeroing in on the deadly quiet
feel my eyes on your face
and turn like a dancer remembering love
in the madhouse dark

Chapter Twenty

The inner glow I usually experience while watching a sunset turns to dismay as the 737 dives into the red circle of smog surrounding Santa Monica Bay that never fails to remind me of the ring around a dirty toilet bowl.

We touch down during rush hour, when the clogged arterials put all freeway commuters at risk for heart attack. I pick up my rental and take the surface streets north, passing dirty beaches and oil wells that I had forgotten lined the coast near the airport.

The Cornings live in a medium-to-largely ostentatious mansion just a few blocks north of Rodeo Drive. The house lacks Greek columns, but the front yard is crisscrossed by green marble walkways and a rock garden that boasts more boulders than the South Dakota Badlands. When I ring the door bell, the motion sensors do their work, and I stand, fully illuminated, swiping at my unkempt hair and hoping I look presentable on the TV monitor.

Leslie answers the door and pulls me inside, giving me the warmest hug I've had since I found Mrs. Emerson's poodle slumming in Anaheim ten years ago. Two dinner candles are aglow on the dining room table. Michael pours me a shot of the best single malt Scotch I've ever tasted.

"Leslie, I need to ask you—were you being truthful when you told Alicia you had a jealous boyfriend?"

"I know it was childish to refuse to tell her who it was, but it's embarrassing to be dating your boss." *So that's what Daniel Rose was hiding.*

"At least you weren't dating a kidnapper."

"Yeah, I heard what happened to Larry Tollway." Leslie shakes her head as if trying to erase that memory. "He never took off that ski mask or said a word to me the whole time I was in captivity."

"Getting back to Daniel, can you think of a reason why his fingerprints would be on the key to your window gate?"

Leslie's laugh is rueful. "We had a picnic on the fire escape the night I broke up with him. He knew where the key was. He must have used it to open the gate."

"Why did you break up with him?"

Leslie looks like she'd rather not answer, but her finishing school training wins out. "Part of my job was to balance the checkbook. There were a lot of withdrawals on the AMT card that didn't have any receipts, and Daniel wouldn't explain. He said it was just petty cash, but when I added up the numbers, I decided to put some distance between us."

It doesn't look like Daniel Rose will come out of this smelling like his namesake.

Eleanor glides downstairs, a new woman, relaxed and self-assured. "You'll be glad to hear that we put in a new security system. We keep it on, except for the motion detector, when we're at home during the day. That's how much our life has changed."

"What really changed your life were those visits from Sal Salvatore," I say, talking to her, but looking at Michael.

"You're right," says Eleanor. "It's Sal who told us about the internship at New Beginnings." She seems puzzled, but Michael knows what I'm talking about. "Jo, would you come into my office for a minute?"

"He probably wants to give you a bonus," says Leslie.

Michael's office contains all the expected accoutrements—award plaques, signed photographs from actors—most of them famous for their brawn rather than brains—and an old movie projector for "atmosphere."

"So you had no idea what Sal was up to?"

"Not a clue. Do you think I would have let my daughter go to New York on his recommendation if I'd known he was a crook?" Michael lights a cigarette, the first I've seen someone smoke inside their own home for a long time. "On the other hand, if you're asking if I feel responsible for what happened to Leslie, the answer is yes."

That's probably why he hasn't asked me about retrieving the

ransom money. "How did you and Sal meet?"

"When Sal's father was alive, he invested in films, some of them mine. Two or three years ago, he brought his son with him to Los Angeles for a movie premiere. Sal told me he was in recovery. He was very open about it, like someone you could respect for turning their life around. When I heard he'd gotten involved in philanthropy after his father's death, I sent him a check. He dropped in from time to time when he was in town. Told me he was fund-raising for Sunflower House. Come to think of it, that's exactly what he *was* doing. I admired him, fool that I was, but what really haunts me is the possibility that he might have engineered what happened to Leslie. After all, he knew she came from a wealthy family, and it was *his* car they used to take her."

"It was probably used without his knowledge. Meanwhile, you should know that the ransom was salvaged from the bottom of Storm King Lake, along with Gloria's van. After the coins are used as evidence, the police will return them to you." Michael nods an acknowledgement, still brooding.

There's a light knock on the door, and Leslie asks if I can stay for dinner.

"Sure she will," says Michael. "It's not every day we get to dine with an investigator like Jo Epstein. No one pulls the wool over this lady's eyes."

Yeah, well, tell that to the devious lady I'm going to visit tomorrow at the State Prison for Women.

* * *

The small motel in Santa Monica is a little mildewed around the edges, but who cares when you can wake up and take a walk on the beach? When I check my voice-mail back in New York, there's a message from Stan. He says he's located Khurram Saleh's friend, Diane Sullivan, but she won't talk to him on the phone. This is understandable, given Khurram's fear of being detained by the INS. Diane's address is in Topanga Canyon. Surprisingly, when I call, she agrees to meet with me. Topanga is due north of Pacific Palisades, and I can cut through the canyon afterwards, and then take Interstate 405 towards Chowchilla and the Central California Women's prison.

I head north on the Pacific Coast Highway—PCH as everyone calls it. I pass all those little houses on the edge of America,
until I get to Topanga Canyon Boulevard and turn right.

The two-lane road, widened in a few places since I last came
this way, winds through sagebrush covered hills for several miles
before houses start to appear on the ridges above. Diane's house is
up a steep road near the Fish Market. She comes out to meet me,
wearing a starched white blouse and silk trousers—not at all typical
of informal Topanga attire. "I leave for work in fifteen minutes," says
Diane, sizing me up, probably regretting her agreement to the
interview. She leads me onto the patio, which overhangs a sheer
cliff, one side of a wide ravine dotted with houses.

"Samarah gave this to me," I say, showing her the photo of
Khurram and his mother. "You can choose to talk to me or not,
but I want you to know I'm here on his family's behalf."

Diane looks at the picture while twirling a blond braid
around her finger. "I didn't invite him. He just showed up with no
luggage, looking so sad.

"Was he frightened of being imprisoned or deported?"

"No! He was infatuated, that's all. Khurram doesn't care
about all the propaganda, the persecution of Muslims. All he wants
is to make money in America and find a wife. It's one of the reasons
I broke off with him. Ironic, isn't it?"

Two hawks circle overhead. I wonder what they're hunting.
"Where is he?"

Diane throws her hands up in frustration. "I wish I knew! A
week after he came, he convinced me to drive up to Mammoth and
go skiing with him."

"Skiing? In June?"

"This year there was snow up there until the beginning of July."

She folds her arms across her chest, maybe not liking the
memory.

"As soon as we got there he started pressuring me to marry
him. It was crazy. We weren't even sleeping together—it's against
his religion. I stopped arguing with him once I knew what I was
going to do. When we stopped at the inn, I let him get out of the car
with his pack, and then I took off. Left him standing there with his

mouth open."

"And that's the last time you saw him?"

Diane nods. "I figured he'd go back to New York. Then this private eye calls me. I thought maybe Khurram didn't want to be found, so I stonewalled the guy. Do you think something's happened to Khurram?"

"It doesn't look good."

* * *

Three hours later, I'm observing that my former client Amy Bingham's golden hair is a few shades darker than Diane's, cut short and glowing with health. Can inmates in the Central California Women's Facility shop for tea tree oil shampoo in the prison commissary? On closer inspection, I see that five years have sketched some character lines on her freckled face.

Taking note of my scrutiny, she grimaces. "The crow's feet are from squinting. I stopped wearing my contacts—ironic, given how the prisoners here manufacture lenses—but there are too many things going on here that I'd prefer not to see." It's food for thought, the way that imprisonment often makes people more thoughtful. My smile prompts her to ask, "Are you here to gloat?"

"I thought that was *your* department."

She mulls this over. "So you bought the prosecution's case that I planned to kill him all along, that I used you to give me the justification I needed."

"That's about it."

"It's true, I wanted desperately to confront him with hard evidence, but that afternoon…in his office…I didn't expect him to react the way he did."

This is the first time we've spoken face to face since the day I handed her the envelope. At her trial I testified for the prosecution, playing the painful part of the savvy investigator taken in by a client. I remember her voice as being high-pitched and disconnected, but today she pushes out one painful word at a time, steeped in regret.

"He said his infidelity was my fault. That I was stupid and boring and unattractive. I knew this wasn't true, but he was a lawyer. His words were persuasive weapons. He said if I got ugly over the divorce and tried to recoup the money I spent putting him through law school or demand a share in his practice, he'd make sure he got custody of our daughter. I had no doubt that he could do this."

"Even if he got custody, Amy, you would have seen your daughter more often than you do now." *If she planned to kill him, she would have tried to cover up the murder in order to stay out of jail and keep her daughter.* I didn't see it then, but now the dots are connecting.

"You're right. I should have thought of Elaine. And I should have realized there was no need to kill him. His heart was beating, but he felt nothing. He was dead already."

We finish the visiting hour talking about her appeal, but there's nothing I can do. It's in the hands of the Appellate Court now. On the five hour drive from Chowchilla to Los Angeles, I have plenty of time to plan how I'm going to stay in touch with this lady and what to include in the care packages I'll be sending.

* * *

It's a five-hour trip from Chowchilla to Mammoth Lakes, including a two-hour drive through Yosemite National Park. There's lots of beauty passing by. Unfortunately, I'm too preoccupied with what I'll find at the end of the road to notice.

My first stop is the Mono County Free Library, where I look through the archives of the local paper for the month of June. It doesn't take long to find the accident I'm looking for—the one involving a small avalanche and an "as yet unidentified hiker."

At the Sheriff's office, I tell the officer on duty I've got some information about the hiker they found in June. The Sheriff sees me right away. He's tall and bulky, wearing a hat two sizes too big for him. I show him the photo of Khurram and his mother. "Why don't you sit down," he says, taking his own advice. "He didn't have a speck of ID on him. We checked every hotel room occupant in town, every lift ticketholder. They were all accounted for."

"His girlfriend dropped him off. They had a fight. It looks like he decided to walk off his anger on the trails."

"The back country is no place for beginners," is the Sheriff's only comment.

I give him all the information I've got. He's not ready to make

188

a positive identification, but I know from the expression on his face that they've found Khurram.

* * *

The hot Santa Ana wind breathes down my neck as I walk from my parking spot on La Cienega to the steel and glass monolith that houses Stan Reese's new offices. West Hollywood is a long way from Torrance. He's got a busy staff of investigators and an administrative assistant who looks like he could run Universal Studios. From the looks of the carpets and artwork, it seems the business is now worth much more than the $60,000 he paid for my insurance clients five years ago.

The conference room where we munch donuts and drink chai lattes is awash in steel and glass, except for the raven in full flight, carved in koa, looking down on us from atop the ceiling-high totem pole. Stan's bright yellow polo shirt and deep tan set off his effervescent blue eyes, which are carefully examining yours truly.

"Are you happy for me or are you thinking about how all this could have been yours?" Stan's always been able to read my mind, more or less.

"You'll get no complaints from me, Stan. I would have built a business, but you've created an industry. I just talked with Amy Bingham and feel like a weight's been lifted off my shoulders. It wasn't my fault."

"I tried to tell you that ten years ago."

I choose to ignore his *I told you so* tone. "I want to thank you, Stan, for your help locating Diane Sullivan." I tell him about the accident at Mammoth. "Some people can't take rejection," is his only comment. Typical Stan, I'm thinking. Then he pulls a fast one.

"While you're here, I've got a proposition to make. We're opening a New York office. How about coming in as a partner?"

I do a quick reality check on his face. He's serious. I try to put it as gently as I can. "It's a more-than-generous offer, Stan, but if I return to detective work full-time it won't be to make insurance companies rich by busting fraudulent claims. I seem to be drawn to cases where the stakes are a little higher. Besides, I'm facing some charges myself in New York that could make me ineligible for a New York investigator's license. I was framed on a drug charge."

189

"All that work you put in on solving the Johnson murder, doesn't it give you some leverage with the NYPD?"

"Possibly. But the police could just as easily swing the other way. There was an old friend involved in the case who I tried to protect."

"I see."

"She killed the person who set me up on the drug charge."

"Ah, Josephine, I forgot what a disaster area you can be." One of Stan's ops knocks at the door and pulls him out of the conference room. I follow and in the hallway Stan gives me his *it was so nice seeing you again* look. I get even by giving him a hug in front of his staff. Most of them are still grinning when I leave.

Ask the dead
sightless eyes
take us inward
motionless arms
hold the answer

Chapter Twenty-One

Groggy as I am from the red-eye, I take a moment to enjoy the familiar chaos outside Terminal 7, the honking horns, anxious relatives waving pick-up signs, and cabbies jockeying for position near the curb. The steamy unpredictability of New York, where smiles have depth and profanity is delivered whole-heartedly, is a pleasant change from the impenetrable surface of politeness that blankets Southern California.

The honeymoon ends abruptly when I call the car service and the dispatcher curtly informs me that the driver is stuck in traffic on the Queensboro Bridge and running at least a half hour late. I'm on the verge of taking a chance that the driver of the next taxi in line is capable of finding a route to Manhattan that doesn't involve a side trip to Newark, when Hasim calls on my cell to say he's at the airport. A few minutes later, he swings open the passenger door of his blue Golf and says, "You look different." I don't think he's talking about my tan. I decide not to tell him about Khurram until we get to my place.

" I've made a decision to get my New York P.I. license and open an office in Manhattan. That is, if I don't go to jail instead."

"No worries," Hasim says. "The Department of Corrections conducted an investigation of Larry Tollway's extracurricular activities. The inmates he recruited for the smurf operation at Sunflower House were also busy running drugs for him at Rikers. You've been cleared of all charges and might even get an apology from the DOCS Commissioner."

"In return for my silence, no doubt."

"Still the cynic."

"No handy proverb to teach me how to behave?"

"I seem to have accepted your uniqueness." This may be the nicest compliment I'll ever get from him, and I tuck it into my memory for safekeeping.

He parks in front of the fire hydrant three doors down from my house, and we walk back. "Why so quiet?" he asks in the elevator, ever the policeman.

It's my turn to brew the peppermint tea and slip in some honey. "I've brought back some news about your nephew." He looks away, and I leave the room to give him some time to pull himself together. When I return and tell him what I found out in California, he says, "You didn't have to do any of this, Jo."

"Then it must mean we're friends," is all I can think of to say.

* * *

I look around the apartment after the Lieutenant leaves. It looks the same, but there's a feeling of potential in the air that wasn't here before. Maybe I'll buy a house plant. Just one.

I'm too tired to check messages. Running the bath water, I monitor a couple of calls. When I hear Silas Harding's voice, I pick up the phone. He'll want to know about Khurram.

"Jo, I'm glad you're back. I've been retained by Gloria Kelly, and we need you as a defense witness. Gloria believes your testimony will justify her actions on the night of the shooting." This is not what I expected.

I decide to let Hasim tell Silas about his nephew when the time comes and agree to show up at Harding's office at 10 a.m. tomorrow to make a statement. I'm not sure how favorable to Gloria my version of events will be. My efforts at damage control on her behalf have been a disaster, and I prefer not to think about what I'll say when Silas starts asking the questions.

The phone rings again, and this time it's Paul, using the same words he does every time, asking the same thing. "Why won't you give me a chance to explain?" He makes me so angry that, before I realize it, I've taken the call.

"You're very good at explaining. Just not good at telling the truth."

"Let me come over. I'll bring dinner. I'll bring a damn polygraph so you'll know I'm telling the truth this time. I made a mistake. Don't make me pay for it forever."

I let the silence hang between us for awhile before saying, "Alright. Seven o'clock." It's hard to say why I relent. It might be to find out just how far he'll go in seeking forgiveness, or maybe I'm hoping to learn what actually happened to Beverly and why. I already know she lost her job because of her sister Chloe's convenient disclosure, but was that enough to drive her to suicide? I did make Beverly a promise, and Paul might be the one who helps me keep it.

* * *

On the phone, I'd visualized Silas Harding as a middle-aged, worn-out liberal, with thinning hair and an unfortunate tendency to wear spotted bow ties. The man I meet in the suite of respectable but sparsely furnished offices on 14th Street is strikingly handsome in his starched pin-stripe pink shirt, with aristocratic features and a bountiful supply of light brown hair cascading down his shoulders. So what if it's dyed?

Silas faces me across his impressively cluttered desk. "Who would have thought that Larry Tollway… I worked with that man for years."

"It's the people we think we know that have the best chance of taking advantage of us," I say, and I'm not just thinking about Larry. "So what kind of time is Gloria facing?" I ask him.

"She's looking at manslaughter and five counts of money-laundering, for a possible total of forty years in prison." Silas adds that bail is set high, at two hundred thousand dollars, and if she's unable to post it, Gloria will spend the six months leading up to her trial in Rose M. Singer Center for women on Rikers Island.

I can tell from Harding's melancholy expression that he's well aware of the pitfalls he faces in trying to obtain a statement from me that will work in Gloria's favor. Ambiguity has colored my relationship with her for so long that I have no steady barometer with which to judge her weather, no scale to measure her intent that doesn't tip both ways. Did she fire before realizing that Larry was unarmed? Or was I an inconvenient witness to her crime, to be disposed of, perhaps regretfully, so she could escape with two million dollars worth of gold coins?

"Do you believe your life was in danger at the moment Gloria Kelly shot Larry Tollway?"

"Yes."

Silas' pen scratches on his legal pad. "Where was Tollway's gun at the moment he was shot?"

"I had knocked it out of his hand. It was on the floor about six feet away from him."

"Did he go after the gun?"

"Yes, but Gloria got there first. Then he started walking toward her, and she shot him."

"So Gloria Kelly may have saved your life."

"That's one way of putting it."

"Did Ms. Kelly threaten you in any way after the shooting?"

"Not explicitly, but it was implied."

"So you left the house with her of your own free will." He makes it sound like we went for a Sunday drive.

"Did you believe she presented a danger to you?"

"Not until she drove the car into the river."

My answers aren't going down easy, but neither are they giving Harding indigestion. After the interview, he tells me he thinks he can establish that Gloria shot Tollway to protect me. Having looked down the barrel of Gloria's gun myself, I don't buy this story one hundred percent.

On the way out of his office, it occurs to me that I might make a good prosecution witness. Something worth thinking about, considering all the death and destruction Gloria's "good intentions" have caused.

* * *

Paul's due at seven. I locate my tape recorder and am in the flow of dictating some final notes when the doorbell rings.

He's brought two bottles, red wine plus champagne. I'm guessing it's his peace offering. He's dressed for the occasion in torn jeans and one of those blue work shirts that went out of style twenty years ago and seem to be back in vogue. With a shock, I see that he's shaved his head. Baldness somehow makes his facial features look thicker and stronger than I remember.

Sipping the bubbly, we pack away the chicken stir fry from the Wild Wok, along with a Japanese salad wearing a tasty rice vinegar dressing. Paul seems eager to talk about my "triumph" as he calls it. "You solved two murders and a kidnapping and made it look easy."

"It's not me we should be talking about."

"You're right, Jo. I know you think I'm a habitual liar. But when I saw how much you felt for Beverly, how much you cared about her even though you'd never met." He leans towards me over the remains of our meal, eyes intent on selling his story.

"I was afraid that if I told you that Beverly and I were lovers, you'd think I was callous, walking out on her like that. And worse, you'd think that I'd do the same with you."

It makes sense. So why don't I believe him?

Paul senses my discomfort and pulls away, then sinks back into his chair with an exasperated sigh. "She wasn't the innocent kindergarten teacher everyone thought she was. She made up stories and hurt people. And she did drugs. Did you know she overdosed on Oxycontin?"

I don't answer, because I'm listening to the school nurse's words playing in my head. *It was never reported in the paper, but my nephew's on the force and he told me about it.*

How could he know about that?

"The police told me about the drugs when I was interviewed." Paul has answered my unasked question without skipping a beat, but my heart has started to pound. There's no way he could have known about the Oxycontin, unless he was there when Beverly died.

To buy some time, I offer to make us coffee. When I rejoin him, Paul has opened the Merlot and refilled our glasses. He proposes a toast. "To Jo Epstein, who has a gift for seeing through people."

I applaud this sentiment with one sharp clap and take a few sips of the wine, a little bitter for my taste. In the kitchen, my pulse had been racing, and my muscles tensed up for a confrontation, but I feel relaxed and calm—heavy and at peace with the force of gravity pulling me downward and inward.

"You've probably got some questions, and since you'll soon

be unable to speak, I'll presume to answer them for you." Part of me is wondering what he's slipped in my drink. The rest of me is already too fuzzy to care. Paul's got himself a captive audience.

"If you could move the muscles in your face Jo, I know they'd show surprise. I've always been able to fool people, especially women. It wasn't hard with Chloe Sterling. She was so blinded by her hatred for Beverly that she was happy to tell that school nurse all about their pathetic childhood—just enough to make sure her sister got fired. After that, I knew it would be easy to make her believe that she'd succeeded in driving Beverly to commit suicide. Probably her intention all along. No remorse tugging at those tough heartstrings. And not very intelligent either."

He studies me closely before he goes on. "But not you, Jo. You're a very clever gal—a lot smarter than Chloe. And when we met I could see you had your head on straight, not like Beverly. She had delusions. She was completely obsessed with that little girl. But not you. You live in the real world, and you've got a nose that won't quit sniffing around until you find the truth. And that's something I can't let happen, Jo. You of all people understand that."

So it was Paul who broke into the apartment that first night we met, to frighten me, and later attacked me in the hallway *to get me to stop nosing around.* How foolish you were, Beverly, to give him a key.

His face is moving in and out of focus; his soft, menacing voice barely cutting through the descending fog. "I should have left her clothes on. Did you know that people, especially women, never get undressed when they're going to drown themselves? It's because they don't want to be found naked. I know that now. I won't make the same mistake twice. Stupid of the police not to pick up on that when they found Beverly in her birthday suit. "

He's watching me closely as he talks, expecting me to lose consciousness at any moment. I decide that now would be a good time to flutter my eyes and drape myself over the chair, spineless as boiled spinach. If he thinks I'm unconscious, maybe he'll drop his guard.

Before I can fall all the way to the floor, Paul grips me under the armpits and drags me into the bathroom. He dumps me in the bathtub and turns on the taps. As water rapidly rises over my legs, I squeeze my eyes shut. I feel chilled in spite of the warm water rising around me. Careful to keep my ribs down, I take as deep a breath as I can, trying to spread air to the back of my lungs. Then I slip under, praying that Paul won't have the stomach to stay and watch me drown. I count to thirty, all I can manage in my weakened state, and raise my thousand pound head out of the water.

He's gone. I'm sure he'll be back to check his handiwork, so I listen and wait. It seems like forever before I hear his footsteps. I slip back under the water and, in my mind's eye, I imagine him carrying a wine glass and an empty prescription bottle, getting ready to set the stage for my sad demise. A woman mistakenly combines drugs and alcohol while relaxing in a hot bath.

I lie perfectly still and play the drowned victim, eyes open. Paul leans over the tub. With my lungs about to burst, I break the surface. I grab the back of his neck with my right hand, jabbing the heel of my left upward, hard, into his Adam's apple. Glass shatters as he staggers back. I grab the heavy metal towel rack, the one Mom gave me that's always falling off the wall, and smash it down on the back of his skull. He's on his knees now. He's screaming and holding his head. The next blow packs a lot more wallop, and he collapses on the tiles, motionless.

I stand shaking and deep breathing. I'm not sure how much damage I've done to my would-be assassin. So, to keep him in the bathroom and not at my throat, I drag a chair from the dinner table and wedge the high back-rest tightly under the door knob. Somehow I retrieve Hasim's number from my fogged up brain.

"Help me!" My croak sounds like it came from the bottom of a jug.

Something tells me I'd better throw up, so I stumble for the kitchen sink. Just thinking about the poisonous Merlot turns my stomach, making it easy to get rid of the damn chicken and the other crap. Then it's lullaby time.

* * *

"You should be in the hospital."

"I'll be okay. I mean, what are the chances of two women dying in the same bathtub in an apartment on West End Avenue anyway?"

We're speeding down Broadway in Hasim's cruiser. You'd think heads would turn, but when you're in a cop car folks tend to see right through you, hoping to stay invisible themselves. Paul's in the cage behind us, barely conscious. I hope his concussion results in a brain tumor. Hasim's looking grim.

"If you suspected him, you should have told me and I'd have set you up with a wire. We could have moved in as soon as you were in danger."

"He was my friend, for God's sake. I just thought we'd have dinner and resolve some of our differences. How in the world could I know I'd end up fighting for my life?" Anger swirls around me. I want to hit someone. I want to hit Paul but have to make do with the smug satisfaction that I have him cold. He isn't going to worm his way out of this one.

"You'll be glad to hear that I caught it all on tape. Do you want to hear his confession? The only thing he left out was the sound effects."

"I'm impressed, Jo."

"Are you saying you underestimated me?"

"Sometimes the nut doesn't reveal the tree it contains."

"There's room for interpretation here," I mumble. Hasim smiles.

* * *

Nikolai answers the door, wearing a threadbare smoking jacket of purple velvet that Mom would donate to a thrift shop if she could only get him to take it off. "Your mother's at her opera class." The thought of my mother singing *Un Belle Di* in her gentle falsetto provokes a smile that Nikolai uncharacteristically returns.

"They don't sing. They watch performances on film. Have some pickled herring with sour cream."

This is the first time he's offered such hospitality, and I'm not sure how to react. The kitchen is cleaner than usual. The table where Nikolai spears herring from a jar to serve on Ritz crackers is covered with a vinyl cloth, Pennsylvania Dutch today, repetitive fleur de leis tomorrow.

198

"Your mother hasn't been feeling well. She's been to the doctor, but he can't find anything wrong. Still, I think you should visit more often."

"Thanks for telling me. I know how well you take of her."

Nikolai looks down at his plate, embarrassed by my sentiment. "She needs you." He takes two small glasses from the cupboard above the sink, splashes them with vodka and orange juice, and hands one to me. It's not a request. We sit quietly, aware of the delicacy of this truce. After a while, he refills our glasses and launches into a lengthy but fascinating story about how several members of his string section threatened to defect while touring western Europe during the Cold War. Just when it's getting good, the clicks of multiple locks being opened signal that Mom has come home.

Her eyes light up when she sees me, but not so quickly that I fail to notice the sad story written on her face. "What's wrong?"

"Della Strindberg, the woman in 3B, had a stroke. She's paralyzed on one side. I saw her daughter in the elevator. She was crying."

Nikolai guides her gently to the table while I put the kettle on. She seems to recover, for my sake I'm sure. "Our teacher played a Puccini aria for us today. So lovely, like falling water."

After dinner, I can see she's exhausted and will be turning in early, so I walk downstairs to the second floor to see what Sasha and Ludmilla are up to. They've lived in the United States for twelve years—the two children they raised here now live in New Jersey—but when you enter their apartment, there's a pervasive sadness, a nostalgia for Russia that persists, even when their apartment is filled with music, which it usually is.

I first met the Vlyodyas when Mom sent me downstairs to complain about the invasive noise from one of their Saturday night concerts. I found fifty people packed into rows of rented folding chairs. Giant mirrors and shiny silver wallpaper transformed the small living room into a Czarist concert hall. A rosy, diminutive woman presided at the piano—Ludmilla accompanying a disheveled male singer with a beatific voice. They attacked Russian folk songs at a tempo that made ragtime sound like a waltz.

Ludmilla agreed to lower the volume if I'd eat some cake. I remember stumbling upstairs four hours later, my head ringing with sentimental ballads, feeling like someone who had discovered a secret room in a house where they've lived for decades.

Tonight it's Sasha who opens the door. "Ludmilla, look who's here." It's been months since I've come by, but their warmth is undiminished.

"I set your poem to music," coos Ludmilla, "and our friend Vladimir is going to perform it at the *Paradiso* tonight. You've got to come."

* * *

Today's the day I make my choice. There's only one side I can testify for; if called by the other, I'll be considered a hostile witness. Thanks to Gloria, a watery grave came close to checking me in and posting a "No Vacancy" sign. So why do I hesitate? Why should one generous gesture by her younger self carry more weight than setting the stage for murder and profiting from a kidnapping?

The District Attorney's office has called twice, Silas only once, and that was yesterday, before I stopped checking my voice mail. Without my testimony, the case against Gloria is surprisingly slim. Sal set up the cash cleaning operation and opened the bank accounts, but I'm the one who saw her driving the smurfs around the city. Michael Corning can testify that she knew about the gold coins and the case, but I'm the one who knows that she helped Larry to steal the ransom. If I don't testify, and if Miroslav and Spike choose to keep her name out of it, she just might walk.

I'm sitting at a table outside the café in the Village where Gloria and I used to people-watch before taking in Kurosawa films at the Bleeker Street Cinema. They still serve acidic coffee in thick enamel cups, with slices of rum cheese cake that take off the edge. It's easy to visualize Gloria sitting opposite me, wearing her skimpy orange mini-dress with the paisley patterns, the one she lived in that never seemed to fade.

"You can't tell me the world's okay the way it is and that I shouldn't try to change it."

"How about drawing a line between activism and crime?"

200

"When corrupt people make the laws, it takes true citizens to break them."

For Gloria, to compromise is to show weakness. Her single-mindedness and willingness to sacrifice others for the cause would carry her far working for the CIA or a political party of most any stripe. But the anarchist's road is lonely, and in her case there's only room on the path for one.

In California I heard a sage, resplendent in a pin-striped suit and hemp sandals, speaking to a rapt audience on Santa Monica Pier. He was talking about the nature of power. He said that every action we carry out creates a ripple effect, like a pebble thrown in a lake. If we're aware of the ripples, that gives us the power of understanding; if we lose track of them, our world spins out of control. He confessed that he'd come to this realization in a prison cell.

Maybe Gloria will do the same.